BLIND FOLD

Best Wishes

Jack Stirling

BLIND FOLD

JACK STIRLING

Matador
9 Priory Business Park
Wistow Road
Kibworth Beauchamp
Leicester LE8 0RX, UK
Tel: (+44) 116 279 2299
Fax: (+44) 116 279 2277
Email: books@troubador.co.uk
Web: www.troubador.co.uk/matador

ISBN 9781783060313

British Library Cataloguing in Publication Data.
A catalogue record for this book is available from the British Library.

Ths is a work of fiction. Characters, companies and locations are either the product of
the author's imagination or, in the case of locations, if real, used fictitiously, without any
intent to describe their actual environment.

Printed and bound in the UK by TJ International, Padstow, Cornwall
Typeset in 11pt Bembo by Troubador Publishing Ltd, Leicester, UK

Matador is an imprint of Troubador Publishing Ltd

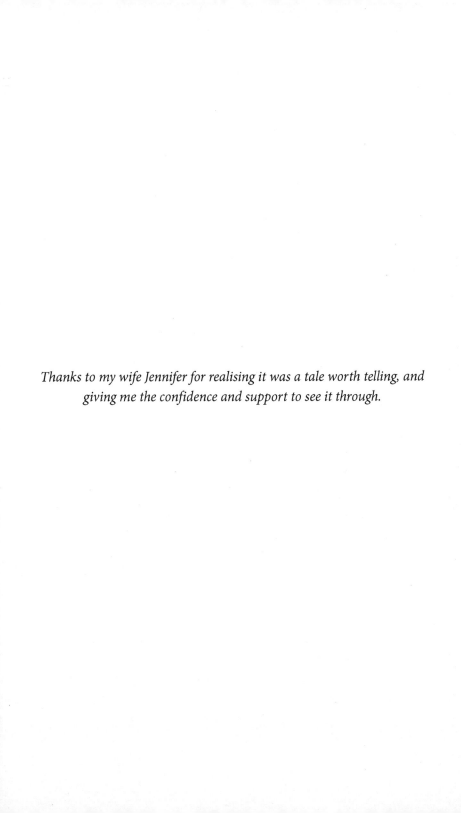

Thanks to my wife Jennifer for realising it was a tale worth telling, and giving me the confidence and support to see it through.

Preface

This novel is a work of fiction. However, much of the background is based on fact. Places mentioned are entirely accurate and do exist. Names and characters are entirely from the author's imagination. Any resemblance to actual persons, living or dead, is purely coincidental. There are very obvious exceptions and, in fact, the two terrorists Midhat Mursi and Anas Al Liby (both these men have several aliases) are an example. Both were still at large at the time of writing this novel. Both with a bounty on their heads of $5,000,000. Further, at the time I began writing this book, Al Qaeda did not possess any type of nuclear device. This situation has drastically altered and a chilling factor has emerged. All the major intelligence agencies are firmly of the opinion that Al Qaeda has, now, obtained some form of nuclear weapon. What they intend doing with it is anyone's guess. Perhaps not Hawes but you can be absolutely certain that they have every intention of wreaking terrible havoc. Sometime. Somewhere! The clock is ticking. You have been warned, but will anyone take heed?

CHAPTER 1

Wednesday 23rd January 1525 hours, present day

There are few places more beautiful than the Yorkshire Dales. However, in winter the icy particles blown on a freezing northerly wind sting hands and faces like a thousand needles. It is miserable and depressing for man and beast alike.

A pheasant shoot is drawing to a close. The shooters are thankful that this is the last drive of the day. The beaters more so! Icy cold hands and wet, freezing feet are pleading to be defrosted in front of a blazing fire.

'Dale Two to Dale Three!' the Head Keeper radioed his Under Keeper.

'When this drive's over tell Tom to take his dog and look for any runners.'

'Will do.' replied Dale Three.

'Be nowt for the pot unless they bloody well hit a few more,' grumbled Jeb Metcalfe to Tom Prescott his long time friend, two of the day's beaters. Tom and Jeb were chalk and cheese. Tom, highly intelligent and smart, even in working clothes. Jeb tended towards scruffiness. His only attempt at neatness being a tendency to pick up anything carelessly left lying about by its legal owner. However, the alliance worked and the two seemed to complement one another.

A salvo of shots indicated the frightened birds had flown causing Dale One to operate his clicker making it sound like a demented geiger counter coming across a motherlode of pitchblende. The landlord's finger purposefully stabbed at his clicker to ensure not more than a handful of shots was fired above the 1200 limit. The piercing sound of a whistle indicated the drive was over.

'Dale Two to Three! Let the beaters go. Fluff remind Tom to take his dog and check for any runners.'

'Did you hear that Tom? We'll wait for you at the Druids car park. There are a few fluffing runners just behind you. Give it ten minutes or so,' advised Dale Three.

'No, don't wait for us. My car is in Knowle Lane. It's going to be a bugger finding them amongst the briars. We'll drop any off at the yard on our way home. I don't think there's much chance of finding them all. It's also getting pretty dark. I'll leave the walkie talkie in the gunroom.' responded Tom.

'OK Tom, well do your best. See you next Monday half past eight. Don't fluffing be late and make sure you bring that dog o' yourn she's a good 'un. Cheers mate.'

'Come on Tom – let's collect our Sunday dinner,' said Jeb.

'Jeb Metcalfe! I'm ashamed of you. You don't mean to say you would deprive his nibs of one of his birds.'

'One? Not just one. I've a couple lined up already.' Laughing, the two walked back into the wood.

'Go, Rusty fetch.' The ever eager Springer, bounded off in pursuit of a runner. Her docked tail wagging furiously as she returned with a cock pheasant. Tom took the still flapping bird from the dog, deftly wrung its neck to put it out of its misery and subsequently into his cooking pot.

'I've a brace to pick up just above the Druid's Temple,' explained Jeb.

'You sneaky sod, I didn't notice you hiding any earlier.'

'I don't tell you everything. A couple that flew back over the wood, shot by Master James. Probably died of fright when they heard his gun go off. I convinced him they had managed to escape – silly sod him. One for you and one for me, fair enough?'

At the top of the slope, just above the Temple Folly, Jeb plunged into a plantation of young trees to retrieve the two birds he had previously concealed.

'Shit, my bastard foot,' called out Jeb painfully.

'Now what have you done Jeb?'

'Fallen arse over tip over a bloody great lump of metal and banged my fluffing toe, as Keith would say.'

'Come on you dozy pillock! Let's get going and leave off nature walks in the middle of winter. I want to get home and into a nice hot bath. I'm bloody frozen,' said Tom.

'Humph, thanks for your concern! Anyhow I've got the birds. What the bloody hell is this?'

By this time Tom was standing over his still prostrate buddy who was clutching a plump hen pheasant and a much more prized woodcock.

'Thank you Jeb, I'd love the woodcock, very kind of you,' chuckled Tom.

'Over my dead body – this hen is yours but I know where I can get a couple of quid for the woodcock. Look, what's this?' queried Jeb.

He stared at a circular grey metal lid secured by a lock. Jeb frantically tugged on the lock Wet feathers from the dead birds were clinging to his fingers like stringy lumps of stubborn snot making the task even more impossible. The lock refused to budge. Jeb stood up cursing and perspiring.

'Damned thing! Let's come back tonight with a hacksaw and have a look inside. We might find summats to flog at a car boot,' panted Jeb.

'Waste of time there won't be owt left in it. I'm going as far as the fire in the pub tonight. No way am I coming out here in the dark,' insisted Tom.

'I'll buy you a pint if you come back with me later tonight.' Seeing the look on Tom's face, 'OK a couple of pints.'

'You're on. Mind you if it is snowing or sleeting you'll be on your own,' Tom muttered back with little enthusiasm.

In the fading light they saw a lid about thirty inches across and half an inch thick. Very firmly secured by a very businesslike Chubb lock. Their decision to return later, to open the lid, was to prove to be a very, very bad choice. Particularly as far as Jed was concerned.

CHAPTER 2

Tuesday 12th January 1960, Moscow

Russia was, and still is, well known for its extreme policy relating to secrecy. However, a Most Top Secret meeting took place, in the Kremlin on January 12th 1960. Only four persons attended this meeting. Not another person, apart from these four, was aware that this meeting was taking place. Present were Premier Nikita Sergeyevich Khrushchev, Defence Minister Rodion Yakovlevich Malinovsky. KGB Chairman Aleksandr Shelepin and Igor Kurchatov, the leader of the Soviet A Bomb project.

Each of them had been given explicit instructions not to mention this meeting to anyone. So far they had no idea why there was such extreme secrecy over a meeting. None of them knew who else was going to be there. Prior to the start of the session The Premier had stated that NO written record would be taken. This meeting had never taken place. Before they got down to the actual purpose of the gathering Khrushchev had a question for his KGB Chairman.

'Comrade Shelepin, are the capitalist Americans continuing to fly over Soviet Russia with total impunity from our air defences?' demanded Khrushchev.

'I regret I have to tell you yes. Comrade Chairman, They use a highly classified aircraft known as a U2. It can fly far higher than any of our fighters can reach. They fly where they wish and photograph our most sensitive areas with a complete lack of concern. They know we do not have the means to intercept them at present.' Khrushchev stood, walked slowly towards the window and gazed out over Red Square for some time before turning round. He approached Shelepin and almost in a whisper, but with a voice heavy with menace said: 'Comrade, the KGB is allocated virtually unlimited funds. What is being done about these affronts to our sovereignty?'

'Comrade Premier, our agents are making excellent progress regarding the flight specifications of this accursed U2. We hope to have pleasing results very soon now'. His face the colour of beetroot, Khrushchev brought his fist crashing onto the table.

'We know what the aircraft can do already. Outfly anything we have. I am asking what you intend doing about it?'

'A new SAM is being developed and test firing has proved highly satisfactory. Production has begun on a handful of these missiles. We are confident we will achieve the required accuracy and altitude enabling us to rid the skies of this American machine. If we can shoot just one down the Americans will cancel further flights over our air space and be restricted to flying along but outside our borders.'

'Let us hope you are right Comrade Shelepin and that positive results are soon forthcoming. The Americans are making us look foolish in the eyes of the world and we cannot do one damned thing about it. I suggest you and my Defence Minister work together on this. I want something doing about it and fast, or heads will roll.' In the Soviet Union there was probably more truth in that phrase than if it had been said in the UK. Composing himself the Premier opened the meeting.

'Now, Comrades, we will get to the purpose of our meeting. It is no secret that what is known as a Cold War exists between the Soviet bloc countries and what we call the West. Should this develop into a Hot War we need to be one step ahead of our enemies. Defence Minister Malinovsky approached me some time ago with a suggestion that I feel we are now able to implement. Comrade, if you please.' Malinovsky rose to his feet as he began to outline his idea.

'Gentlemen, it is no secret that I am opposed to nuclear weapons being used except as a deterrent. However, we have to face facts. This cold war is warming up and Soviet Russia must be prepared and able to, not only defend herself, but also to strike back at any aggressors.' Taking a sip of water he continued.

'Some time ago I was speaking with Igor! He happened to mention a phenomenon that occurs when a nuclear device is detonated. It was discovered that electrically operated equipment failed, within a second, due to what they call EMP or Electro Magnetic Pulse.

The pulse is a high-energy emission and it can kill electric equipment, even if it is switched off. The electric cable acts as a giant aerial to conduct this EMP to the appliance. Comrade Kurchatov has had a team working on this particular side effect of a nuclear explosion. They have developed a way to enhance this pulse, sufficiently powerful to kill any unprotected electrical equipment within a very wide range.' Malinovsky paused to take another sip of water, allowing time for the information to sink in.

'If we could detonate several nuclear devices we could virtually destroy all communications systems in use by our enemies. These devices need not be large yield weapons. It would, in effect, render them deaf, dumb and blind. Aircraft, ships at sea, ground forces would be unable to communicate with one another efficiently. Radar would cease to work. Forces could not be mobilised effectively.

Meanwhile, ensuring our own equipment would be fully protected against this EMP. It is not too difficult to safeguard our own comms equipment. Without efficient communications in the West, Russian forces would easily overwhelm them as we would be able to coordinate our attacks.'

Thanking the members for their attention Malinovsky sat down and Khrushchev invited Kurchatov to speak.

'What Comrade Malinovsky says is perfectly feasible. What is more, as he pointed out, we need use only weapons with a very small yield. However, for them to be successful they need to be sited inside countries of the Western Alliance.'

At this Shelepin interrupted.

'I presume you mean, dropped by Russian aircraft over enemy territory. While we are attempting to do this I assume the allies will just sit back and allow us to proceed.' This was said with some derision.

'No Comrade. Firstly, we could not rely on sufficient numbers of our aircraft getting through. Secondly, the whole point of this new system is based on the fact that they would be unprepared and taken totally unawares. The weapons need to be sited inside the borders of our potential enemies long before we need to use them, ready to be operated by remote control or by a mechanical timer.'

'Oh, so we simply walk up to the various Governments and say 'please may we store the odd atom bomb here and there in case we have a war' and they will, of course, welcome us with open arms.'

Shelepin had little time for Kurchatov and took any opportunity to show it. It also rankled that, until this present meeting, he of all people had been kept in the dark about this new war plan.

Premier Khrushchev intervened saying, 'Be patient Comrade, all will be made clear shortly. This plan has been well thought out. Please continue Igor.'

'Thank you Comrade Chairman.' Kurchatov continued.

'To reaffirm, these devices must be positioned at strategic points where enemy communication strong points are known to exist or where new ones are being planned. My people have now created, for want of a better name, a "suitcase bomb". One has been designated RA 115. It weighs a total of 50/60 pounds. Initially we wanted to design, if you like, a portable nuclear device. Whilst I was discussing this with Comrade Malinovsky, I happened to mention the EMP side effect. This idea appealed to him so we redesigned our present weapons to accommodate his wishes. We have modified it to be slightly larger and somewhat heavier, but with a greatly enhanced EMP output. This new design requires TWO containers but each one will be comfortably portable. As I say, each complete device comprises two units that when linked together complete the device. The units weigh approximately 70lbs each. A simple but foolproof method of remote control, or a plain mechanical timer would enable us to detonate the bombs.

Are there any questions? If not I suggest our Defence Minister explains how this can be achieved.'

Despite his misgivings Shelepin had to admit to being somewhat mystified as to how this venture could be successfully carried out. For the meeting to come to fruition the Premier must have been convinced that the idea was a distinct possibility. He would not have authorised further research if he had not had total confidence in the scheme. Khrushchev was renowned for keeping an eye on the purse strings when it came to spending roubles.

At this stage Khrushchev announced a short break for some light refreshments. Pressing a hidden button under his desk he had summoned a trusted waiter. As if by magic he appeared wheeling in a trolley laden with various delicacies. Liquid refreshment comprised scalding hot tea from a huge silver samovar, a decanter of mineral water and the omnipresent iced vodka.

Scotland has its *uisge-beatha* or water of life. France its *eau de vie* in the form of brandy and the Soviet Union has *zhizennia voda*, its very own water of life. Nikita Khrushchev's favourite tipple was a heavily chilled bottle of Stolichnaya or Stoli as the Russians affectionately call it.

Clapping his hands the Premier called the men to order,. telling them to resume their seats while Malinovsky said his piece. They did so with some of them still finishing off the mouth-watering sweets.

"Thank you Comrade Chairman! Now, the method of delivery for our suitcase bombs. In the United Kingdom and other parts of Europe a massive building programme is underway, I will concentrate on the UK as that will be the hardest nut to crack. Two World Wars led Britain to develop a system known as The Royal Observer Corps, for spotting and reporting enemy aircraft. During the past few years this role has changed with the emphasis being on reporting information relating to nuclear weapons. This is due to their perceived threat by the Soviet bloc countries.'

'Can we get to the matter in hand Comrade? We do not need a history lesson.' A further interruption came from the disgruntled Chairman of the KGB. Disregarding Shelepin's comment Malinovsky continued.

'As I mentioned earlier! A huge building programme is underway in the UK. Underground bunkers are being constructed all over mainland Great Britain and the offshore islands. One of these bunkers will be constructed every ten miles or so. We can use the British Government's secrecy to our own advantage. With such a vast building programme underway we have realised a foolproof way in which we can build our own smaller bunkers. To house, gentlemen, our 'sleeping' suitcase bombs deep inside the United Kingdom. Due to the restricted information available to the British public the majority will not know the location of these bunkers, and even if they did they would show little or no interest. So a few of our own would pass unnoticed! Apart from members of the Royal Observer Corps, Police and a few other organisations no one will be really interested.

In addition, as these buildings will be underground, the general attitude of the British will be that they couldn't care less. The majority of these underground bunkers will be in isolated locations in any case. This is where Comrade Shelepin plays his part. The KGB with his vast resources throughout the world, particularly his sleepers will at long last get off their backsides and earn their pay. A sleeper will approach a land owner or his representative informing them that the British Government wish to construct a small underground bunker for use by the Royal Observer Corps. The matter is subject to the Official Secrets Act, so consequently the landowner will be paid in cash for the right to build on his land in order to keep things quiet. There will be very little inconvenience to his land and no unsightly mess. An annual fee will be made to pay a rental for the use of the small area. I think any land owner will be delighted to think he is doing the British tax man one in the eye and will be more than willing to cooperate, never dreaming in a million years that the new bunker will be for Soviet use. Our structures will be less than half the size of the official bunkers but no one will realise. We will ensure there are prominent "Government Property" signs so sightseers will be firmly discouraged.'

At this the Defence Minister resumed his seat leaving the Premier to sum up. 'I am going to repeat myself. This meeting did not take place. There is no record of it. It never happened. No one will discuss it out of this room. We will meet here again in one month precisely 9th February at 1000 hours. A final word before you go your own ways.

For reasons that should now be perfectly clear to every one of you I have decided to call this venture Operation Blindfold.'

No one at this most secret meeting could have foreseen the outcome some fifty years hence. Blindfold was about to place a nuclear device into the murderous talons of the most heartless and effective terrorist organisation of all time. Unwittingly our very own early defence warning system had provided the basis for a new Soviet Battle Plan. The concept was both brilliant and potentially devastating. Operation Blindfold was about to be born.

CHAPTER 3

Wednesday 23rd 1705 hours

'Come on Jeb let's get this lot back to Fluff before he goes home,' ordered Tom.

'Tom, what do you reckon that thing is?' queried Jeb.

'From what I remember it looks like one of those Observer Corps bunkers.'

Little did they realise that the eventual discovery of what was beneath this metal lid was to set in motion a situation as potentially threatening and terrifying as World War Two. Culminating in the largest covert manhunt in British history.

'They used to have, like sheds, on high ground so they could see planes for miles around. Then the Russians were becoming pushy so they decided to build underground bunkers for the Observers in case the Russkies lobbed an atom bomb at them,' explained Tom.

'How do you know about this?' enquired Jeb.

'Don't you remember Basil Marriott poncing about in a RAF uniform saying he was working on secret government business' responded Tom.

'Aye, that's right and that lass from the shop in the Market Place was the same. I remember now. If it had been me it would have been more monkey business in that bunker than government business,' said Jeb. The two friends laughed at the thought of it.

'It goes back to the Cold War days. The Government was worried about a nuclear attack and so prepared for it. How about this tidbit of info – the Government built 1563 of these underground places.'

'You are bulling me now. How would you know that?' asked Jeb disbelievingly.

'Anyway we are here now. Give me a hand with these birds and bring that walkie talkie.' directed Jeb, looking questioningly back at Tom.

'Nah then lads. Did you find many birds?' asked Fluff.

'Better then we thought, but the falling snow made it darker early,' said Tom.

'You've not done badly, though. Here, gimme the walkie-talkie to put on charge.' Both Jeb and Tom, with great difficulty, kept straight faces. If only Fluff knew how many pheasants were stuffed under the seats of the van.

'Ay, we did the best we could Fluff. Anyway see you Monday. Cheers.' Once they were moving in the van the two reprobates burst out laughing.

'Hear that Tom? We've not done bad.' This set the pair off laughing again.

'Go on brains, how do you know how many of these secret places were built,' demanded Jeb. 'There was a series of programmes on the telly about the end of the Cold War. In 1989 George Bush declared 'the Cold War is over' and new words like glasnost and perestroika were the in words. Just after this the Observers were dumped. The Government said they were no longer needed.'

'Clever bugger! How do you remember all this stuff? Or are you making it up.'

'I told you. I watched this series on TV and I thought it was interesting. I remember the bloke saying 1563 of these posts had been built because the last numbers of my phone are 1563. He also said they were built at ten mile intervals.'

'I still don't see how you remember all these things.'

'I'll tell you something else he said.'

'Go on, what?'

'Even today there will be one of these places within a few miles of every person in the UK. So the place we found is very likely to be an old Observer bunker.' Driving into Masham Jeb pulled up outside Tom's house.

'I will pick you up later so we can go back and see what they left for us. Don't forget your birds,' added Jeb.

'Ay, OK if I have to. You know it will be empty so why go back on a night like this?' asked Tom resignedly, but he was talking to himself. Jeb had rattled away. It wasn't exactly a Royal Observer Corps bunker but Tom's suggestion was closer than anyone could imagine.

CHAPTER 4
11th January 2008 Derunta Training Camp, Afghanistan

Derunta was an important training facility. It was initially jointly run by British Intelligence and the American Central Intelligence Agency. They used the facility to help train locals and others opposed to the bad guys in that part of the world. In 1995 the British and Americans decided they had no further use for it. So, ironically enough, they handed it over to the good guys. It just happened that these good guys turned out to be none other than Al Qaeda, meaning 'The Base'. Admittedly not fully appreciating who the new tenants were going to be. Al Qaeda made full use of Derunta to train followers to their cause from all over the world, including America and the United Kingdom. Control of Derunta was passed to one Ibn Cheikh who, as it turned out, was the Libyan leader of Al Qaeda. Meanwhile back in the States President Bush had decided that Muhammar Ghaddafi was now 'a good guy'. To appease the West, after the Lockerbie aircraft crash, Ghaddafi issued an Interpol warrant for the arrest of Osama bin Laden. This was a step ahead of America who had not issued any warrant, Interpol or otherwise. So, Libyan leader Ghaddafi was welcomed into the good guys camp again. Derunta camp was still in use by Al Qaeda. A meeting of high-ranking members was taking place there.

'Our intelligence reports that the Americans now realise exactly what goes on here. That means we can expect some sort of attack at any time,' Mohammed Jamal Khalifa said to Midhat Mursi. Khalifa being a Saudi financier for Al Qaeda and also the brother-in-law of Osama bin Laden. His job to raise the millions of dollars needed to finance their huge terrorist organisation. Not only raise the necessary finances but also to ensure the funds were safely distributed to where they were needed. Much as Osama bin Laden abhorred America and all it stood for, it was the American dollar that made things happen. It is the only currency recognised and accepted the world over, apart from gold. So like it or lump it Al Qaeda was compelled to use American dollars to further the terrorist organisation with its, malignant, spidery tentacles touching every part of the globe.consequently placing Khalifa high on the list of Americas Ten Most Wanted. However, even his position is dwarfed by the reputation and abilities of Midhat Mursi, known also as Abu Kharab al Masri. Out of earshot he is also better known as 'The Mad Bomber of Derunta.' This terrorist has a bounty of five million US dollars on his head, dead or alive. Five million dollars being the going rate for top ranking Al Qaeda terrorists! OBL, himself, is reputed to be valued at anything between twenty five and fifty million dollars. Born in Egypt in 1953 Mursi was head hunted by Al Qaeda for his skills in chemistry and bomb making. Initially Mursi had served a spell in prison suspected of helping plot the assassination of President Anwar Sadat. Although not aligned with Al Qaeda's policy on America, the great US dollar did the trick. Mursi was enrolled into Al Qaeda. For a time he ran the Derunta terrorist camp giving eager recruits hands on instruction in bomb making. He even wrote several handbooks on the subject. However, his forte is designing and trying to obtain weapons of mass destruction. With WMD in their arsenal OBL and his cronies could wreak untold havoc throughout the western world, or any other place frequented by non Muslims. Whilst at Derunta Mursi experimented with methods of delivering cyanide. He frequently exposed dogs and other animals to its effects to determine quantities needed. The final effect, however, always being an excruciating death for the animal or animals involved in his cruel experiments. It is also rumoured than any human transgressors were also incorporated into his testing programme. After all, a real live human made a far better specimen to experiment on than a mere dog. At this line of work Midhat Mursi was not only considered the best, he was the best.

'We know the Americans are aware of what we do here. With our reward money being so tempting I am not sure if we can rely on our presence here being kept secret,' said Mursi to Khalifa.

'Yes, to many of our followers five dollars is a lot of money, never mind five million. I have to be in Algeria very soon to help promote our cause with Al Qaeda in the Islamic Maghreb so the Americans will need to move sharply to catch me here,' replied Khalifa.

'All the same my friend, I intend leaving here shortly. I suggest you do the same. We can never really trust anyone not to betray us to the Americans. Separately we are both worth millions to the west – together it would be a huge blow to our cause and a massive temptation for us to be betrayed.'

'Mohammed, you can count on it. I will be leaving in the early hours. God willing. I have already briefed Ahmed to take over. I instructed him on what training needs to be done and he is most capable. Right now our men are in desperate need of correct small arms training. They need to aim more carefully to conserve ammunition. Far more annoying is their custom of exuberantly firing dozens of rounds into the air at the least provocation. They fail to realise just how much each round costs us. I have stressed to Ahmed that, Insh'allah, he must control this ridiculous and wasteful ritual.' It wasn't as if Al Qaeda needed to join a dole queue yet, but Mursi could not deny his interest in taking good care of the finances. Although not an accountant every penny counted. This was Midhat Mursi's philosophy however wealthy the organisation.

'Ah well, we will see but I will bid you goodnight as I also plan on an early start to Jalalabad.'

'Goodnight my brother! Sleep well and may you travel in safety.' Very early the following morning Mohammed Jamal Khalifa set off on his journey to Libya. Midhat Mursi was leaving shortly after on his way to Algeria. Both of them had breakfasted lightly on succulent dates and fresh camel's milk. These men were wanted worldwide and even in their own countries. Being wanted men their journeys necessitated great care and secrecy. Although Khalifa was a Saudi he was relentlessly hunted throughout the world but nowhere more so than in Saudi Arabia, his country of birth! Large amounts of dollars lubricated their travel routes. Seagoing freighters closing into some remote coast, light aircraft landing at small, private airstrips all requiring many palms to be greased. Despite the huge rewards offered the two men felt relatively secure. Very few people crossed or tried to cross Al Qaeda. Anyone attempting such a foolhardy transgression was dealt with ruthlessly and mercilessly. Any 'traitor' would experience a very long, slow and painful death, but not before he had watched every member of his family being tortured abominably. Their screams would echo as a grim warning to others. For these unfortunates death could not come soon enough. When their lives had eventually expired his turn for a slow and agonising end would follow. Death's icy fingers a very welcome release.

CHAPTER 5

Wednesday 23rd January 2010 hours

After a long soak and a hot meal Tom telephoned Jeb to tell him he was ready.

'OK Tom see you soon. Er, I can't find a hacksaw or anything, can you help?' enquired Jeb.

'Bloody hell Jeb you are hopeless. OK I have one, I'll look it out and also bring some spare blades. Those Chubb locks are a bugger to open.'

Sometime later Jeb's old van rattled slowly up Knowle Lane towards Druids Wood car park. Jeb suddenly braked to a halt.

'Bugger what's up now?' he muttered.

The battery charging light had come on. Taking a torch he climbed out and opened the bonnet. He poked around and was rewarded by spotting a battery lead flapping around. He pushed it back onto the terminal as tightly as he could, with his fingers.

'Come on I'm freezing in these inclement climatic conditions. This van is no bloody good and too bloody cold called out Tom.

'Let's get out of here and get that tin lid opened so you can have a shufti. Then perhaps we can go to the pub.'

'See, there you go again. Bloody long words,' complained Jeb.

Minutes later Jeb drew up at the Temple car park. The pair soon walked the few hundred yards to the Druids Temple. With such a hard frost the ground was like stone so there was no need for rubber boots.

Both men knew the history of the temple. A local philanthropist named William Danby, round about 1770, had decided to provide unemployed men with some meagre income, if only a shilling a day, to erect a mini Stonehenge. Despite knowing this, both of the men shuddered involuntarily as they passed the huge rocks of the henge. Particularly as a dark cloud chose that very moment to blot out the moonlight! Neither one either cared or dared to own up to the fact that he was feeling decidedly apprehensive at being so close to the temple. Even though it was not an ancient monument, with no real history attached it still had a foreboding presence. This was felt during the day, never mind a blustery night in midwinter. Immediately past the temple the duo turned left to climb a small slope. It brought them to the edge of a fir plantation. Jeb's torch flicked on until he spotted the metal cover.

'Here hold this so I can see what I'm doing.' With that he thrust the torch into Tom's hand. He had thoughtfully brought a plastic sack to kneel on. Within seconds Jeb was furiously trying to saw through the hasp of the lock. Tom kept the torch beam on where Jeb was working. After a few minutes a sweat-lathered Jeb stopped and passed the hacksaw to Tom.

'Your turn mate, I'm knackered.'

'These are clean jeans.' protested Tom. Then he knelt on the plastic sack and started to saw at the hasp, muttering under his breath something about anything for a quiet life. Mr Chubb's lock was proving to be very stubborn but some moments later, with blistered fingers and much cursing Jeb's second attempt finally succeeded. Putting the lock to one side Jeb tugged the handle on the lid. To their surprise a well-greased counter-balance helped them raise the lid.

'Go on then Tom, there's some metal rungs. You have the torch, so go down first.'

'Piss off. No way I'm going down there. You found it so you go down. I'll wait here.'

At that moment a loud noise of something crashing through the saplings and getting nearer put Jebs' heart into overdrive. However, the sound diminished away into the night. It was probably a deer or a marauding fox in pursuit of a rabbit. Tom's shoulders were shaking with silent laughter at seeing the startled manner in which Jeb had jumped.

'Very bloody funny,' muttered Jeb as he grabbed the torch and slowly disappeared into the bowels of the earth. Some seconds later.

'Here, look at this lot,' Jeb called up.

Aided by the moonlight and the subdued glow of the torch Tom reluctantly descended into the dimly lit void. Anything to get away from here sooner than later. As his eyes adjusted to the light Tom noticed the chamber was about six by eight feet. It contained a small table, a couple of stools and in one corner what looked like a new chemical closet. He also spotted a light switch. On pushing it, to his further surprise, a small but bright bulb illuminated the small room. Meanwhile Jeb had opened some small metal containers and was taking out packets and placing them on the small table.

Opening them he discovered the packets contained an assortment of biscuits, cigarettes and bars of chocolate, all wrapped in strangely marked wrappers. Other containers held cans, some of which indicated that they held soups, stews and a variety of sweets. Both men looked at each other and without saying a word hastily began to stow various items into their coat pockets.

It was at this point that Tom noticed two larger containers lying alongside one of the walls. There was a carrying handle on top with which he lifted one of the bulky containers off the floor.

'Ere Jeb, shine the light over here.'

Seeing the possibility of more and better goodie's Jeb shone his torch onto one of the metal cases. He lifted one by its carrying handle.

'It's funny? This one isn't a case or a box. It looks like some sort of machine. Look, this other one has a little green light flashing on it.'

'Hold that light over here Jeb. Just there! Shit, I don't know what this is and I don't want to know. I have just realised what that writing is.'

'Go on then what about it?'

'What it is about is the fact that it is Russian.'

'Russian. Don't be daft, what is a Russian thing doing up here?'

'Did you notice how very clean and tidy this place looks? As if it has been tidied fairly recently. Did you also notice the hatch cover was greased and opened easily? Thirdly, this light is also bright, so how is it the batteries have held their charge all this time?' questioned Tom.

'OK. What do they need this place for?' asked Jeb.

'I don't know and I don't want to know. I wonder if we ought to tell someone about it though? Let's go now. Forget this place ever existed and no mention of it to anyone, and I mean anyone, until I have had a good think. There is something definitely odd about the place. I don't like it one little bit.'

With that Tom began climbing from the underground chamber closely followed by Jeb who had paused to grab a few more of the unopened packets.

'What is all the rush about?' grunted Jeb as he hauled himself up the metal ladder.

'There are still a few more boxes to look in. Maybe more fags. We don't want anyone else to know about it. We found it so let's keep it to ourselves.'

'I just don't like it. Why is this place hidden way up here and why is everything in Russian? I don't want to talk about it anymore and those other boxes can stay there as far as I'm concerned. Just let me think about it for a bit. Something very odd about it.'

The two carefully closed the lid and placed the lock in position so that it would appear locked if anyone else stumbled over the cover. The remoteness meant there was virtually no chance of anyone else being up there. They then proceeded to conceal the lid with small branches and twigs.

'We are out of here now. Put that bloody light out, the moon's bright enough.' If anything Tom was even more shaken up on the return journey to the car park than his journey up. All thoughts of the eeriness of the Temple had vanished. This hidden bunker now filled his mind to the exclusion of everything else.

'I'm not going to tell anyone about it Tom. No fears there. I still want to get the rest of that gear out.'

'Jeb, listen. You are not to go back there until I tell you. We don't know what is going on. So stay away. I mean that. OK?'

'OK I'll wait a bit but I don't want some other bugger finding the stuff.'

What on earth was a hidden bunker doing up here? It also appeared to be connected with the Russians somehow. Another question. Who was keeping it in working order?

It was obvious that someone was maintaining the bunker. Charged batteries. The greased lid! The clean state of the chamber. Grateful to be climbing back into Jeb's boneshaker Tom reminded Jeb.

'Remember Jeb, not a bloody word until I have thought about what to do. I know you. Don't do anything stupid like going near that place again until I say so. I mean it. Someone has been up here not too long ago. I fucking mean it Jeb. Stay away.'

CHAPTER 6
Tuesday 9th February 1960, Moscow

'Welcome Comrades to our second, meeting. It is with the deepest regret that I have to inform you of the sudden death of Comrade Igor Kurchatov. He passed away two days ago. His death was due to a blood clot to the brain.' Although Kurchatov headed the Soviet A bomb programme he was totally opposed to Operation Blindfold. Fine to have a nuclear deterrent, even a nuclear retaliatory strike capability. Placing devices, however small, in Britain's backyard did not appeal to him one little bit. Since the first meeting he had, expressed his extreme disapproval to Premier Khrushchev. It was probably not a wise thing to do. Bearing in mind the methods Russia uses to deal with dissenters it seemed incredibly convenient that Kurchatov should suddenly suffer a fatal blood clot to the brain!

'Without his invaluable contribution to the Atomic Bomb programme,' continued Khrushchev.

'Russia would still be struggling to become a nuclear power. He will be accorded the Soviet Union's highest honour and his ashes will be entombed in the Kremlin Wall.' It is a fact of life, or more probably death, that in Russia if you kick over the traces you will find yourself in deep trouble! You are liable to either end up in a Gulag in Siberia or suffer a blood clot to the brain' or a motoring accident. At one time the USSR was a very 'accident prone' place to live. Crocodile tears were included in the package along with the job of members of the Politburo.

'You will also be aware that we are still four in number. For those of you who do not know him I am honoured to introduce Comrade Andrei Sakharov who worked closely with Igor.' With that Khrushchev seated himself at the head of the table, indicating that Sakharov should introduce himself.

'Good morning Comrades! I shall greatly miss Igor's influence and leadership. He was also a very dear personal friend of mine. He taught me much of what I know. He willingly gave advice and encouragement to those under him. However, I am delighted to be invited to join your group. The Premier has outlined what he expects of me. I just hope my limited knowledge will be of some use to your daring scheme.' Sakharov sat. The Premier rose.

'Gentlemen, I fear Comrade Sakharov is being overly modest over what he calls his limited knowledge. He is now our leading nuclear physicist and is currently working on what he calls the Hydrogen or H bomb. If his figures are correct the H bomb will make the A bomb seem like a Chinese firecracker by comparison. I am sure we all wish him well in his research. It goes without saying that this information is of the absolutely highest security category. As with our own purpose for being here, no word of Comrade Sakharov's project is to be discussed out of this room.' History was to utterly disprove Sakharov's attempt at modesty. He led the team that designed the Russian H bomb. Even though it took almost thirty years to perfect. This weapon, when detonated in October 1991, proved to be the world's largest ever explosion. It gave Russia a clear lead over every other nation. Continuing, Khrushchev invited the Chairman of the KGB to enlighten the group as to his progress.

'Gentlemen, during the past month my people have been scouring parts of Europe, but in particular Great Britain, in an attempt to locate suitable sites for our suitcase bombs.In this short time we have identified five locations in England alone.' Still smarting from Khrushchev's withering attack the previous month Shelepin was doing his best to show his organisation, and himself, in a more favourable light.

'My top sleepers in Britain have worked tirelessly to identify suitable sites.Not only have we identified these sites but we are also pursuing builders to carry out the work of constructing the underground bunkers. Potential builders and landowners are being told that these bunkers are subject to The Official Secrets Act. Consequently the entire matter is to be conducted with a high degree of secrecy. I will, of course, be pursuing this with the utmost vigour and will bring you fully up to date at the next meeting.' Cat-with-the-cream face sat down thinking, let Khrushchev pick the bones out of That. Malinovsky rose.

'Comrade Sakharov, I appreciate your newness to this group but can you bring us up to date on the proposed suitcase devices?'

'Certainly, Comrade Minister! I am new, as you say, but I had worked with Igor on this weapon. I am happy to inform you that we have already developed quite a number that will be ready to transport as soon as the bunkers are ready. With the Chairman's permission I can tell you that BEFORE your first meeting we had already produced a number of these suitcase bombs. Comparatively minor modifications were needed to enhance their EMP output. At this moment seven enhanced units are completely ready for use. This matter was not given priority but if necessary we can have a further dozen or so ready within a few weeks.' This information niggled Shelepin but he dare not show it. Much as it griped him he felt he had to congratulate Sakharov. If only for appearance's sake!

'On behalf of myself and the KGB I must offer my sincere congratulations to Comrade Sakharov's team! You have proved most capable already.'

'You are too generous Comrade. We are only trying to do what we can for the Motherland. Let me know when you are ready to take possession of any of these units and we can guarantee delivery. I would add, delivery to a destination in the USSR. It is not part of our task to transport them to the United Kingdom. That, Comrade, is your unenviable task.' With other pressing matters on his agenda Khrushchev called the meeting to a close.

'You have done well Comrade Sakharov. We will meet here in a month's time. I hope by then that the head of my KGB has better news regarding his progress with bringing these American flights to a stop.'

Secretly, no love was lost between Khrushchev and Shelepin and the Premier could not resist his digs at the KGB chief. He could not deny, however, that Shelepin was doing a fine job and would be difficult to replace.

CHAPTER 7

Tuesday 26th January 1960, North Yorkshire

The previous Tuesday a senior British Government official had telephoned to make an appointment with the owner of a particularly large estate in North Yorkshire. It just happened that this Government official was also in the pay of the Soviets.

'I am sorry but the owner is away. I can put you onto Mr Stanton if you like. He is the Estate Manager,' the receptionist told him.

'Thank you young lady you are most kind. That will be ideal.'

'Good morning Stanton here! How may I help you?'

'I was hoping to speak to the owner on behalf of a Government department but I am told he is away. It is quite urgent.'

'If you tell me what it is you wish I can pass it on. I telephone him each evening at six to keep him up to date with things here. He is 'taking the waters' at Cheltenham.'

'We wish to build a small underground bunker. It will be most unobtrusive and well away from everything else. All of this is subject to the Official Secrets Act so should not be discussed with anyone not directly concerned. I assure you it will not be noticed once the shrubbery has recovered. We will also be paying cash to maintain the secrecy. Plus an annual rental. All cash of course.' The official, Soames, had dangled the bait. It was now up to the owner to bite.

'Well, the estate is vast and I am sure the owner would have no objection. I will put it to him this evening. You did say cash didn't you. What amount do you have in mind?'

'We are limited to £2,500 and a yearly rental of £100. You know how the government tends to look after its money,' added Soames.

'That sounds most generous. I am sure the owner will accept.

Particularly as it is a cash transaction and you did say the bunker would not be visible. If you wish I will telephone you in the morning to let you know the decision.'

'Thank you but do not trouble yourself, I will call you tomorrow about ten.'

Promptly at ten the following day the telephone sounded in the receptionist's office. 'Mr Stanton! That nice Mr Soames is on the line.'

'Good morning Mr Soames, you will be delighted to know that the owner has agreed to help the government in any way he can. There are one or two provisos. The estate does not want a lot of people wandering about and we do not want a lot of disruption.'

'Please thank the owner on our behalf. Would it be possible to meet you on Friday morning about this time?' enquired Soames.

'I will be here and perhaps we can drive round the estate to find you a suitable location,' suggested Stanton.

'A drive round would be most helpful. Thank you and I look forward to meeting you on Friday morning,' replied Soames. He had, already, carried out a quiet recce and had already spotted an ideal site. He just had to persuade Stanton to agree.

At exactly one minute to ten on the Friday morning a new Rover pulled into a parking slot outside the Estate Office. A smartly dressed man stepped out carrying a briefcase suitably embossed with a gold crown surmounted over the letters EIIR. Entering the office he approached a small but open sliding window marked reception. A rap on the glass brought a young office girl to the window.

'Good morning, my name is Soames I have an appointment with the Estate Manager.' He beamed at the flustered young girl who had noticed, and been suitably impressed with, the official marking on his briefcase.

'I will take you to his office sir.' With that the girl came out of a side door almost curtseying as she led Soames into the Managers office.

'Good morning Mr Stanton' said Soames, presenting his

impressive business card taking care to return it to his pocket after Stanton had checked it out.

'It is most kind of you to meet me at such short notice. If I may, these are the plans of the small bunker we wish to site on the estate. I must emphasise the necessity for secrecy to be maintained. You will, therefore, also be required to sign a copy of the Official Secrets Act if we decide to go ahead here.'

'Why would you not wish to go ahead?' asked Stanton, concerned about losing out on some additional revenue for the Estate.

'Oh I am sure it will be perfectly suitable. It is merely that the location has to be ideal for our purposes and secrecy is vitally important.'

'I have the Estate Land Rover here if you wish to drive round for a while.'

'Excellent Mr Stanton. I was looking at an ordnance survey map and I have seen what may be the perfect location. Near a spot called the Druids' Temple,' suggested Soames.

'That is a well isolated area and I am positive the Estate would certainly be in agreement with that location,' added Stanton.

Stanton, with Soames beside him drove out of the Estate yard. He had decided to go directly to the Druids' Temple car park. It was well out of the way and if Soames wanted his bunker built there so much the better.

'Here we are Mr Soames. Where do you wish to look?'

'Would you mind if I had a look at the Temple? It sounds so fascinating.'

'Of course not! It is not too far and the ground is frozen so it is not going to be muddy,' advised Stanton. Arriving at the temple site Soames said.

'What an interesting collection of rocks! It must have been a huge task to get them up here. However, to business! I would like to look up this small slope if I may?'

'Certainly. Anywhere here would suit us completely. You go ahead and I will wait here,' answered Stanton.

As Soames had visited the area a week earlier he now confirmed, in his mind, that this was the correct spot for the bunker. It was just over the brow of the small hill. Out of the way of prying eyes and at a good elevation.

Returning to Stanton Soames announced, 'Just at the top of this small hill would be ideal for our purposes. If that is acceptable to you?'

'I could not have picked a better spot. No one goes there except gamekeepers or foresters. They rarely have any reason to be up there. Yes, I will inform the owner.'

'Assuming all is well can we return to your office now to sort a few small details out. If you are completely happy I can also give you the money now. There is one thing I want to point out we would prefer it if none of your estate workers interfered whilst the building is in progress. Once it is complete we would like to put notices up indicating it is Government Property and trespassers will not be allowed.'

'We insist visitors keep to the paths. A number visit the site of the temple and there is a public footpath that passes directly in front of the temple. None of them would have any reason to wander off the track,' said Stanton.

Back at the Estate Office car park Stanton walked inside to organise some coffee whilst Soames sat in the office and opened his briefcase. He smiled nicely at the receptionist as he entered Stanton's office.

'Coffee will be here shortly. Please take a seat. What do we do now?' asked Stanton.

'Well, assuming you are satisfied and you feel the owner will also be satisfied I now give you some money and two documents to sign.'

A tap at the door and in walked the young Shirley carrying a tray with coffee, milk, sugar and biscuits. 'Here you are sir.' Placing the tray on Stanton's tidy desk.

'The boss phoned to tell you he has decided to come home early. He will be up at the house in about ten minutes if you need him for anything.' She was talking to Stanton but could not take her eyes off Soames. Mm, he was such a nice looking man!

'Oh, thank you Shirl. I wonder what prompted him to come home early?' muttered Stanton almost to himself!

When the girl had left and closed the door Soames opened his briefcase. He took out bundles of money and placed them on Stanton's desk.

'Here we go. One thousand, two thousand and here is six hundred. That is the payment of two thousand five hundred plus the first years' rental of a further hundred.

My department is grateful for your assistance and would like you to take this as a token of our goodwill and appreciation for your extra work on our behalf. Soames passed over an envelope containing £50.

'Mr Soames, it really is not necessary but if you are sure?'

Soames waved the protestation aside and Stanton hastily slipped the envelope into his pocket. If you will sign this as a receipt for the money it will keep things straight at my end. There will be no other record of our dealings. So you may find the cash useful for Income Tax purposes…! If the owner is like me he will jump at the chance to do the taxman one in the eye once in a while. Check it if you wish but I can assure you that Her Majesty's Government does not make mistakes when handing out money.'

'I am sure that will not be necessary Mr Soames. If we can not trust a gentleman like yourself who can we trust?' said Stanton picking up the bundles of notes and placing them in his desk drawer.

'Nice to have met you,' said Soames rising,

'It is reassuring to know that we have patriots such as yourself and your employer! I will be up at the temple site with a builder early next week. Please remember, we do not want anyone nosing round. Obviously with exceptions for you and your boss. Oh, one more thing.'

Taking a sheet of paper from his briefcase he placed it in front of Stanton. 'Please sign this here. Remember once it is signed you are subject to the requirements of the Official Secrets Act. I do not need your employer to sign. Your signature will suffice.'

Shaking hands the two men parted company. Soames gave the blushing young girl one of his nicest smiles. His next job was to find a telephone kiosk and confirm the fact that the KGB had just acquired its first underground site in the United Kingdom.

The minute Soames left his office Stanton took out the money and carefully checked each bundle. Once he was satisfied he telephoned his employer. 'Hello sir! Nice to have you back. That Government chap has just left. Sitting on my desk is two thousand six hundred pounds. What would you like me to do with it?'

'That is the sort of news I like to come home to. Put it in a large envelope and have it sent up to the house right away. Did you have any problems with a suitable site for him?'

'None at all sir! Better than we imagined. He picked a place near the temple.'

'Hmm, that is a bit out of the way but if he is happy I am. Send the package up now and help yourself to twenty five pounds. Call it a bonus for your good work.'

Taking out his 'bonus' Stanton thought that today had been one of his better days. A neat £75. I bet the taxman does not hear anything about his employer's bonus either. Just then Shirley walked in through the open door.

'I will take your dirty cups and stuff if you have finished.'

'Yes thank you Shirley! Oh, one other thing. Take this envelope up to the Big House. Here are the keys, you can drive the Land Rover.'

Shirley picked up the brown envelope, almost skipping out of the office. She would probably meet her latest boyfriend who worked up at the Big House. A few minutes slap and tickle during working hours would fit in very nicely!

CHAPTER 8

14th January, Mediterranean Coast off Algeria

Mursi and Khalifa had gone their separate ways from Aleppo. Khalifa had re-boarded the Gulfstream after it had refuelled. Staying low, about two hours later it kissed the tarmac at Sirte on the north Libyan coast. A small strip used primarily by oil company personnel. Unfortunately it still left a good distance to Bejaia, Algeria but there were no suitably safe landing strips nearer. Other arrangements, however, had been made for the rest of the way.

Although Al Qaeda had strong supporters in Libya the Libyan Air Force guarded its air space zealously. Muhammar Ghadaffi was also doing his best to remain in the West's good books so these covert flights were not as welcome as they would have been years earlier.

The moment Khalifa had disembarked the Gulfstream was rolling for takeoff, heading to the north-east into less hostile airspace. A car took Khalifa a few miles along the road to where Khalifa stepped aboard the fast Sunseeker sea going cruiser.

'Welcome my friend. Abdul will show you to your cabin. The weather is good so you will enjoy an easy journey.' Like the Gulfstream, the skipper of the Predator 108, a very fast seagoing motor cruiser wanted to clear Libya's twelve mile limit as soon as possible.

The gentle rocking motion soon had Khalifa snoring heartily until he was woken some hours later by a tapping at his door.

'We will be dropping you off in about thirty minutes. Would you care for something to eat or drink?' asked Abdul.

'No thank you! I prefer nothing until I am ashore but I will come up on deck now.'

'Greetings my brother! It has been a great honour to be of some small assistance to you,' the speaker was the owner/skipper of the fast cruiser!

His usual work was smuggling hashish and other drugs to and fro across the Med. Obviously, in his case, crime did pay. His craft was a Sunseeker Predator 108 with a range close to 500 miles and a book top speed of 42 knots. However, a boat yard in Italy had 'tweaked' the engines and added an additional seven or eight knots. This made it one of the quickest vessels in the Mediterranean. It was easily capable of outrunning any naval or customs boats it might encounter.

'Thanks to Allah the sea has been blessed. It has been calm. I am not a good sailor,' replied Mohammed Khalifa, the AQ financier.

'My tender will land you near the coastal road where you specified. It is a spot a few miles west of Bejaia. You arranged a car to wait there to take you to your destination. I do not know where you wish to go and it is best that way.'

'The movement is grateful for your cooperation. The contents of this envelope will enable you to refill your fuel tanks many times over,' said Khalifa.

'It is not necessary my friend. My crew and I are only too happy to be of service,' replied the skipper, at the same time stuffing the bulky envelope inside his jacket pocket just in case Khalifa took him at his word.

'Prepare the tender for lowering,' ordered the skipper as he eased the throttles back. He could see the occasional lights of a vehicle as it sped along the coast road.

Closing the throttles brought the boat to a halt where it rocked in the gentle swell. The low hum as an electric motor lowered the small inflatable tender at the rear. The lines were freed and Khaaifa stepped gingerly into the little dinghy. He had spurned the offer of a lifejacket but wished he had not.

Whilst the dinghy burbled quietly towards the nearby shore, the skipper tore open the 'unnecessary' envelope. A brief count indicated twenty thousand US dollars. Not bad for a taxi fare but not as good as the drugs runs. Best to keep in with Al Qaeda though. On top of the twenty thousand dollars there was still the thousand kilos of hash he would be delivering in a few hours.

Some twenty minutes later the inflatable gently bumped the stern and was quickly winched out of the water.

'Did our guest find his transport?'

'No problem skipper, it was waiting where we were told it would be.'

'Let's get underway. The rest of you top up the fuel tanks from the barrels on deck. Then throw the empty drums over the side. I will set a course for Almeria to meet Manuel's fishing boat. The sooner we are rid of that cargo the happier I will feel.'

On shore Khalifa stepped through the open door of the car whilst the driver safely stowed his luggage in the boot.

'You know where to go?' Khalifa asked.

'Yes sir, I know Tizi Ouzou well.' It is one of the training camps run by AQLIM. Al Qaeda in the Land of the Islamic Maghreb! The next largest AQ camp after the Middle East. A short drive brought Mohammed Khalifa to the caves where Mokhtar Belmokhtar was waiting to meet him. On 16th January 2013, Belmokhtar would spring to worldwide prominence. He was the leader of a gang of militants responsible for kidnapping over 100 workers of many nationalities from a gas plant in Algeria. They slaughtered over 40 of these workers, several of them, British!

'Allah be praised my brother. Another day in Derunta camp and you would have been killed by the American dogs,' said Mokhtar, head of AQ in Algeria.

'The Americans are confident that I was killed there with Midhat Mursi and other vital members. Allah must have smiled on us enabling us to escape before the raid. It will take the pressure off us a little if they continue to believe we were killed. It is well known the Americans have to kill us many times. Remember that they claimed to have killed Mursi in 2006 with a drone attack or a missile.'

On 13th January 2008, only hours after Mursi, Khalifa and other high ranking leaders had departed, the Americans bombarded

Derunta camp, killing a large number of the terrorists, trainees and instructors still located there. Personal documents were discovered convincing the allies they had managed to eliminate several of Al Qaeda's high-ranking members. Mursi and Khalifa included. Unfortunately for the allies, events proved them to be terribly mistaken. Mursi was about to commit one of Al Qaeda's greatest coups of all time. Nevertheless the camp was out of action for some considerable time for fear of further air raids.

'Do you think some son of a hyena has betrayed you my friend?'

'No, the camp was known to the West before we took over, and in fact was used by the British Secret Service and the American CIA. I believe we were probably observed by American reconnaissance satellites. After all we were experimenting and detonating bombs, even though small, during our research. It was inevitable the authorities would take an interest in us sooner or later! Spy satellites are so sophisticated nowadays that faces can be recognised from a hundred miles or more. Hence our heads remaining covered. You can be sure the Americans are watching us this very moment, but unsure of our identities.'

'We are delighted and honoured to have you enjoy our humble hospitality. You will have seen we have an ample supply of nubile young girls from Mali and Niger to entertain you in any manner you so desire. Treat them as your own and use them as you wish.'

'You are too kind to me Abdullah. I have much to do and little time in which to do it. I must keep moving so as to confuse our enemies. The longer they believe I am dead the better it will be. I need to be in Paris in a few days. Much as I would enjoy the pleasure of your girls I regret I have too much work to do to allow them to distract me.'

Obviously Mokhtar was not aware that Mohammed Khalifa, and Midhat Mursi were more interested in young boys than nubile young girls. Khalifa loved nothing more than breaking in young boys. In any case his business here would be completed within a day and work was more important to him right now. Paris was next on his agenda and then the United Kingdom. Getting into France was not too difficult and once there entry to Great Britain was a doddle with their virtually non-existent immigration controls. Mursi had enjoyed a relaxed journey all the way to Calais.

Khalifa had flown out of Islamabad, on the first leg of his journey, in a Gulfstream IV! To the rest of the world Afghanistan appeared to be working hard to rid the country of terrorists and any association with them. However, all the time Mursi was residing there, with his family, next to an army barracks! As was OBL himself.

There are always officials and others looking for an extra dollar. A greased palm or two ensured the Gulfstream flew in and out with only cursory checks being made.

The luxurious jet touched down at Aleppo in Syria. Again, there was no hassle of any description. From here Khalifa travelled by taxi and train all the way to Calais without the slightest hitch. He chose rail because he was never entirely happy flying and the sleeper trains meant he was well rested when he reached Calais.

Both Mursi and Khalifa had 'British' passports and spoke very good English so they never had trouble entering and leaving the UK, as a rule.

On the ferry from Calais, for some reason Mursi felt very apprehensive. He had used this passport many times without a hitch. He had no cause to be uneasy yet he was. A voice announced, over the tannoy, that they were approaching Dover and passengers with cars should return to their vehicles. The ferry slowly edged in and was swiftly moored. As Mursi joined the throng ready to disembark, a young woman was having difficulty controlling three lively youngsters. One little girl appeared uncontrollable and despite her mother's shouting totally refused to do as she was told. With his maximum charm Mursi saw his opportunity. Lifting the little girl he smiled nicely at the young mother.

'They can be such a handful at this age. My young ones are just the same.'

His smile and manner put the mother immediately at ease.

'She can be a right little madam when she wants to be and in this crowd I am afraid she will get lost or crushed,' answered the harassed mother.

'She is fine now. I will carry her if you wish. See, she is perfectly happy with me.'

'You are so kind. Would you mind carrying her until we get safely ashore! My husband will be there to meet me.'

'It is a pleasure madam. She is as good as gold now.'

Indeed she was. Mursi's charm worked on everyone. The little girl was smiling into his face as if he was her best friend in the whole world.

Although the little girl had quietened down she suddenly let out a yell and burst into tears again and struggled violently. Not surprising really when you consider Mursi had administered quite a nasty pinch to the back of her legs. Approaching passport control Mursi held up his UK passport with the little girl wriggling and crying. Playing the long-suffering father, Mursi held her so that she also shielded his face.

He was waved through with the passport officer looking sympathetic. Little children could be a real pain at times. Once through, Mursi visibly relaxed. As expected, it had been so very, very easy.

'Thank you! I do appreciate that. She will be fine now,' said the grateful mother.

'Think nothing of it. She is a lovely little child and I can see she gets her good looks from you. Are you sure you can manage?'

'Yes, thank you so much. I can see my husband now.'

Mursi smiled farewell and lowered the young child to the ground and walked confidently out of the port, the little girl glowering at his back.

He immediately spotted the car that had come to collect him. Recognising the face of the driver.

'Hello, my brother! Did you have a good journey?' asked Ahmed.

'Yes, it went perfectly. No trouble at all.'

'Did I not see you carrying a small child?' enquired Ahmed.'

'That child, Ahmed, was better than any passport. That child ensured my safe passage through customs and immigration.'

With no further explanation Mursi entered the car and they set off to London.

Ahmed was left puzzling how a troublesome child could be better than a passport.

CHAPTER 9
20th January 1963, London

I do not know if there is a collective name for a bunch of spies, perhaps a Cloak of Spies might be an apt title. However, some years back a group known as the Cambridge Five were unmasked.

'Nick, thank you for coming so promptly.'

'A pleasure Chief! Why all the urgency?'

The Chief being none other than the Head of MI6! Known generally as "C".

'You are going on a short holiday. To Beirut! I am now convinced Blake was spot on. You are to bring Russell back to the UK. Don't tell him why but phone him to make the arrangements to meet him.'

Harold Adrian Russell was undoubtedly better known by his code name. Kim Philby. He was soon to be proved the man responsible for the deaths of more British Secret Intelligence Service agents than any man before or after. The name derived from Rudyard Kipling's book Kim, about a young Indian boy who spied for the British. In Philby's case it was the other way round. He spied for the Russians.

'Nick, I appreciate Russell is a good friend of yours but you are the only man he would trust to meet. Sorry and all that but I want that bastard so badly it hurts!'

'WAS a friend. If you recall I sat in with some of the sessions with George Blake. I did not want to believe him but it all checked out. It will give me the greatest pleasure to bring him in. Just on the offchance he does not wish to return…?'

'I'd prefer him undamaged in order to learn who his contacts are but I would not be unduly concerned if he met with an unfortunate accident.'

Although suspected, and questioned at the time that Burgess and

MacLean were, some years earlier Philby convinced his masters he was not involved. Because of this he continued to work for SIS and was ultimately responsible for the untimely deaths of a large number of British and allied agents.

In 1956 he was posted to Beirut as a correspondent for The Observer and The Economist. Amazingly he continued to work for SIS!

A telephone call was put through from London to the offices of the Observer in Beirut. The switchboard operator put the call through to Philby's office. Fortunately he was sitting at his desk busily putting the finishing touches to a story he was working on.

'Hello Kim, this is Nicolas Elliott. I will be in Beirut in a couple of days and wonder if we could meet up for a drink?'

'Hello Nick, it is a bad line but yes I'd be delighted to meet you old chap. When did you say you would be here?'

'Great Kim! I expect to fly in on the 21st and should be there about 10pm local time but you know how unpredictable these airlines are.'

'Fine Nick, telex me the details and I will arrange for a car to meet you at the airport.'

'Excellent, Kim, look forward to meeting you. The fax is being sent at this very moment confirming my flight details. I am booked in to The Al Bustan.' The Al Bustan being Beirut's newest hotel. The name means garden' in Arabic.

Two days later Elliot's aircraft touched down at Beirut International, only forty-five minutes behind schedule As good as his word, Philby had a car waiting at the airport. Elliott was whisked from the airport to the Al Bustan and settled in for the remainder of the night. The driver had assured Philby that he would let him know when Elliott had arrived safely.

CHAPTER 10
Monday 22th February 1960, Druids' Temple

'Rightho, this is the spot. Remember to be careful and not make too much mess or noise. I do not want any hassle from the Estate Office.' Soames was issuing orders to Walter Wiseman, the building contractor.

'Make sure your men do not fool around the Temple site. Above all, remember this work is subject to the Official Secrets Act. If you want further contracts keep this to yourself and the same goes for your workmen as well. If I hear a whisper about this you will never do another single job for the Government, this includes Council work as well.'

Considering Soames was, in reality, a high ranking KGB officer, it was unlikely the Soviet Union would have any further need of this contractor. Any British Government work coming the way of Wiseman would be sheer coincidence.

'Don't worry about us sir. We have done a few jobs for the Government at places like RAF Leeming and the army camp at Catterick, and know how to keep our mouths shut,' explained Walt Wiseman the main contractor.

'Just make sure you do. I will inform the Estate Office that work has started. Phone me when you are about half way done so that I can check all is as it should be. Everything has to be is in line with the specifications.'

With that Soames drove down to the office to meet Stanton.

'Good morning. It is Shirley isn't it,' stated Soames.

'Yes sir! Mr Stanton is in his office if you want to see him,' said Shirley, fiercely blushing. Delighted that such an important visitor had remembered her name. He was so good looking and polite. Just like that film star David Niven.

42

'Thank you, I hope he is not too busy.' Soames gently pushed the estate manager's door open and stuck his head round it.

'Hello Mr Stanton! Am I interrupting anything?'

'Not at all Mr Soames! Nice to see you again! Is there anything I can do for you?'

'I have just been up to the site with the building contractor. A local man called Wiseman. I wanted you to know he will be starting work this week. Please remember we need to keep this quiet. Did you ask your estate workers to stay well away?'

'I certainly did. The only people I am allowing up there are the foresters, naturally, and the gamekeepers to keep an eye on their birds. They have been instructed not to go any nearer than is necessary.'

'Thank you Mr Stanton! It really is important to keep this under your hat. If word got out we would have to abandon the project. You know what Government departments are like. They may even want some of their money back.'

'Rest assured! The workers will not say a word. They value their jobs too much.'

'I am delighted to hear that. I will be on my way now but I will keep in touch with you to let you know how work is progressing. It should not take long at all and Wiseman has been told to cause as little disruption as possible. Good afternoon.'

With that Soames left, not forgetting the receptionist. He was fully aware of the effect he had on the young girl.

'Bye Shirley! See you again soon I hope.' He gave her an exceptionally nice smile.

'Goodbye sir, I hope so,' said Shirley, almost wetting her pants in pleasure.

Monday 7th April 1960

Following up on Wiseman's telephone call the previous Friday, Soames met the contractor on site where he inspected the finished article.

'You have done well Mr Wiseman. You completed the work ahead of schedule and it looks to be very well constructed. In addition I am happy to see that there is little evidence of any disturbance. The grass and shrubbery will quickly recover to mask any wheel tracks or other marks on the ground. As agreed here is your money, in cash. You will find it correct with a small bonus for doing the job so promptly. I do hope I do not have need to call you back if I find any faults.'

Wiseman greedily stuffed the envelope into his overcoat pocket. 'Nice to do business with you sir! Everything is in perfect order. You will not need to call me back to put anything right. I always do a good job. Anything else and you know where I am. Here are the keys to the manhole cover.'

'I take it these are the ONLY keys. You do not happen to have held onto one.'

'No sir. I don't work like that. I do a good job at a fair price and ensure I stay in my client's good books in the hope of future contracts,' protested Wiseman.

'Very well, nice to do business. You can be sure I will contact you if we have other suitable jobs for you.'

Later that day a priority signal left 13 Kensington Palace Gardens, London, home of The Russian Embassy! It was directed to KGB HQ Moscow. Soames first bunker was ready for the devices to be delivered, together with a supply of provisions in the event someone might have to remain concealed in the bunker for some time.

'A priority signal for you Chairman Shelepin.' So saying a cipher clerk handed a sheet of paper to the head of the KGB.

'I will wait should you wish to reply.'

Scanning the sheet Shelepin let out a whoop of delight. 'Yes, wonderful news! Just the thing. Take a signal.

'Congratulations. Well done indeed,' sign my name.

Wait until Khrushchev saw this signal. It proved beyond any doubt that the KGB were on the ball. The first bunker completed well ahead of schedule.

CHAPTER 11
22nd January 1963, Beirut

'Good morning, this is Nick Elliott, would you put me through to Mr Philby please?'

The operator in The Observer office quickly located Philby. 'Mr Philby, I have a Mr Nicolas Elliott on the line.'

'Thank you Jennifer, please put him through immediately. I was expecting him to call.'

Jenny Powick was The Observer's highly efficient and stunning maid of all trades. Telephonist, typist, secretary and even would be reporter when the newspaper was pushed. Jenny could be relied on for anything, 'Nice to hear your voice Nick! Hope you had a good trip.'

'Tiring, but a good night's sleep and I'm full of the joys of spring. Or would be if it wasn't for the fact it is still winter. Thank you for sending the car. It saved me battling it out with the taxi drivers. I wonder, Kim, if you are free could you meet me in my room around ten this morning. I have a few things I need to discuss with you. Room 55. Come straight up.'

'Be delighted to meet you to catch up with what has been happening in London. I am not too busy so could be there for ten or just after. What do you need to discuss?'

'Best not to say too much on the phone, they have more people listening in than there are whores along The Gut in Malta. Nothing too serious! Just a general chat in the hope that you can throw some light on a problem or two over here.'

They closed the call and Philby strolled into Jennifer's office, telling her he would be tied up for a couple of hours. Telling her where he would be and which room number he would be in if there were any really important calls for him.

When he offered to give her the hotel telephone number she pointed to a gleaming picture postcard sent by the management of the Al Bustan, with the telephone number prominently displayed. Miss Efficiency, as usual!

'Fine, will you call me a taxi please and let me know when it arrives?'

'OK Mr Philby' replied Jenny.

The forthcoming meeting was causing Philby some concern. An itch in the back of his neck usually forewarned him of any trouble. This morning the itch was in overdrive! He just KNEW something was wrong. He had always been ultra careful to cover his tracks and, so far, had talked himself out of a few potentially serious close shaves. Every time, that is, so far.

Sending Nick Elliott, however, set the alarm bells jangling, despite the fact that he had been friendly with him for a long time. Nick was important in British Intelligence and he did not travel around the world just for a chat. Something was definitely boding ill for Philby.

Arriving at the hotel Philby decided to use the stairs instead of the lift to Elliott's room. It allowed him the luxury of a few more moments to mull over in his mind what he felt sure was coming and to slow down his racing heart.

At his knock, Nick opened the door to invite Philby in. 'You are looking well Kim. All this sunshine must be doing you the world of good. Come on in. What can I get you to drink?'

'A cold beer would go down well. You look pretty good yourself. So what is the meeting in aid of?' No preamble. Philby wanted to know what was going on.

Taking a beer from the minibar in his room Nick removed the cap and handed the bottle to Philby. Elliott selected a miniature whisky and poured it into a crystal glass. 'You want a glass or will the bottle do?'

'A glass please Nick. We have to keep our standards up. Can't let the side down, can we now?'

'No, we Brits set the standard for the rest of the world to follow. Thanks for coming. Grab a chair and we will get on with our little chat. Actually, it concerns George Blake who came over to us recently! I am sure you remember all about that, however. He has been singing like the proverbial. So far it is checking out to be solid gold. Top quality information. He has also hinted, very strongly, that you are overfriendly with several Russian Cultural Attaches in various parts of the world?'

In fact Blake had not hinted. He had made it very clear with dates, times and places. Although Philby and Nick went back quite a way, this time Elliott knew he could not save his friend. Blake had hammered enough nails into his coffin to ensure Philby went down at long last.

'Of course I am. That is part of my job. It is what you pay me for.'

'Let me finish please, Kim. Blake is saying it is possibly more than friendship. If you follow my drift.' Taking a sip of his whisky, Elliott let Philby take this on board.

'Our people feel it would be better if you returned to London. Just to put your side and clarify the situation.'

'Is it really necessary to return to London just for that? Surely you must realise there is not a grain of truth in what he says. There is something else. Right now, I am on the verge of something big. Ivan Bulganin is considering coming over to us.'

'Bulganin?' exclaimed Nick in amazement.

'He'd never.'

Philby had prepared this story for such an eventuality. He was hoping to buy time.

'It is because of Blake. Bulganin has been hearing how regally Blake is being feted and fancies some similar treatment for himself. He is turning it over in his mind. In addition, if he does jump to us, and this sounds to be very important, he claims to have information about something very big called Operation Blindfold. He will not say further until he knows we will take him and that he is assured certain guarantees. I did not inform London as I was not certain! I need just two or three more days. Will you contact London and get the OK. three days at the most then I'll head straight for London.'

Philby did not know what Operation Blindfold involved but he had been consulted about the Royal Observer Corps building programme and asked to recommend sites near to Military and Government communications. The only thing he knew was the name.

'What is this Operation Blindfold about? The West has not heard a whisper about Operation Blindfold. Are you sure he is not merely trying to bull you?'

'He would not say, except that is it something extremely sensitive and could prove catastrophic to the West. It must be extremely important. It is claimed to have been Russia's best kept secret for almost four years. He is 99 per cent certain that he wishes to defect, but he needs various guarantees and full protection. When, and if he does defect, you may be able to extract more information from him then. He insists he will only deal through me, personally.'

'Very well! See if you can convince Bulganin. In the meantime, no promises but I'll put your proposal to London.This, so called Operation Blindfold. You have to find out if it is merely Bulganin trying to emphasise his usefulness to us or is it a genuine threat. If so we need to know exactly what it is all about. It in unbelievable that we, in the West, have never heard a dicky bird about any such thing as Blindfold! Bulganin would, indeed, be a feather in your cap if you could pull off his defection. I will contact you as soon as I have some news. In the meantime, as they say, don't leave town.'

If there was, in fact, something known to the Reds as Operation Blindfold this was the very first SIS had heard about it. Elliott and British Intelligence had realised at long last that Philby had been fooling them for God knows how long. Elliott now wondered if this was another of Philby's red herrings or the genuine article.Chuckling at his humour but said with more than a hint of steel Elliott knocked his whisky back. The words, however, sent a chill down Philby's spine. Seeing Philby had hardly touched his drink he asked if he could get him something else instead.

'No thank you Nick! I'll be getting along and see if I can pin Bulganin down to make a decision one way or the other. I think, in view of what you just told me, that it is vital that I get things moving as quickly as possible. I'll let you know soonest. I want to get this settled so I can return to London and clear my name.'

In fact Bulganin would have been shocked at the idea that anyone could ever consider the possibility of him defecting. Bulganin was a dyed in the wool communist through and through. In addition, Bulganin had not heard of Operation Blindfold either. The suggestion, however, did buy Philby valuable breathing space. Nick had decided to allow his old friend a little leeway. Taking his leave Philby decided to use the lift. He entered a phone booth in the hotel lobby and dialled a number. After only one ring it was answered.

'I need a taxi, urgently. I am at the Al Bustan!'

CHAPTER 12

25th January, London

'Salaam aleikum Midhat Mursi and welcome to London. Did you have a good journey?' With that Mahasheer jumped up flinging his arms round Mursi and kissing him three times on the cheeks as Arabs do.Mursi's driver had taken him directly to the mosque. He had changed from a suit to full Arab dress on the way up in the car from Dover, the headgear adding the finishing touches to his disguise. Their destination was, the now named North London Central mosque. Three years earlier it had been known as Finsbury Park Mosque. However, following police raids where forged passports, CS gas canisters, guns and knives had been found, the new management thought a fresh name and image was called for.

The new management were now doing their best to create harmony and understanding and repair their hugely damaged reputation. Abu Hamza, or 'The Hook' formerly in charge of the mosque had, eventually, been arrested for his extremism. Inevitably, Al Qaeda agents, unknown to the New Order, continued to frequent the mosque. Over the years the attendance had tripled with cafes and shops in nearby Blackstock Road providing an attraction for many of the Muslims.

'Thank you Karim, my brother! The honour is all mine in meeting you again after all this time. How is your new daughter, Ameerah the Princess? I believe she must be almost a year old now?'

Mursi was well served by an efficient staff. They made sure he knew all the personal details of anyone he was meeting. It was good for 'business relations'. Unknown to Karim and others like him, Midhat Mursi could not have given a toss about Karim or his little Princess. Mursi was a user of people. He found that it worked to show concern and interest in any underlings. After all it did not put him out in any way. His staff officer did all the research to arm Mursi with so much personal knowledge. Consequently his contacts worshipped him for showing so much 'interest and concern'. Most would willingly have laid down their life for him. After all, as we all know, such concern was good for 'business relations'.

'You have a fine memory Midhat. Thank you, all my family is doing well and, yes, Ameerah is doing very well.' *Ameerah* being the Arabic word for Princess.

'She is just a year old. Much as you honour us with your presence, I fear you will have to move on very soon. British Intelligence covertly photograph every single visitor here.We have a nice flat nearby. Fortunately you kept your face concealed with your ghutra so they will not have much to go on.'

'Alas you are correct Karim but I need to remain in the UK for a little longer as I have important contacts to meet in the north. What arrangements have been made for my stay?'

'It has all been arranged. We have an Arab mother, with a young son, who will be your readymade family for the remainder of your stay. She will be well paid and will be pleased to have the money as her husband was killed a month ago in a car accident.' Mahasheer continued, 'I received your message stating you had meetings in the north. Accommodation has been booked for you in a pleasant hotel called Stone House just outside the small market town of Hawes in North Yorkshire. You will be on holiday as a family. Even during the winter, the Dales are popular with tourists. Wensleydale probably more than many of the other Dales! In addition, other Arabs, Italians, French and so on are also staying in the area for game shooting, so you will not stand out by being a foreigner. Also your spoken English is excellent.'

'Is the woman reliable and able to carry off the fact that she is supposed to be my wife?'

'The lady is a teacher, presently on compassionate leave. She is attractive, and highly intelligent. You need not worry about her ability.

51

She will carry out the usual wifely duties and is prepared to sleep with you to ensure the ruse is totally successful.'

'Karim, tell the lady that we will sleep in the same room but her virtue will not be marred by my demands. All that I require of her is that she does what she is paid for without arousing any suspicions. Anywhere.'

'As you wish Midhat. Another identity has been prepared for you. I have a Kuwaiti passport and Kuwaiti driving licence for you in the name of Hamid Al Fadhil. Your car will be a Ford Mondeo which will not draw undue attention to you.'

'Your organising ability is excellent, as always. I thank you Karim. One last question! When do we leave for this place Hawes, wherever it is?'

'You will remain in London this evening. Someone will show you to your flat. We will take you to meet your 'wife and son' first thing tomorrow. She is already packed and you are advised to leave as soon as possible. Your room is booked for one week. If you need more time you will have to arrange it. Finally, this envelope contains five thousand pounds in British notes. Do not draw attention to yourself by being overly generous when tipping. Waiters and similar are usually given a few pounds tip. Certainly not more than £5! In the Dales word would get round about a wealthy Arab and you do not want to stand out unduly.'

Having no further questions and beginning to feel very drowsy Mursi was driven the short distance to his flat where he was pleased to sink into a soft bed where sleep quickly overtook him.

Mursi's sole aim in life was to develop weapons of mass destruction. Hoping to bring about the slaughter of hundreds if not thousands. Despite this, Mursi, like other monsters before him slept, the sleep of the innocent.

Chapter 13
22nd January 1963, Beirut, noon

Waiting for the taxi Philby walked nervously up and down, outside the Al Bustan, trying to marshal his thoughts. A typical battered and rattling yellow and black taxi drew up alongside him, the bodywork belying the fact that the engine and suspension were in tip top condition.

'Your taxi sir!'

Climbing in, Philby smiled with undisguised relief on recognising the passenger in the rear of the taxi. 'Ivan Ivanovich! Good of you to come so quickly.'

'What has prompted you to use the emergency number, my friend?'

'London has sent someone to question me regarding my association with members of the Russian Embassy. Blake is singing like a canary. He has mentioned my name. So far I have no idea what he has said but I have been recalled. It is only a matter of time before they arrest me. I need to get out now.'

'Stay close to your office, I will make all the arrangements. Above all carry on as normal! Do NOT pack anything when you are given instructions to leave. Not even your passport. Remember! Carry nothing that will arouse suspicion. You can be sure the British will be watching you from now on!'

The taxi lurched to a halt outside The Observer offices and Philby climbed out, giving a last pleading glance at the Russian KGB man.Bracing himself he strode into the Observer building trying to appear confident and sure. Outside he seemed calm but his insides were churning away in turmoil.

'A couple of calls for you Mr Philby,' called out Jenny, 'but nothing important. I have left the details on your pad. Oh and don't forget the expat party this evening.'

'Thank you Jenny! I think I'll give the party a miss. I don't fancy a boozy night with a room full of puking oilmen.'

In the meantime a hasty radio signal was being beamed to a Russian freighter, the Dolmatova, some hundred miles away in the Mediterranean. Due to visit Alexandria and then Beirut. The Captain was instructed to make all speed for Beirut first. He was asked for an accurate estimate of his arrival time there.

At the same time the signal was sent to the Russian freighter a high priority coded signal was being sent from the British Embassy in Beirut to SIS Headquarters in London. London quickly signalled Elliott to allow Philby not three days but two days grace. However, he was to be very closely followed and watched round the clock without him noticing. The slightest suspicion that Philby was up to no good and the Beirut Desk had orders to lift Philby immediately and get him back to London under close escort.

Quite often the Secret Service is accused of acting either too late, not at all, or in a slip-shod manner. On this occasion they were right on the ball. Elliott had already given instructions for a team to cover Philby the moment he left the hotel, even before he had received the reply from SIS, London. If he was up to no good they would soon know and might even manage to identify his contacts.

'Mr Philby, a Mr Elliott on the phone,' Jenny announced.

'Hello Nick. Just caught me, I was about to leave for home. What can I do for you?'

'Kim, London have authorised you a further two days. I am sorry, that is all I could swing. They did tell me to assure you that there is nothing for you to worry about. It is mainly for you to clear up your side of things. I vouched for you. I am sure I know you well enough after all this time,' Inside, Elliott was thinking we will soon have you, you treacherous lying bastard. Your time is running out, and fast.

54

'I could have done with the three days. I have not been able to contact Bulganin yet.'

Resignedly Philby added, 'OK, two days it is. See you soon bye Nick.'

He locked his desk and was preparing to go home when his phone rang again. He was on the point of ignoring it, thinking it might be Elliott, but decided to see what he wanted if it was him. Jenny had already gone home, rerouting the phone before leaving.

'Mr Philby? The taxi you ordered will be outside in five minutes,' a man's voice said.

Catching on, immediately, 'Thank you, I will be right down.' It was customary for him to walk home so the taxi could only be from his Russian friends.

'Night Mr Philby,' called out the night porter.

'Goodnight. I hope you have a quiet night.'

Stepping into the bright sunlight Philby walked casually up to the only taxi at the kerbside and climbed in.

'I will drive you home Mr Philby. Listen carefully. You will be going to the expat party this evening.'

'Oh, I was going to give it a miss. They are usually excuses for a booze up and invariably fights start.' said Philby.

'Mr Philby, listen! You will go to the party and make out you are drinking a lot of vodka. Make sure it is mostly water. You are to act drunk and be in your apartment by eleven this evening. You MUST look convincingly drunk. Once in your apartment do your usual toilet activities. It would help if you could make out you are vomiting. Put your bedroom light on and after about ten minutes switch it off as if you were going to bed. Without switching on any lights get dressed and leave by the rear entrance at precisely eleven-thirty. Someone will be waiting there to guide you to the docks. We are getting you out tonight. Have you got all this?'

'Tonight is it? That is marvellous.'

'Mr Philby,' said the driver raising his voice.

'I said have you taken all that information on board?'

'Er, yes I have. Go to the party. Home by eleven and meet your man outside at eleven thirty, whilst playing the drunk. Yes, got it thank you.' The taxi pulled up outside his apartment and Philby was about to walk away.

'Sir, your fare please.'

Philby pulled a few notes from his pocket and handed them to the driver.

'Mr Philby. That was extremely careless,' hissed the driver through clenched teeth.

At eight Philby called a genuine taxi to take him to the small hotel where the function was already well under way. Remembering his instructions he helped himself to a measure of vodka that he promptly diluted with water, allowing the glass to overflow onto the sopping table top. He circulated to chat with the few people he knew, making certain he was seen to be knocking the vodka back and becoming, apparently, increasingly drunk. He staggered down to reception and had them call him a taxi. The taxi dropped him outside his apartment at about ten forty. Maintaining his drunk act Philby threw a handful of notes into the taxi.

He looked amazingly convincing as he entered his apartment. Two steps back or sideways and three forwards!

22nd January, 2255 hours

'Bloody hell look at that. I would not like to be his head in the morning.' George and Peter had been tailing all evening. They had not been spotted. They were both experts and it would take an exceptionally alert man to realise he was being tailed by this pair.

'I'd better call the boss. Keep him in the picture.' Pressing the transmit button of his transceiver which was answered immediately by Nick Elliott.

'Mr Elliott! Nothing out of the ordinary! Philby has been to a party for British expats. He had a tankful and had to be almost carried home. There will be nothing from him for some time.'

'Thank you George! But drunk or not, two of you are two remain there all night. Stay awake, he is a crafty bugger. At six in the morning I want the team up to four people again.'

'Understood sir. Goodnight,' replied George, laying the radio at his side.

'Bloody suit from London! Shitting himself in case we lose Philby. Little chance of that after the state he was in. I can't see him coming round until lunchtime. That is us stuck on the graveyard shift.' George complained to his colleague, Peter, as they settled down in the car for the rest of the shift.

'We will take it in turns to doze. I'll do the first two hours awake.'

'George.'

'What's up now?'

'Do you know where the term graveyard shift came from?'

'No, but I'm sure you are going to tell me. Just remember it is your sleeping time you are eating into.'

'Hundreds of years back graveyards were filling up. So, the church authorities agreed to dig old coffins up. Send the bones to somewhere suitable.'

'Battersea Dogs Home wouldn't say no to a few old bones.'

Ignoring George's attempt at humour Peter, was not to be deterred. 'They would replace the bones with recent bodies. But when they opened some of the coffins they noticed scratch marks inside some of the lids. Obviously the person had been buried alive.'

Continuing the morbid tale Peter went on. 'After that when a person was buried a piece of string was tied round his wrist that led to a bell above ground. This, of course, is where the phrase 'dead ringer' originates. Anyway someone had to sit all through the night to listen for the bell. That person did the graveyard shift.'

With a smug look on his face Peter sat back smiling to himself.

'Peter,' said George.

'Yes mate what?'

'Fucking shut up. You now have an hour and fifty minutes left.'

With a hurt look Peter turned on his side and tried to get some sleep. Not helped by the fact that as soon as he dozed off the gear lever kept sticking up his arse. Well, he assumed it was the gear lever. He was sure George was not that way inclined.

However, both Peter and George would not have felt so relaxed had they noticed how quickly Philby had sobered up. Philby had done a first class job with what everyone believed was vodka. He had followed his instructions and was drinking nothing stronger than mineral water.

Around midnight the Dolmatova glided alongside the docks in Beirut to be unloaded. The unloading was done quickly and haphazardly with the dockworkers threatening to strike if the Russian seamen did not slow down. Ignoring them the Russians simply carried on and offloaded the ship's cargo onto the dockside. The cargo should have guaranteed the dockers a good eight hours work. It was done in less than three, much to the chagrin of the disgruntled dockworkers!

Philby left the apartment block quietly by the rear door, adjusting his eyes to the darkness.

'Mr Philby. Come with me please. Ivan wishes to speak with you before you leave' It was his former taxi driver associate. He led Philby along a darkened street to where his taxi was parked. The pair entered the taxi, which drove to the suburbs on the outskirts of Beirut. They stopped in the drive of a pleasant detached house.

'This way please,' the driver escorted him through a side door, along a passageway into a sumptuously decorated room where Ivan Ivanovich greeted him with a lead crystal glass of Russia's best.

'All is ready Kim. Soon you will be on your way to Moscow.'

'Thank you Ivan! I appreciate you moving so quickly to move me out of Beirut. I am sure that my people would have pulled me in later today.'

'They are no longer 'your people' Kim, but I know what you mean. Drink up and we will take you to the ship. You will not be noticed in the hustle and bustle. Put these clothes on so you look like a docker. Speak to no one and follow me up the gangplank and straight onto the vessel.'

Stepping into the clothes Philby knocked back his vodka. He was eager to be on his way now that the decision had been finally made. The three left in the taxi encountering no hold ups or checks to draw up alongside the Dolmatova. They were not noticed due to the frenzied activity with the offloading of the cargo.

The argument between the dockworkers and the shipping agents was still in full flow. Ivanovich stepped confidently up the gangplank, closely followed by Philby and they made their way to the captain's cabin.

'Captain, this is Comrade Philby. Please take good care of him, he is probably the most valuable cargo you have ever carried' announced Ivanovich.

'Welcome, Comrade. I have prepared a cabin for you. If you need anything please ask my steward. Do not go on deck until I inform you that we are well clear. I have work to do so will leave you.'

During the early hours of the 23rd of January 1963 the Dolmatova quietly slipped her moorings. Like some grey wraith she slowly faded into the night, unnoticed by the few remaining dockworkers. Curled up, in a comfortable cabin, Kim Philby was already sound asleep. Comforted in the knowledge that every turn of the propellers thrust him that bit closer to Russia and safety.

Operation Blindfold was to remain a secret for many years to come.

A little before noon the same day, Ivanovich had arranged for a car to collect 'Philby' from the front of his apartment. The KGB were making doubly sure that Philby had made a clean getaway by tossing this red herring to the British agents. The car drove steadily north followed by the four SIS officers. It eventually drew onto the forecourt of a roadside café. As the passenger stepped from the car he looked directly at the men in the SIS car and grinned broadly at them. Very clearly this man was not Kim Philby! The same suit, hat and general appearance had worked. The KGB had well and truly duped Britain's best.

On March 3rd 1963 the Soviet Union announced that Political Asylum had been granted to Kim Philby!

CHAPTER 14
Saturday 26th January

Mahasheer had obtained a car for Mursi and called round at his flat to take him to meet his ready made family. Hanan was ready and waiting as Mahasheer pulled up with Mursi.

'Hanan I would like to introduce you to Hamid al Fadhil. You must remember to use that name at all times. Hamid this is Hanan your new wife.'

'I am delighted to meet you. Thank you for being so kind as to help me out. I am so sorry to hear of your recent bereavement. And this must be your son Eid. I do hope this is not too great an imposition on you at this difficult time.'

'I am pleased to do something to take my mind off things and a break will do me the world of good. Little Eid misses his father terribly.'

'I will leave you two to get on your way and hope to see you on your return. I can walk from here, it is not far and the exercise will do me some good,' said Mahasheer, patting his ample stomach.

'Thank you for what you have done for me Karim. We will return as soon as my work is done. May I help you with your luggage Hanan?' asked Mursi. Ever the charmer!

By ten thirty Mursi or Hamid al Fadhil was driving up the A1, more romantically known as The Great North Road, with Hanan his readymade wife and her five-year-old son. He had a dislike of British motorways and thus had opted for the A1 instead of the faster M1,taking great care not to speed or draw attention to the way he drove he, nevertheless, made good progress.

'Hamid, would you mind if we stopped for a while. Eid and myself would like to have a comfort break?'

'Oh I am so sorry, it never occurred to me. I will pull into the next service area. In any case I do not like my fuel tank to drop below half full.'

Sometime later they pulled into a service area just outside Grantham in Lincolnshire. Whilst they ate the usual soggy, tasteless sandwich and drank what the service station called coffee, but looked and tasted like used engine oil, they chatted like any normal married couple.

'Our son Eid has been very good. No tantrums or crying for anything. You must be proud of him. He is a lovely little child,' said Mursi.

'Yes, he is a very wellbalanced and easygoing little boy for his age.'

Before resuming their journey Mursi gave Hanan money to buy young Eid sweets, comics and whatever else he fancied for the final lap of the journey.

'I have money Hamid. Karim paid me in advance for accompanying you.'

'I insist. I appreciate your help and I want to pay for everything. Keep the money Karim gave you and try to relax and enjoy yourself, as much as is possible under the circumstances. Here you are, fifty pounds for your personal spending. When that has gone I will gladly give you more.'

Hanan treated herself to a couple of women's magazines and, noticing a guide-book to the Yorkshire Dales, decided to buy it as well. Mursi's only purchase was a better road map than the one that Karim had placed in the car for him.

Just under an hour after stopping they climbed back into the Mondeo for the next leg of the journey to Hawes. Eid, now wide awake and having seen only streets in London was eagerly taking in the new sights. As they passed Dishforth, Eid excitedly pointed across to the east. The sun was clearly showing up the White Horse near Sutton Bank some twelve miles away.

Looking at the new, and better detailed map, Hanan had taken on the job of navigator. 'Hamid, a little further along and take the B6267 to Masham. It looks a faster road to Hawes than going through the place called Bedale.'

'I will follow your advice Hanan, here is the B6267.' Mursi turned left off the A1 and headed towards Masham which they entered over a hump backed bridge.

'Look, Hamid, can we please stay here awhile? It looks so nice.' Seeing a large grassy area on their left Hamid slowed the car and turned left onto a narrow track. They saw some picnic tables and decided to sit out for a few minutes to enjoy the unexpected warmth of the January sun. After being cooped up in the car Eid ran round wildly like any five–year-old.

'Eid, do not go too near the water,' called out Hanan as she decided to read a little of the history of Masham.

'Hamid, this is about this small town. It is pronounced Massam and not Masham.'

Being a teacher she found it thoroughly interesting. Although a Muslim, Hanan found one section particularly interesting. Many years ago the Archbishop of York did not relish the thought of a long journey to Masham in order to carry out his duties. As a result he pronounced the small town would be a 'Peculier.' In effect Masham would be responsible for administering both ecclesiastical and civil law. Even today the Archbishop of York cannot order the Vicar of Masham to York but has to send a formal invitation.

More up to date is the fact that two very well-known breweries are based in this small market town. Oddly, both of them called Theakston's but not linked in business. One of them being the Black Sheep Brewery, so named due to a family member going his own, and very successful way.

Deciding to press on Mursi ushered his 'wife and son' back to the car. With Hanan still navigating they drove through the historic town of Middleham with its many world famous race-horse training stables. All the while Hanan kept pointing out interesting things she had read in her Dales book. Middleham Castle being one.

They crossed the ancient River Ure, or Yore, via the delightful castellated ancient Middleham Bridge. Taking the next left they entered the hamlet of Wensley where they turned left to re-cross the Ure.

Even Mursi with his jaded perspective of the world began to perk up when he saw the beginning of the magnificent Wensleydale scenery. A dusting of snow was apparent on the hills. Entering Hawes they turned right and headed towards their hotel. Eid, in the back of the car, yelled and pointed up. They saw half a dozen intrepid paragliders hovering above the fells. Looking like giant butterflies, turning and soaring with the sun clearly showing up their brilliant assortment of colours.

Arriving at Stone House hotel, Hamid left Hanan to book in whilst he removed their luggage from the car. A young man helped carry the cases and showed them to their rooms. They were informed of the facilities the hotel had to offer and presented with a list of meal times. Being accustomed to dealing with a wide range of nationalities the hotel assured them that, should they so wish, halal meat could be made available.

Their room was large, airy and well heated. Looking out of the window Hanan was delighted to see the view across the valley to Hawes and the majestic fells beyond.

Apart from unpacking and settling into the comfortable hotel they did little else except eat a tasty meal, accompanying it with a glass of red wine. Muslims or not, they both had a taste for alcohol in moderation. Hanan decided to put Eid to bed to get some rest, after the long journey. The following morning Mursi opted to drive into Hawes to savour some of the local atmosphere whilst Hanan lounged about the hotel with Eid.

Parking in the market place he strolled along the one main street looking at the varied shops and other places of interest, eventually entering the bar of the Board Hotel where he bought a small glass of beer from one of the famous breweries in Masham.

Being a Saturday, the bar was quite busy with walkers tucking into some of the tasty and filling dishes provided by the country pub.

Luckily, finding a seat Mursi idly glanced through some of the tourist guides for the area. Reading about a celebrated rope maker and a local cheese factory being made even more famous by someone called Wallis and Gromit, whoever they happened to be! No doubt Hanan and young Eid would find some of the things interesting. With the heat from the blazing open fire and the effect of the alcohol Mursi began to feel drowsy and tired from the long drive. Drinking up, he set off to join his family.

Knocking politely before entering their room, Mursi was far more apprehensive than Hanan was at having to spend the night in close proximity to a stranger and a member of the opposite sex. He quickly showered, took some spare blankets that had been provided and settled down to sleep on the floor. Being accustomed to sleeping on the ground, under the stars, this was no hardship. Bidding Hanan goodnight, Mursi fell into a deep sleep within minutes.

He awoke early and gazed at Hanan still sleeping peacefully. He was struck by how attractive she was, not having really noticed her before. As if sensing his presence, she opened her eyes and for a moment was surprised to see a strange man standing before her.

'Good morning Hamid, I trust you slept well and were not too uncomfortable sleeping on the floor. You were welcome to use the bed you know.'

'Thank you for your concern and a special thank you for remembering to call me Hamid. Especially as you only just woke up. I think this artificial family of mine will work very well indeed.' Even little Eid had accepted Mursi after he had been given the sweets and comics.

'Have you any plans for today Hanan? if not I read last night about some caves not too far from here called White Scar. Perhaps you and Eid might like to look round them.'

'Thank you Hamid! That is most thoughtful of you. Speaking for myself I would love to see them and I know Eid will also.'

After breakfast they checked they had maps and guides and drove into Hawes where Hamid stopped the car near a row of telephone kiosks.

'Excuse me Hanan, I need to make a telephone call. I will only be a few moments.'

He entered one of the kiosks and dialled a mobile number. After two rings, 'Hello, Ahmed's Dry Cleaning Service, can I help you?'

'Hello, I am calling to see if my dry cleaning is ready to collect. Reference number 2411.' At the same time giving them the number of the kiosk.

Replacing the handset Hamid waited and within a minute the phone rang. 'Hello, this is Hamid.'

'Thank you for calling sir! Your dry cleaning is ready and we have been waiting for you to contact us. Ideally we could do with two more days. Please let us know where you wish it to be delivered to.'

'Thank you for being so prompt! I will be in touch but I think possibly next Wednesday morning. I will confirm the exact time and where I wish to receive it.'

With that Mursi climbed back into the Mondeo and drove eleven or twelve miles to The White Scar caves where the three of them had a very interesting and pleasant guided tour of the breathtaking underground world. The rest of the day was spent walking almost to the top of Great Whernside to enjoy the sweeping panorama of the snow-dusted hills before them.

Monday was spent taking things easy. They visited the Hawes Ropemakers, where they were fortunate to see ropes actually being made. This was followed by a visit to the Cheese Factory, where Eid quickly brought Mursi up to date on Wallis and Gromit. Being the mother of a lively youngster Hanan had heard of Wallis and Gromit. They decided to wander round and see how Wensleydale cheese was made.

'Hamid, before we return home would it be possible for you to bring me here to buy some different cheeses to take back home?'

'Of, course Hanan. I have people to meet but I expect we will be here for about a week. Will that be acceptable? My first meeting is going to be on Wednesday so we will have lots of time to see the area and enjoy ourselves.'

To see and hear Mursi, no one would have dreamed how badly the West wanted him or that he had a huge bounty on his head. Dead or alive! Preferably dead. It made life easier for everyone.

CHAPTER 15
Tuesday 29th January

Tuesday turned out to be wet and miserable.

'Hanan, I am going out for a ride into Hawes, would you and Eid like to join me?'

'It is kind of you to offer but I think today is a day I prefer to remain indoors. I am reading all about the area and its history.'

'As you wish. I will not be away too long. Is there anything you wish me to bring?'

'No thank you Hamid, we will be fine.'

Mursi decided to drive into Hawes. Being Tuesday it just happened to be market day. Due to the wintry weather only a few of the more hardy stallholders had decided to give it a go. Feeling cold and not overly inspired with the market Mursi opted to try The Board hotel. Seating himself near the welcoming open fire he ordered coffee and a sandwich. He soon began to thaw his frozen bones and idly listened to some of the customers discussing the price of cattle, sheep and other farming matters. Sitting at the same table were two other men. One, he noticed, had a packet of cigarettes in front of him, next to his half-empty glass of beer. What fascinated Mursi was the fact that the cigarette packet was marked, not in English, but Russian!

For some reason Mursi's curiosity grew, particularly as the man was quite definitely English. How would an English man come to have a packet of Russian cigarettes? The other interesting factor was that the packet was obviously pretty old. The writing seemed to date it at least thirty or forty years. The man's friend stood up and made to leave, saying, 'you know what you can do with your cigarettes. No way I'm buying any of them, they taste like horse muck. Smell like it too. Anyhow, see you Jeb, bye.'

Jeb drained his glass and Mursi deciding to have another coffee asked if Jeb would care for a refill. Warily looking at the foreigner next to him Jeb asked 'Why would you buy me a pint mate?'

Putting on one of his most disarming smiles. 'I am on holiday here and do not know anyone. It would be nice to talk to someone local to learn more about the area. However, I do not wish to trouble you and I will sit and mind my own business. I am sorry to have bothered you. I thought you might sell me some of those packs of cigarettes. I overheard your friend mentioning them.'

Seeing his free pint about to disappear, and the possible sale of some lousy cigarettes looming, Jeb soon changed his attitude.

'That's OK mate. I'd love another drink. Can't beat a liquid lunch can you?'

Catching the barman's eye Mursi ordered more drinks to be brought over. 'Cheers mate.' Jeb to Mursi.

'Oh yes, cheers to you also.' After a few sips Mursi casually brought up the matter of the odd looking cigarette packet.

'That looks unusual writing, what is it?' Knowing full well it was Russian.

Looking round Jeb replied, in a quiet voice, 'Russian, my mate told me. Got em for nowt but they taste like shit.' Realising his error, Jeb quickly added, 'I mean they don't taste as good as English ones but you can have them for two quid a pack. Good value at that as well.'

'Do you mind if I look at one of the packs?'

'Help yourself mate. You can have one if you want but you can't smoke it in here. This bloody government banned smoking inside public places.'

'Thank you! They do look interesting. How did you manage to get them?'

'I've got a lot more at home, and other stuff.' Jeb,offered, taking a good swig from his glass. It was almost empty again.

'That sounds fascinating. What sort of other stuff?'

'Why d'you wanna know?' Jeb slurred.

'My business, not yours.'

'It seems so unusual here in the Yorkshire Dales. Here your glass in empty, can I offer you another?'

'I pay my corner, it is my round,' Jeb grunted almost belligerently.

'I insist my friend. You have been most interesting.'

'Ay, go on then. Last one then I'll have to go.'

Mursi returned with a measure of whisky and a further pint. Both the drinks were for Jeb.

'I got you a short as well to keep the cold out.'

'You're a real pal you are. Bottoms up.'

The whisky disappeared down Jeb's throat without even touching the sides.

'So, Jeb, you were about to tell me where you managed to find these cigarettes.'

'I can't tell you. My mate says not a word to anyone.'

'Before you go, here. Ten pounds for five packs if you can spare them,' said Mursi.

'Course I can. I told you I got lots.'

'They seem so old, that is what interests me. I just wonder how you came across them. Does your mate want to keep them for himself?'

'Nah. He don't smoke, it is just that he thinks it is odd finding this place where they came from.'

'You make me curious Jeb, what sort of place?'

'You won't find it. Nobody will. It is well hidden, in a hole in the ground.'

'Jeb, you joke with me. You found these things in a hole in the ground?'

'Not joking. We found this concrete place buried in the ground. Lots of Russian things in it! There was also a couple of big boxes but we could not open them.'

Something was niggling away at the back of Mursi's mind. He felt it could be important but he did not know why. What, what, he kept asking himself?

'Jeb, would you show me this place?'

'No. My mate said not to mention it to anyone,' answered Jeb loudly.

'I would not want you to fall foul of your friend. What if we did not tell him about it? Just you and I. Of course I would pay you for your trouble. I am on holiday for the week and it would be something for me to do.'

'Don't know. Anyway how much would you give me? It would take an hour or more of my time?'

'I do not know how much to offer. Ten, twenty pounds?'

'Make it twenty and we have a deal, but keep it quiet.'

'OK Jeb, twenty it is. You have my word, I would not dream of telling anyone.'

Sealing the deal Jeb gobbed enthusiastically onto the palm of his hand. Insisting on 'shaking' on the deal, and grasped Mursi's hand. Not noticing Mursi's look of horror at having to share Jeb's handful of beer, flavoured spit.

'When can we do this Jeb, my friend?' asked Mursi.

'Mebbe, Wednesday, but it will have to be at night. My mate plays darts so will not miss seeing me as I can't throw an arrow for toffee.'

What do arrows and toffee have to do with darts, thought Mursi. Toffee?

'That will do fine. Anytime that suits you. Where do we meet?'

'Do you know where Masham is?'

'Yes I drove through it on the way here.'

'OK Masham market place, Wednesday half past seven.' Mursi's only concern was would Jeb be sober enough to remember.

'You won't change your mind will you, or forget about it?'

'Not where there is thirty quid involved.'

'Thirty? We had agreed twenty.' A half protest from Mursi!

'Very well thirty it is. I do not want you increasing our agreed thirty pounds. Do you understand? until tomorrow evening my friend.'

'No, thirty it is. Don't be late. I will be in my van waiting.'

With that Jeb finished off his pint, stood up and walked unsteadily from the Board.

Racking his brain Mursi still could not bring to mind what was niggling him but instinctively knew it might prove to be of vital importance.

Eventually he left his cosy fireside seat, which was immediately claimed by a large ruddy faced man. Mursi strolled though the small crowd of shoppers and crossed the road to a telephone kiosk.He dialled the same number saying, 'I would be grateful if you could deliver my dry cleaning tomorrow morning at ten to the Stone House hotel.'

In fact, Mursi's dry cleaning was merely a way of having schedules and locations of meetings handed to him in person. Tomorrow's arrangement was to meet an old friend of his, face to face, telephones and mobiles being dangerously prone to interception. Using the same procedure he replaced the phone, which rang almost immediately.

'Hello, this is the Dry Cleaners. Please confirm your reference number.'

Mursi did so and was informed, 'Delivery confirmed for ten am tomorrow.'

CHAPTER 16
Wednesday 30th January

Wednesday dawned bright and clear but with a lazy icy wind. Lazy because it went straight through you instead of going round. Just before ten Mursi was in the hotel lounge glancing through the various newspapers. A minute before ten in walked Mohammed Jamal Khalifa. Khalifa was with a tall, fair-skinned Arab with a scar on the left side of his face.

'Good to see you again my friend,' smiled Khalifa to Mursi, and looking knowingly into Mursi's eyes.

'This is an associate of mine, Mansour Al Bakry.'

Shaking hands with both, Mursi invited them to sit with him where coffee and biscuits were brought to them. It had not dawned on Mursi straightaway but he now realised Al Bakry was, in fact, one Anas Al Liby. There was a mystery surrounding Al Liby.

Why had British Intelligence allowed him to live freely in the UK for so long? At this moment he was back on the 'wanted' list. The FBI offering a reward of $5,000,000 had necessitated Al Liby having to shave off his full beard. He was never normally seen without a full beard. The disguise worked well as even Mursi had failed to appreciate who Al Bakry really was. Little did the hotel management, or anyone else realise that sitting on three chairs was the sum total of fifteen million US dollars.

Mursi had previously chosen a quiet area of the lounge so the trio soon got down to business. Khalifa was primarily in the UK to raise money, covertly, for Al Qaeda.

Khalifa was en route to Scotland and had chosen to have an impromptu meeting with Midhat Mursi. When he deemed it proper Mursi would ask Al Liby why he had been given full political asylum in the UK where he had lived for some time. The only logical explanation was that Al Liby had been helping British Intelligence!

'Would you care for more drinks and something more substantial to eat?' Mursi enquired.

'Not just now thank you We had a very filling breakfast. More coffee will do just fine,' explained Khalifa.

After discussing various matters Mursi happened to mention the fact about the old packet of Russian cigarettes supposedly found in a hole in the ground. 'Midhat. You say the packets were very old and printed in Russian. Your contact also stated they were found in, what you call, a hole in the ground.'

'Yes, Mohammed! It is what I was told but the man had been drinking quite heavily.'

'Midhat. Midhat. You of all people! Do you not realise the potential significance of what you say?'

'There is something at the back of my mind that I feel I should know but I can not recall what.'

Glancing furtively round, Khalifa was glad to notice they were the only people in the lounge, but he spoke quietly nevertheless.

'Cast your mind back to the Cold War between Russia and the West. There was talk that the Soviets had a plan to situate small nuclear devices throughout Europe and Great Britain.'

'That is it,' gasped Mursi. 'Now I recall, little wonder I failed to remember. It was almost fifty years ago. Surely there cannot be any of these devices still in situ. Not after almost fifty years. That is, if the Soviets even got round to attempting this in the first place.'

'You did mention, my friend, that this Jeb had said something about finding two large containers that looked like some sort of electrical equipment.'

'Allah be praised. Do you think Allah is really smiling down on our cause? It is too much to hope that this hole could possibly be concealing one of these weapons. Just imagine what we could do with such a device. No, it is too much to hope for.'

'Midhat. You say you will be meeting this Jeb tonight. I am going to postpone my visit to Scotland until you see for yourself what these cases actually are. Like yourself I do not believe we could be so fortunate but we need to know. I suggest you take Anas with you. Anas and myself will book into the hotel in Middleham. We stopped there for coffee and it is a very pleasant and friendly family run hotel. It is not too far from you here and I know they have vacancies.'

'Anas, is that alright with you?' asked Mursi.

'Of course it is my friend. It will give me something to do. I am not too keen on these quiet little villages. What time do you suggest?'

'I have to be in Masham for seven-thirty to meet this man. If he turns up. I am a little concerned that he may not remember. I know where your hotel is in Middleham. I will be there at exactly ten minutes past seven. Wear something warm as it is in a wood of some sorts.'

With the coffee and biscuits consumed the trio parted for the time being. All three of them had only one thought on their mind. What was the significance of the two strange looking containers! Still as yet unidentified. Surely, fifty years later it could not possibly be a nuclear device still left in situ! Even if it was, by now it would surely be utterly unserviceable.

CHAPTER 17
Wednesday 30th January 1925 hours

After collecting Anas from his hotel Mursi drove into Masham's ancient market square. He drove slowly round, staring into the various parked cars. Stopping near a battered looking old white van he saw the pale face of Jeb.

'Who else is in the car with you?' demanded Jeb.

'It is a colleague of mine. Is it OK for him to join us? We will pay you extra if you wish, but he is most interested in your find. I assure you he will not tell anyone.'

'It will cost you another twenty and I want the cash here and now. Don't say a word to anyone else mind you. My mate would go spare if he knew.'

'Thank you Jeb, it shall remain our secret. I can promise neither of us will say a word to anyone. You have my solemn word on it.'

With that Mursi handed over the fifty pounds total from a thick wad of notes in his wallet. As he counted the money Jeb was cursing for nor asking for more. After all, the bloody wog seemed to be loaded.

'Where are we going Jeb, is it far?'

'Not far, it is close to an old ruined temple that people used for carrying out weird rituals. It is a bit creepy but it will be OK.'

'What sort of old temple and what sort of rituals?' enquired, Mursi.

'Some say they used to sacrifice people and animals up there, on the altar's but it is just a load of old cobblers. Anyhow follow me.'

With that Jeb's old van spluttered out of Masham travelling slowly uphill to Ilton and the Druid's Temple car park.

A watery moon provided some light as Jeb led the way past the old temple. 'Ah, it is like your Stonehenge ruins.'

'Ay, summat like that. Don't go flashing your torches round there could be gamekeepers about,' warned Jeb.

'Up here, come on it is only a small slope. Here we are. We sawed through the lock so it is not locked. But we covered it with a few branches.'

Arriving at his 'treasure chest' Jeb lifted the lid and told the two Arabs to follow him down.

'Here we go,' said Jeb as he switched the small light on.

'That is most helpful Jeb. Thank you. I am glad I thought to bring a torch though.'

The small room smelled damp and chilled them to the bones but Mursi only had eyes for the two containers. He had brought a digital camera, which he used to photograph the boxes from different angles. A buzz of excitement, almost electrical was flowing through him. Whilst he did this Jeb was busy filling his pockets with the contents of more of the boxes. The flash from the small camera startled Jeb.

'Here, why do you want photographs of those things?' demanded Jeb.

'This is marvellous Jeb and so interesting. I just have to have some pictures that I can treasure. Do you think we could come back again sometime for another look?'

In actual fact nothing could prevent Mursi from returning. With or without Jeb's approval! However, at this time he felt it prudent to keep in Jeb's good books at least until the pictures had been checked and verified. Deep inside Mursi knew that he had discovered the ultimate weapon for Al Qaeda. He had not even had to smuggle it into the UK. It was here, ready and waiting. On a plate as the British would say. Allah had, indeed, been bountiful in his blessings. When the weapon, if that is what it turned out to be, was ready to be moved it, would probably need three men to manoeuvre it up the shaft of the bunker. An extra few pounds would undoubtedly secure Jeb's muscles.

'It is cold here Jeb, shall we go? I have seen all I need to see.' With that Mursi led the way back up the few feet of the shaft to the surface.

'Don't you want any fags or chocolate mate? You've been fair with me so I don't mind you taking a few,' Jeb called up to Mursi as he climbed clear of the bunker.

'It is most kind of you Jeb, I still have some you sold me, and, after all, it is your find so they belong to you and your friend. My friend would like to buy some packs off you if that is acceptable to you.' In actual fact Mursi did not even smoke, but it was another way to keep in with this idiot Englishman.

Al Liby handed over £10 for some packs, which would end up in a litter bin. 'My mate won't touch these fags. He says they are rubbish. Nor the chocolate so there's enough to spare you a few. Anyhow your choice mate.'

With that they carefully covered the metal lid, Mursi taking extra special care to ensure it was well hidden from view. Even so he felt most reluctant to leave the bunker unguarded. What if it was a nuclear device? He could scarcely contain his excitement.

'That will do. Nobody ever comes up here, especially now the shooting season is just about over. Safe as houses.' Jeb assured the two Arabs.

'Jeb, you can be sure we will keep our word not to mention this to a soul. You also must do the same. If your friend found out he might be very cross with you. We would not want to be the cause of you quarrelling.'

Walking back to their vehicles Mursi's mind was working furiously. He needed the photographs confirming and, more importantly, the two containers moving to a safe place at the earliest possible moment. Arriving back at the Druid's Temple car park.

Mursi turned to Jeb. 'Jeb, my friend, I would very much like to look at this place again. How soon can we do it?'

'I'm not sure of that and I do not like deceiving my mate.' Deceiving his mate Tom Prescott was furthest from his mind. Jeb was mulling over how much he could fleece these wogs for. Remembering how bulky Mursi's wallet was.

'I will pay you well Jeb and it has to be night-time as I am busy all day.' What he really meant was – they would be less likely to meet anyone else if they came back at night.

'So what do you say? And how soon can you return here without anyone knowing?'

'Maybe, but not tomorrow! I don't know about Friday but it will cost you more than £50 next time! It is difficult for me to get away at night.'

'I agree Jeb, you should be paid more money for your time, especially as you will need to work at night. Did you have a figure in mind?' Mursi was doing his best to keep Jeb sweet, knowing full well that they would need a third hand to manhandle the containers out of their resting place. He also had to persuade Jeb to part with them.

'I reckon it is worth at least seventy-five quid,' stated Jeb.

'Jeb, I think that is a little expensive don't you?' Mursi was perfectly happy paying that sum but he did not want Jeb to think he was going to keep forking money out left right and centre.

'I am willing to pay you sixty pounds and if I am entirely happy I may consider giving you an extra ten, but no promises. How does that sound?'

'OK then, give us the sixty for now.'

'I will give you £20 now as a sign of my good faith.'

Sod it, thought Jeb. Oh well, Mursi had not quibbled too much. He would co-operate in the hope of getting his hands on the rest. Perhaps they might need further visits so there was always the chance of screwing more out of them.

'Do you have a mobile phone so I can contact you when I will be free again. I would like it to be soon. That is also considering when you will be available.'

Fishing a grubby Morrison's shopping receipt out of his pocket Jeb obligingly scribbled his number and handed it to Mursi who checked it to ensure the numbers were clear.

Before driving out of the car park Mursi handed Jeb another ten pounds. 'This is a bonus as you have been so helpful. Remember, it is our secret Jeb. I will contact you in a day or so. You are sure no one will stumble upon the bunker?'

Eagerly pocketing the tenner Jeb realised he was onto a better thing than he had originally thought. Money for old rope! Bloody oil sheikhs.

'No problem, no one will wander up here. It is off the usual path and does not lead to anywhere. People tend to look at the temple, take a few pictures and carry on with their walk. Even the gamekeepers have no reason to come up here. Anyway, give me a call to make sure it is OK for Friday.'

On the drive back to Hawes Mursi handed his camera to Anas Al Liby. 'Take this, first thing, tomorrow to the car park at White Scar Caves. I will arrange for someone to collect it from you. I need the films printing and the cases identified.'

He explained how to find the caves car park and the approximate driving time.

A phone call from a kiosk in Hawes market place to the dry cleaners ensured someone would be at the White Scar car park at 9am the following morning.

CHAPTER 18
Thursday 31st January

Driving into the White Scar car park at 0845 Al Liby saw only three other vehicles. A red Vauxhall drove slowly into the car park. The rear doors opened and two young Arab boys climbed out and began kicking a ball around. A tall male Arab left the car and joined the boys playing football. Recognising Al Liby as another Arab he 'accidentally' kicked the ball towards Al Liby's car.

'I must apologise for my lack of skill. Are you hoping to look round the caves?'

Realising this was almost certainly his contact Al Liby said, 'No. Just stopping for a break from driving. I am on my way to collect some laundry for a friend. It is most pleasing to see another Arab.'

Al Liby alighted from his vehicle and shook hands with the other Arab-looking man. 'My name is Abdullah, it also pleases me to meet another Arab. Do you have a reference number for your laundry?'

'Yes, number 2411.'

'Is the package ready now, if so pass it to me when we shake hands to part.'

Al Liby surreptitiously took the small digital camera from his pocket and carefully handed it to Abdullah. 'It needs to be processed quickly. Please contact Mursi the minute it is ready and we will arrange to collect the photos. If you know of a sympathiser who would know about the pictures you may show them but no one is to ever speak of them except to Mursi.'

The two of them smiled at the young boys who were obviously enjoying kicking their football around. Al Liby waved his goodbyes to the two young lads, climbed back into his car and drove steadily off in the direction of Hawes.

Just before noon Midhat Mursi, Hanan and young Eid were parked at the Buttertubs Pass gazing down into the bottom of the void, about a hundred feet below.

'Yukk' from the boy who was pointing into one of the 'buttertub's, 'Look there.'

Mursi and Hanan looked to where the boy was pointing. Amongst the empty Coke cans and other detritus of thoughtless visitors he had spotted a dead sheep. No doubt killed by falling into the deep hole. They were still examining the various 'buttertubs' when Mursi felt his phone vibrate. Recognising the number Mursi accepted the call. The usual rule was One mobile. One call. Then dispose of the phone to avoid being traced. Expecting nothing incriminating whilst using this mobile Mursi had hung on to it.

'Are you calling to say my laundry is ready?' asked Mursi.

'That is correct sir.'

'You are sure it is mine?'

'Quite sure sir. The chitty is number 2411.'

'Can you deliver it this afternoon to the same place it was collected from?'

'Certainly sir! As you need it urgently my driver will be there by 2pm. It is most important that you collect it in person.'

'Thank you. I will be there on time.' Mursi closed the connection and turned to Hanan.

'We need to be going soon if we are to eat, in order for me to keep the appointment.' At the same time he wondered why it was considered important for him to be there in person. Most irregular.

'A couple of miles down this road is a village called Thwaite and the guide book says it has a delightful hotel that serves splendid home cooked food. Please can we go there to eat? It is only a mile or so further,' begged Hanan.

'Of course, if that is your wish.' Mursi was so pleased with the way

Hanan had played her part, so far, that he was more than willing to consent to her request.

Very soon the three of them were enjoying the delicious food and at the same time taking in the stunning view from the rear window of the dining room.

'It is amazing, the amount of beautiful scenery in this part of the world,' Hanan stated, wistfully.

'In other circumstances, things could be so different.'

After thanking their host and leaving a generous tip they returned to the car and set off to the White Scar car park again.

'Hanan, you are excelling yourself with that guide-book. You have discovered many places of interest and most agreeable locations to dine.'

No more was said and they drove in companionable silence to Mursi's rendezvous.

CHAPTER 19
31st January 2008

As Mursi was about to turn into the car park a car flashed its lights. Acknowledging with a flash from his own lights Mursi drove alongside the red Vauxhall. Lowering his window the Vauxhall driver gestured to Mursi, mouthing the words.

'Please follow me. This could be of the greatest importance.'

With that the Vauxhall exited the car park heading in the direction back towards Hawes.

Staying a reasonable distance behind, Mursi was surprised to eventually see the car signal and pull into a lay-by. Several other vehicles were parked there. Quite obviously a popular rendezvous spot for walkers. A mobile snack van appeared to be doing a good trade in bacon butties and other similar gastronomic delights.

'This place is called Ribblehead,' Hanan indicated with a nod of her head, 'It is a well known structure called the Ribblehead Viaduct.'

By now the driver of the Vauxhall, also an Arab, was walking towards Mursi's car. 'Shall we walk a little? I have much to tell you.'

Mursi explained to Hanan that he would not be long and with that he left her and Eid to their own devices. Mursi then set off in step with the other man along the path towards Great Whernside. They looked like any other ramblers out for a pleasant afternoon's stroll.

'This is most irregular, meeting like this. What is so vital?'

'I have the prints and your digital camera which I will give you when we return. Bearing in mind what you had said about the containers I showed the photographs to a retired University lecturer who supports our cause. His field of expertise included physics and electronics. Firstly, he is convinced that your boxes are genuine. However, you may have a serious problem, a very serious one.'

Mursi felt the blood drain from his face. 'How do you mean? Have we been discovered or what?'

'No, but our University friend looked on the internet in order to learn more about these 'items,' It seems that they may be up to almost fifty years old, powered by small batteries. Now what does that tell you?'

'I'm not sure I follow you. Batteries, so what?'

'Midhat, batteries tend to run down. You, yourself, said the light in the bunker was bright, as was the light on one of the devices. These batteries send out a coded signal when they are running low. This tells someone they are in need of replacing. It is thought the batteries may last up to three to five years. Are you with me now?'

'By the beard of the Prophet! You mean someone has to replace the batteries every so often.' The sudden realisation hit Mursi a gut wrenching blow to the stomach.

'Precisely my friend, and we do not know the state of the existing batteries. Which means you will have to move the containers almost immediately. Assuming it is a Russian sleeper, which it must be, there is no telling when he is likely to visit the site again. Also, he is more than likely living not too far from the bunker. Now the stores have been pilfered and the lock opened he will realise immediately and set the cat amongst the pigeons.'

'I must get back straight away and arrange their removal. I assume you have a secure location to store them until we are ready to use them. I keep saying them, as it is two containers, which, if I remember correctly, make up one complete unit.'

'Yes, once you have the boxes I will arrange to meet and take them off you. I assume they will fit into your Mondeo.'

'Yes, I measured them roughly. One in the boot and the other on the rear seat.'

'Do you need help in getting them out of the bunker?'

'No thank you, a greedy Englishman will help.' The two began walking briskly back to their cars.

'One other thing! Midhat. Can this Englishman be trusted?'

'Most definitely indeed! There will be no problem, believe me. I have considered a way to ensure our secret remains with us.'

Arriving back at their cars, the Vauxhall departed and Mursi treated the three of them to an ice cream from the van. He ate his deep in thought and seeming to be engrossed in the wild, looking moor land scenery, but in fact not taking any of it in. He had a problem, indeed.

Setting off towards the Stone House hotel he once again parked adjacent to one of the telephone kiosks in Hawes Market Place. Consulting the scrap of Morrisons' receipt he called Jeb.

'Hiya, Jeb here,' came Jeb's voice at the second ring.

'Jeb my friend how nice to catch you! Are you alone so we can speak?'

'Yep, I am just walking home from the shop with a few groceries. What can I do for you squire?'

'Jeb, I realise it is a little soon but do you think we could return to your secret place this evening? Any time convenient to yourself.'

'Ah, sorry that won't be any good. I am meeting my mate tonight. He will be busy tomorrow night. I could meet tomorrow say about half past seven in the market place.'

'Thank you Jeb, that would be greatly appreciated.' Inwardly seething that Jeb could not make it tonight, Mursi was becoming more agitated by the hour at the thought that someone might visit the bunker before he had liberated the two containers. He even considered trying tonight with Anas Al Liby but ruled against it due to the difficulty that would face just the two of them manoeuvring the boxes from the hole.

CHAPTER 20
Thursday 31st January, 2030 hours

'Jeb, where did you steal that lot from?' queried Tom Prescott. Money tended to drain out through the holes it had burned in Jeb's pockets. Yet Jeb was openly flashing a number of ten -and -twenty pound notes.

'A bloke owed me some money for a load of scrap and he paid up today,' Jeb blustered.

'Scrap?' exclaimed Tom.

'The only scrap you have is that crappy old van of yours. Come on give!'

Realising that he had been a little foolish allowing all and sundry to note his usually empty wallet he muttered, 'Well, that is where you are wrong. I got some lead last week and the bloke has just collected it today.'

Jeb now appeared to have gone into a sulk. Curious, but realising that he would get no more out of Jeb tonight Tom let the matter drop. For now!

After another pint Jeb was back to his usual chatty self but Tom decided to let the matter rest. He knew that sooner or later Jeb would let it slip out.

'You still smoking those shitty Russky fags? You tight sod, with all that money in your pocket you could afford some decent smokes.'

'Waste not, want not my old granny used to say!'

'You had almost run out last weekend. Did you go back to that bunker again on your own?' demanded Tom sounding annoyed.

'I told you to lay off going there. You are stupid. All that Russian stuff can't be up to any good.'

'I was careful and made sure nobody was about but I wanted some more ciggies. I bought extra ones and, if you must know, sold some to a pissing Arab on holiday from his oil wells. That is where I got some of my extra cash from. He was in a pub in Hawes.'

'Of all the idiots Jeb. Just let's hope he does not mention those fags to anyone.'

'Right, I'm telling you now for the last time. Do not go back there ever again. I mean it. I am seriously thinking about going to the police and telling them. I could phone them anonymously.'

This outburst startled Jeb and sobered him up slightly. Shit, he thought, if Tom goes to the police tomorrow my seventy-five, or so, quid has gone out of the window.

'Sorry mate I didn't think. I promise not to go there anymore. I give you my word, but don't go to the police, they might find out it was us there. You know, with fingerprints and other things they do these days, 'pleaded Jeb.'

'You give your word? That'll be the day. I'll think about it over the weekend and see how I feel later. Come on, it is my round now. You've been buying all night. A pint and a whisky chaser, how about that.'

Inwardly Jeb gave a huge sigh of relief. At least he would have another opportunity to wheedle more money out of the poxy Arabs.

CHAPTER 21

Friday 1st February

Following their initial procedure Mursi and Anas Al Liby drove slowly into Masham market place.

'There he is Midhat' Said Al Liby pointing to Jeb's white van.

Mursi was relieved to note Jeb was already waiting with his engine running. Following his fright over realising the bunker had a current caretaker he was more than anxious to return to the site as soon as they possibly could. A brief nod as they motored past and Jeb set off. The two terrorists trailing along behind. Ten minutes later Jeb pulled to a halt in the Druid's Temple car park. Mursi drew up alongside.

'Jeb, we plan on removing those metal containers tonight. Would it be possible for me to drive my car nearer to save a long and arduous carry?'

'Hey I never said you could have them. You did not say anything about taking those things out of the hole. Why should you have them? Me and my mate found them so they are rightly ours?' Jeb questioned sounding somewhat disgruntled. Not wishing to antagonise Jeb, Mursi quickly countered any further protests with an offer he knew Jeb would not refuse.

'Jeb we will leave them for you if you wish but you said you had no use for them. In any case we would not leave you out of pocket. How much would you take for them?

I only wanted to see if I could make use of them. But you are right. They are yours and we will leave them for you and your friend.'

'What are you doing?' demanded Al Liby.

Catching his eye Mursi gave an imperceptible wink.

'Jeb is right. He found them, they are his. I was going to offer him money for them but I do not really think they would be of any use to me.'

Quick on the uptake, Anas Al Liby said, 'Yes, we are sorry Jeb. I don't know why my friend wanted them in the first place. I think they are a load of rubbish! I can't see any use for them. As you say, you found the boxes and they are rightly yours.'

'Well they might be worth something for scrap and I could get a few quid for them. I might consider letting you take them off my hands for a few notes. It would save me lugging them to a scrap yard. What are you offering?' whined Jeb.

'It is as my friend says, Jeb. I do not think they will be any use to us after all. They can't be worth anything or they would not have been left here.'

'Here, I didn't say you could not have them. I reckon fifteen quid would do me.'

'Well. I do not really want them but I agree. Fifteen pounds but only if you help get them into my car as well.'

Jeb's mind was on the petrodollars, 'Fifteen would be OK for me but my mate would need a tenner as well.'

Jeb had decided that as Tom would eventually discover he had returned against his express wishes, a few pounds would mollify him. After all it was only a couple of old boxes of old radios or electrical equipment.

'OK Jeb, but you drive a hard bargain. Here take this. The extra is because you promised to help get the cases into my car.' So saying Mursi placed a couple of twenties into Jeb's grasping hands.

'Great, thanks a lot. I'm sure my mate will be happy now.' At least Jeb hoped so.

Tom could be an awkward bugger when he was crossed. 'Right, I'll shift the barrier and you drive your car in, but sidelights only and don't rev up too much,' instructed Jeb, hoping that the gamekeepers were enjoying a night with their feet up. Driving up the narrow lane Mursi quietly whispered a prayer to Allah asking him to help make sure they were not walking into a trap. On the off chance the break in had been discovered.

Parking adjacent to the Temple the trio climbed the small hill to the underground bunker. Jeb hastily removed the leaves and branches to reveal the metal manhole lid. Jeb went in first, quickly followed by the others. The small light continued to burn brightly when it was switched on, thus convincing Mursi that the batteries were well charged. The Arabs began to drag one of the containers to the bottom of the hatchway. With foresight Mursi had brought a short length of stout rope.

'Jeb, will you go to the top and pull this rope whilst we push from down here?'

'OK mate give us the end of the rope.' With that Jeb ascended the short ladder and climbed out of the shaft. Not before pocketing the remaining cigarettes and a few bars of chocolate.

'Are you ready Jeb?' Mursi called from below.

'Ready when you are,' replied the Englishman.

Surprisingly the first container came up much easier than expected and as it exited the opening Jeb lifted it to one side. A thought flashed through Mursi's mind that they could have managed without Jeb and collected the cases the previous evening after all.

'Coming down,' called Jeb as he lowered the end of the rope.

'Thank you Jeb.' Securing the rope to the last device Mursi called up to Jeb, 'pull now my friend.'

This final container proved to be more awkward than heavy. It took a considerable amount of pushing, pulling and cursing to finally free it from the bunker where it had rested for almost fifty years. Mursi realised they would never have managed to free this case without Jeb.

Heaving themselves from the void Mursi and Al Liby got their breath back whilst Jeb closed the hatch, covering it with twigs and grass. Not that anyone was likely to pass this way. Satisfied, Mursi and Al Liby set off down the hill with the first container. They slipped and slithered on the wet ground. Now Mursi had them in his possession he wanted then stored safely, well away from this area. With a greater effort Jeb decided he could manage the second metal box on his own and staggered off after the others slithering on the uneven and greasy hillside ground.

Mursi and Al Liby approached their vehicle and gently lowered their burden onto the soft earth. Gasping at the effort Mursi proceeded to open the rear door and the boot of his car. A heavy thud indicated, Jeb had arrived and unceremoniously let his container drop heavily to the soft, peaty ground.

'Careful you fool,' snarled Mursi, 'You might damage it!'

'No need to be like that,' protested Jeb.

'I wish I'd let you carry it yourself.'

Disregarding Jeb, Anas Al Liby turned to Mursi.

'I hope that it is worth it after this struggle and that it does turn out to be the bomb.'

Alarmed, Jeb exclaimed – 'Bomb, what bomb? I am not having anything to do with anything like that. My mate was going to the Police about it as he was not happy with those boxes being Russian and all. I've a good mind to report it to them now.'

Placing his left arm round Jeb's shoulder, Al Liby tried to calm Jeb. Al Liby's face had a demonic appearance from the red tail lights.

'Jeb, my friend I was only joking. These containers are merely radio equipment of some sort, you can see that for yourself.'

Al Liby's arm unnerved Jeb. He was a man's man and not into this touchy feely stuff.

The Frogs were bad enough, men kissing each other's cheeks, but the Arabs were even worse. In addition to kissing they could be seen walking along hand in hand. Suddenly Jeb's eyes bulged and a look of sheer terror and disbelief spread across his face. Something cold was slicing into his chest. He looked down as quiet whimpers escaped from his lips. In his last seconds of life on this earth what Jeb saw was unreal. Al Liby was thrusting and twisting his khanjar or curved dagger slowly and deeply inside Jeb's chest. Methodically slicing through the tissue of the still, beating heart. A sudden explosion of the most intense pain accompanied by a gushing of bright red frothy blood from his mouth and Jeb was dead. Al Liby lowered him slowly to the ground.

'Well done! That keeps our activities to ourselves,' hissed Mursi, 'He might have gone to the police and he would definitely have told his friend about us. It is best this way. We need to get away from here as fast as possible.'

The two terrorists briskly placed the containers into the car. One went in the boot. The second was placed onto the rear seat.

'What about the corpse?' enquired Mursi anxiously.

'Help me, we can hide him in the underground chamber. It may be many months before he is discovered,' suggested Al Liby.

With that the two of them started trying to drag Jeb's lifeless body back up the slope. However, what with the steepness of the hill, the saturated muddy ground and the fact that Jeb weighed close on eighteen stone they had no chance. The duo collapsed, exhausted and filthy, on the ground gasping for breath from the effort.

'We will have to leave him here,' said Al Liby it is just impossible to drag him up that slope'.

'Wait, I have an idea. When the body is discovered here just lying on the ground it will look even more suspicious.' Said Mursi. He briefly explained to Al Liby the history of the temple as related to him via Hanan.

'If we mutilate him on one of the altars it will buy us more time. People will think it is some sort of pagan or other sacrificial killing. Unless you can think of anything better?'

'You may be right there Midhat. Quickly, help me lift him on to one of the altars.'

Once in place the two cut and dragged Jeb's clothes from his body. Jeb's arms were placed straight out, giving him the appearance of a crucifix.

Al Liby, using his Damascus steel Khanjar, butchered Jeb from chest to groin with one, long powerful sweep. He then cut Jeb's throat, almost severing his head. The testicles and penis were sliced off and forced into Jeb's mouth. Although messy and bloody, very little further blood flowed from the new wounds since Jeb's heart was no longer functioning.

'It will buy us even more time if the police are not able to identify him quickly,' Al Liby matter-of-factly said to Mursi. With that he hefted up a large stone by the side of the altar and smashed it into Jeb's face. Again and again he brought the rock smashing down onto the remains of Jeb's head, the bones cracking and crunching as he pounded the face into a mushy pulp.

Breathing heavily and covered in perspiration Al Liby gathered Jeb's clothes and flung them into the boot of the car. 'We will dispose of these somewhere well away from here.'

Al Liby's frenzy had made even Mursi feel nauseous. However, he climbed into the car and drove from the scene. Al Liby followed in Jeb's old van. They did not wish to advertise the fact that Jeb, or anyone else, had been there. The van would be abandoned in a quiet spot in Masham, Al Liby's soft leather gloves making sure he left no fingerprints.

'We cannot return to our hotels in this state,' Mursi said.

'We will stop by a stream and try to clean ourselves up.'

Remembering an earlier stop with Hanan, Mursi drove onto the large grassy area outside Masham adjacent to the bowling club. A lone dog walker was slowly leading her mutt back to the road as Mursi drove into the small parking area. Luckily no one else was about and the two set about ridding themselves of Jebs blood, checking each other until they were satisfied that they were as presentable as the circumstances allowed. Mursi dropped Anas Al Liby outside his hotel in Middleham and, driving into Hawes, stopped next to the same telephone kiosk. He phoned the 'dry cleaners' explaining he needed some laundry collecting urgently.

It was agreed that someone would meet Mursi at the Ribblehead Rail viaduct. Within forty to forty-five minutes. At about the appointed time the red Vauxhall drew up alongside Mursi's Mondeo.

'Once you set off with these cases do not speed. They are vitally, vitally important and you must not be stopped by the police,' warned Mursi.

Two men helped move the two containers into the Vauxhall, also taking Jeb's blood stained clothes in order to dispose of them. Glad to be relieved of the devices and Jeb's incriminating bloody clothes, Mursi had ordered the men to contact Mahasheer, in London. Mahasheer would give them a safe address where they were to take the two cases.

Mursi proceeded to the Stone House hotel. In the car park he waited until it looked clear, then rushed up to his room. Barely acknowledging Hanan he dashed into the bathroom where he showered and scrubbed until his flesh was glowing and cleansed of the infidel's blood. He towelled himself vigorously and called for Hanan to bring him fresh clothes.

Tapping lightly on the bathroom door she entered with the fresh clothes he had demanded. Hanan knew better than to ask what had happened. It was impossible not to have noticed his blood-stained clothes.

Without a word she picked them up from the bathroom floor. One by one, with the help of liberal amounts of washing-up liquid, she rinsed off the majority of the red stains, which were already turning dark brown.

'You will not be able to wear these until they have been properly cleaned. I have managed to get rid some of the stains.'

'Hanan, place all the stained clothes in a plastic bin liner. I will dispose of them when we return to London.'

'As you say, but this suit looks very expensive, are you sure you do not wish it to be dry cleaned?'

Indeed his Ralph Lauren suit had set Mursi back over three thousand dollars. Al Qaeda's top men certainly dressed and travelled in style. 'It will be burned Hanan. Please put it in the bin liner as I asked.'

As the last article disappeared into the plastic bag, so Mursi's memories of the evening's previous events also disappeared.

With one most vital exception! Al Qaeda now had their very own nuclear device.

Chapter 22
Friday 1st February a little after midnight

'Hanan, we will leave tomorrow,' Mursi informed Hanan, 'to return to London.'

'As you wish Midhat. I would like to thank you for the time we spent together. Eid and myself greatly enjoyed the area. One day we intend to return.'

'Would you care for a glass of wine?' enquired Hanan.

'That would be most acceptable Hanan. I think I am in need of one. Yes please.'

Although forbidden according to the Muslim faith, a great many Arabs and other Muslims enjoyed the occasional glass of wine, beer or spirits. It is convenient for terrorists to forget the preaching of the Koran at times. Particularly the sections dealing with killing living things. The evening was getting late as Hanan made ready for bed and Mursi prepared to lie his blankets on the floor, as he had done since they arrived. As Hanan was lying in bed Mursi walked over and gazed down at her.

'I must thank you again Hanan. You and your young son have been of enormous help to me. It would have been so much more difficult without the two of you.'

'It was good of you to allow us both to join you. We both enjoyed getting away from the city but I wish you would have allowed me to pay occasionally.'

Seeing the top of Hanan's firm breasts, above her nightdress, gave Mursi a tingle in his groin. A strange sensation for Mursi as it was usually only young boys who affected him in this manner.

Hanan could not fail to see the growing bulge in the front of his trousers. Drawing back the covers she gave Mursi an inviting look.

With that, Mursi hastily flung off his few clothes and climbed in beside Hanan. Fully aware of his obvious desire Hanan sensed his nervousness, imagining it was because he was uneasy with a strange woman. Never, for an instance, guessing it was because he preferred boys. All Arab girls are taught from a very young age how to pleasure a man. Hanan slowly removed her night attire and gently reached down to grasp his engorged member. Mursi began breathing more rapidly as Hanan straddled him and slid his erect penis inside her wet and moist vagina. Timidly, Mursi reached up to hold her lovely breasts. Hanan leaned forward so that he could take her enlarged nipples between his lips. Moving rhythmically, Hanan kept up a steady pace. She soon sensed Mursi's heightened excitement and speeded up. With a loud groan Hanan felt his seed spurting deep inside her. Lying on top of him for some time Hanan slowly rolled off to lie at his side. Her arm lay across his chest as she kissed him on the lips, smiling to herself as she realised he was already in a deep slumber.

In the early hours Hanan was aware of Mursi fumbling with her breasts and stroking her still wet vagina. Touching him she realised he was fully erect once more. This time Hanan eased herself beneath him, Mursi positioning himself on top as Hanan guided his turgid penis back inside her. Moving slowly at first Mursi began moving faster. With a cry Hanan had a huge orgasm. This spurred Mursi to even greater efforts. Hanan began making repetitive moans and groans as she experienced a series of orgasms. Moving in and out like a piston he once again cried out as his body shuddered with a great orgasm. He slid off in a pool of perspiration and lay at her side. Hanan lowered her head to take his limp penis into her lips. Her expert ministrations soon brought Mursi to climax yet again. This time in her mouth. Swallowing his semen Hanan kissed him and left the bed to shower. Mursi joined her almost immediately and the pair soaped each other off, letting the hot water play on them as they held each other closely.

'Hanan,' Mursi began.

Putting a finger to her lips Hanan said, 'Sshh do not say a word.

You were marvellous.' Being a woman she knew he was about to thank her. It wasn't necessary.

To her surprise it had thrilled her more than she cared to admit. Her husband had been more interested in business than in physical activities with her. Mursi had made her feel a real woman once again, and it felt good.

Saturday 2nd February 0900 hours

'Thank you for your excellent accommodation and service! We have had a wonderful break here in this beautiful part of the country.' At Reception, Mursi settled the account, leaving a twenty pound note gratuity for the staff. He thanked them for their excellent management, expressing the hope he might, one day, visit them again.

Apart from a number of comfort and fuel stops they had an uneventful drive down to London. Mursi said his goodbyes to Hanan and her son as he dropped them off at their home. Helping carry her cases to the door he once again thanked Hanan, he kissed her gently on the cheek. As he handed her one of her jackets he thrust well over a thousand pounds into her hand.

'Hamid, what?????'

'Hush Hanan, you have more than earned it. The organisation I work for is the wealthiest organisation of its kind in the world. I will keep in touch, if I may, and if ever you need money for anything simply speak to Karim Mahasheer at the Mosque.'

With that Mursi turned, waved his farewell to Hanan and Eid and drove to a side street close to the mosque. He carefully placed his *ghutra* and *igal* over his head, folding it to conceal his face. The ghutra is the head covering, also known as a *shmagh* or *keffiyeh*. The igal is a heavy black ring of material placed on top to hold the ghutra in place.

Thus protected, Mursi strolled slowly into the mosque where he immediately encountered Mahasheer. 'Salaam aleikum my brother,' said Mursi.

'Midhat, it is you. Did you enjoy your short trip and was Hanan any help to you?'

'Karim, you did well choosing such a person. Hanan was more help than you can ever imagine. I have told her that if ever she needs money to speak to you. I fear, however, she may be too proud. In which case I charge you to keep in touch with her and ensure she is well looked after and provided for. You are to ensure that she and the boy want for nothing. They were excellent cover for me and even the boy, unknowingly, played his part to perfection.'

'I am pleased to have been of some use,' Mahasheer fawned up to Mursi.

'Now to business! I trust my packages arrived and are safely secured.'

CHAPTER 23

Sunday 3rd February 0915 hours

Blaring sirens shattered the usually tranquil rural Sunday silence of Masham. A police car, lights flashing and siren wailing rocketed through the market place. This was closely followed by another police car. Similarly announcing its presence. Minutes later an ambulance sped past. Its lights and siren ensured its speedy passage.

Passers by speculated on the cause of the unexpected excitement.

'I reckon it'll be one of them motor bikes again. They drive like idiots on these narrow roads,' old Mrs Johnson surmised.

'Every flaming weekend! It isn't safe to be on the streets with them about.'

Meanwhile the trio of emergency vehicles skidded to a halt in the Druid's car park. A group of walkers had stumbled across the mangled corpse of Jeb. 'Up there mate,' one of the walkers indicated as he comforted a shocked and tearful lady hiker. A task he seemed to be enjoying, possibly because she was young, blonde and the sort of girl any man would love to comfort!

The police had the sense not to drive up as they approached the Temple so as to leave the scene as sterile as possible for the Scenes of Crime team. A couple of men, clearly with stronger stomachs than most, were peering at the mutilated corpse. The police sergeant ordered them well away and instructed two of the constables to start taking names and addresses ready for statements.

'Sarge, I was one of the first to see the body,' volunteered one of the hikers, leisurely devouring a Mars bar.

'You do not seem too upset about it sir,' commented the Sergeant with raised eyebrows.

'After serving for fourteen years in the Army in Iraq and Afghanistan I've seen far worse than this. It was obvious the bloke was dead so I kept everyone back.'

'Very commendable sir, but we cannot assume the person is deceased until life has been pronounced extinct by a doctor at the scene.'

'So what are you going to do? Give him mouth to mouth and cardiac massage. It should be easy enough you can see the poor sod's heart from here?' offered the former soldier with a hugely wicked grin on his face.

'Yes, it appears the person is very clearly dead but we have to follow procedures.'

Speaking into his radio the Sergeant passed on as many details as possible and asked how long before the SOC team could be expected.

Just then a pair of ambulance personnel arrived panting with a stretcher and a haversack of emergency equipment. They were disgruntled at having to jog the few hundred yards due to the police preventing the ambulance from driving up.

'Bloody hell, you don't need us. This is a mortuary job. We are not taking him in the ambulance. Injured people OK but not when the bloke is obviously a goner.'

'Yes, you would be better trying to calm down some of the walkers in the car park.

He is not going anywhere for some time. We are waiting for a doctor and Scenes of Crime. Thanks for coming and as you rightly said, not a lot you can do here.'

Taking a last look at the sanguine cadaver the ambulance crew set off back to their vehicle, one of them informing their HQ, by mobile, that they were not needed and were available for other emergencies. Maybe time for a cuppa and a bite in one of the cafés in Masham market place.

Eventually word reached the good folk of Masham. The consensus of opinion was that it was the work of a group of pagans or similar. Masham's gossips were about to have not one field day but an estate full of fields by the sound of it. The murder would earn a few of the locals a free drink or two as they expounded their own theories on the slaughter to the many tourists, every re-telling adding a little more blood and gore. It wasn't every day that Masham had such excitement as this. The last time Masham experienced such excitement was when the famous annual Steam Engine Rally had to be cancelled due to a week of heavy rain, rendering the field unusable.

Even to Old Mrs Johnson the latest event looked as if it was going to be every bit as exciting as the cancelled steam do. It was her bounden duty, surely, to rush off and pass the word on to anyone prepared to give her the time of day.

CHAPTER 24
Sunday 3rd February 1030 hours, London

'Thank you Karim, this flat seems ideal and it is not too far from the mosque. Please deliver any messages by hand. We must be ultra vigilant now. It seems that somehow we slipped up. I heard on the radio the police have discovered our northern friend much sooner than we expected. We had not allowed for hikers to be out so early in the day in that particular area.' Mursi was positive he was well in the clear. No one had seen him and Al Liby with Jeb, apart from the short time in the pub and they would not have been noticed, particularly as it was Market Day and crowded.

'I must remain here until these containers have been positively identified for what I imagine them to be. Did you contact the gentleman I asked you to?'

'Yes, and he will meet you at the time and place you proposed.'

'You have done well Karim. I feel a great urgency to push ahead with my plans.'

'What do you have in those boxes Midhat? Are they very valuable?' questioned Karim Mahasheer.

'Karim, my brother, these are valuable beyond price but it is better you know nothing about them. Certainly do not mention them to anyone. Do you understand? I need someone totally trustworthy in this flat whenever I have to leave it unattended. He must be one hundred and ten per cent loyal to our cause. He is not to examine the containers or touch them in any way whatsoever. I have securely wrapped them in blankets. I repeat, no one is to see them or discuss them. I hope you understand how important this is.'

One moment Mursi was smiling pleasantly, the next second

Mahasheer felt his blood turn to ice. Something in Mursi's eyes sent a huge shudder down Mahasheer's spine.

'Ppplease my brother I assure you your boxes are safe. No one will touch them or discuss them,' stammered Mahasheer. In a flash Mursi's changed attitude had put the fear of Allah into Karim Mahasheer.

'If I suspect someone of being too talkative or inquisitive they will meet Allah sooner than expected! It will be in a most unpleasant manner I promise you this. You, Karim will remain here whilst I go out to meet this person. I will ensure I look like a typical Arab and keep my face well hidden.'

Ten minutes later Midhat Mursi strolled through Finsbury Park and sat on an empty bench near to the tennis courts. He placed the day's Arabic newspaper on the seat beside him, carefully placing his mobile across the headlines.

The Park was fairly quiet apart from the occasional jogger and people exercising their dogs. A stout, middle-aged man walked slowly along the path. He had an eastern appearance and was wearing a grey-pin stripe suit that seemed a little baggy on him. He nodded courteously to Mursi and lowered himself onto the bench. He looked down at Mursi's paper and slowly slid his mobile over the date. Not having met before, this had been a pre-arranged signal to identify himself to Mursi.

'*Salaam*. Do you read Arabic?' asked Mursi.

'*Salaam aleikum,* my friend! Yes I do,' answered the stout man. Perspiration stood out on his brow and above his top lip. He introduced himself as Mousa Al Khasib, 'Wa aleikum es salaam! Would you care to look at my paper?' responded Mursi.

Casually picking up the newspaper the stranger flicked through it. Carefully sellotaped between the centre pages were Mursi's pictures of the containers. His visitor glanced round to make sure no one was close. He began to study them whilst pretending to read the paper. After some moments he leaned towards Mursi and spoke quietly in Arabic.

'My friend I am positive this is, indeed, what you suspected. I will need to examine them physically but I am certain we are correct. How soon may I examine them?'

Mursi could hardly contain his excitement. Soon, very soon, everyone in Great Britain that had not heard of Al Qaeda would know and fear its name.

'The sooner the better thought Mursi,

'Is this evening convenient to you?'

'I will be happy to visit you this evening. I can hardly contain my curiosity.'

'You will make no mention of them to anyone. Is that perfectly clear?'

'You need have no fears there. I realise the extreme importance of what you appear to have acquired.'

Confirming the address and location of his flat Mursi bid his companion farewell, got to his feet and casually wandered out of the park to return to his flat. Although a devout Muslim, Mursi decided not to attend the mosque for prayers. As soon as Mahasheer had left Mursi took out his prayer mat and cleansed himself in preparation for *salah*.

Ironically, when kneeling to Mecca in the east he had placed the two containers before him. As he kneeled down and bowed to Mecca it looked, for all the world, as if he was praying to his lethal packages resting on the floor before him, instead of chatting to Allah.

CHAPTER 25

Sunday 3rd February

Later that evening Tom Prescott was propping the bar up in the Bruce Arms, the obvious topic of conversation being the ritual sacrifice because that is definitely what it was. Old Mrs Johnson had said so. She always knew what was happening and very often before anything happened. She always liked a good gossip. Even if nothing had happened Old Mrs Johnson could come up with some tidbit, the sole reason for her existence being gossip.

'Has anyone seen Jeb about? He should have been here tonight for a few jars. The silly sod is not answering his phone so I can't phone him and I'm not walking all that way to his house,' asked Tom.

'No, not me Tom,' from another customer doing his bit to make sure the bar at his end did not fall over either.

'But he has been flashing the readies about just lately. Has someone remembered him in their will?'

'I wouldn't think so but it is not like him to miss out on a Sunday night. In fact he is usually here before me. Never misses. I'll try his phone again.'

Once again no contact with Jeb's mobile.

'With the money he has he might have taken a bit of skirt away for a dirty weekend,' chuckled one of the men.

'They would not get far in that wreck of a van he uses. No woman in her right mind would go with him. Mind you, what about Old Mrs Johnson.'

At that the bar erupted into guffaws of laughter and all thoughts of Jeb were forgotten for the remainder of the evening.

The media was full of the story on the Monday. The police asked anyone to come forward who had been in the area of the Druid's

Temple over the past few days. The television news stated, the victim had been identified, from his fingerprints, but the name was being withheld until the next of kin had been informed.

On hearing about the Druid's Temple involvement Tom idly thought how he and Jeb had been there recently. Mind you they had not seen anyone or anything suspicious so they would not be of any possible help to the police. In any case the first time they had been poaching game and the second time they had broken into that Russian bunker.

So neither of them would go anywhere near a policeman. No, no way would Tom help the police and Jeb had gone off somewhere, probably to spend his sudden windfall on a woman. Mind you, any woman wanting Jeb would have to be desperate.

CHAPTER 26
Sunday 3rd February 1945 hours

Mursi opened his door at the first knock. He had observed his visitor approach the flat. Looking carefully up and down the street Mursi could see no sign of anyone having followed his acquaintance of that morning.

'Greetings my friend,' said Mursi as he ushered his guest into the room.

'Everything is ready for you. I have uncovered both containers for you to inspect. There they are.' Mursi pointed to them, beaming proudly as if he were introducing his two favourite sons.

Kneeling down, Mousa al Khasib, opened a small tool case and began with the less complex looking container. He used an electric meter to check circuits, verify voltage and the state of the batteries. Then, he minutely traced wires and components, checking to ascertain whether they were in accordance with a diagram he was studying. He hummed quietly to himself as he worked away.

'Well?' enquired Mursi impatiently.

'I will not be much longer my friend. Please be patient a while,' murmured the technician quietly as he concentrated on the task in hand.

Some thirty minutes later he turned and began work on the second container, once again comparing it to other diagrams he had. A further forty-five minutes passed before the man stiffly got to his feet and turned to Mursi.

'Would it be possible to have a tea please?' he asked of his host.

'Tea??' exclaimed Mursi, barely able to contain his own curiosity. 'Tell me what we have?'

'Very well,' smiled the man.

'As you are aware the containers are of Soviet origin. The drawings in my hand show details of what the Russians call a 'suitcase bomb'. If you examine the drawings and the containers you will note they are practically identical. Here, my friend is a Soviet RA 115 nuclear device,' indicating the drawing.

'The two containers are virtually identical to the drawings except certain items are slightly larger. At present I do not know why but I will investigate further. Do you see?'

Mursi was staring at the two containers as if he was witnessing the 'second coming.'

'This is beyond all our wildest dreams,' exclaimed Mursi as he affectionately rested his hand on the largest container.

'So far as I can see it is in working order despite being fifty years or so old. Quite certainly someone has been checking and maintaining it at frequent intervals. Which also means that sooner or later someone is going to realise it is missing. Once I have looked into the blueprints I will try to ascertain the reason for the amended design.'

Taking the tea Mursi had made for him, the man drank it in one go. He replaced the cup on the saucer and thanked Mursi, at the same time rising to leave.

'If you will excuse me I have work to do. I will contact you as soon as I have the information you need. Before I go I will tell you one thing. The device can be operated by a clockwork timer or by a remote control radio transmitter. See, this round knob can be set for thirty minutes to twenty-four hours. I will show you.

First you must push this switch down to energise the system, then simply turn the knob so the pointer indicates the time delay you need. As for the remote control you will need a very simple radio transmitter. I can easily find out which frequency it operates on. Unfortunately I do not know the range of the transmitter but I suspect it to be line of sight. In which case you need to be able to see where the device is located. That is a method I would not recommend. Unless you have a desire to tell Allah in person how successful the device was.' Chuckling away at his black and blasphemous attempt at humour.

'I intend using the timer in order to be well clear of the area,' explained Mursi.

'Yes, nevertheless I will obtain a suitable transmitter for you and I will also write down, very simply, how to operate the device. Incidentally, you can override the timer at any time by the remote transmitter.'

'So, there are two methods of operating the weapon?' queried Mursi.

'Yes, as I said. You can set the timer for, example six hours, but if for some reason you wish to use the transmitter, and feel you are in a safe position you could detonate the bomb just by pressing the button to send the radio signal.'

The technician was as eager as Mursi to learn more and walked to the door. After Mursi had checked the street he bade farewell to his guest and sat in a chair staring dreamily at the devices.

Eventually falling into a deep sleep where he dreamed that his small bomb had not only destroyed London but also Paris and New York. The world would very soon learn of the awesome power in Al Qaeda's armoury and tremble at the mere mention of the name.

CHAPTER 27
Tuesday 5th Feb 1030 hours

Recognising Mahasheer's prearranged coded knock at his door, Mursi cautiously opened it and indicated for the man to enter.

'Salaam aleikum,' said Mahasheer, with Mursi mumbling a brief reply. As a rule courtesy is high up on an Arab's priorities, even if he plans on slitting your throat later. On this occasion Mursi was dying for news from the technician.

'What do you have for me?'

'The technician would like to meet you this evening if that is convenient to you?'

'Of course it is. Did he say anything else? asked Mursi bursting with impatience.

'Nothing, except to tell you Allah is smiling down on you.'

The rest of the day dragged with Mursi willing the hands of the clock to move faster towards the planned meeting time of 1930 hours. Positioning himself behind the darkened window a little before the allotted time Mursi scanned the street, looking for anyone out of place. A couple with a child were the only people out and about. Emerging from the shadows he recognised the shape of his tame technician.

'Greetings my friend,' smiled Mursi, opening the flat door before the man had knocked.

'Mahasheer tells me Allah is smiling on us. Is this really true?'

'It certainly is true. I have obtained further information on the devices. The bomb, although not specifically designed to do too much structural damage, had been adapted to produce an enhanced EMP.'

Seeing Mursi's puzzled expression the man went on to explain. 'During the Cold War, Russia was planning on disrupting the West's communications by planting several of these devices throughout the western alliance countries.'

A look of sheer dismay crossed Mursi's face. 'Does this mean the device will not do any structural damage or kill many infidels?'

'No not in the least,' laughed the technician.

'The damage will be considerable, both to structures and loss of life. You can expect thousands of deaths from the initial blast and heat wave. Depending on where it is activated. Further deaths will occur over a very long period of time due to residual radiation,' explained the man.

Before leaving he handed Mursi simple instruction, on how to operate the device and ran through the procedure on the actual devices.

'See, it is so simple. If you need me further please ask and I will be here for you,' added the technician as he walked towards the door.

'Thank you my friend you have been of excellent service. I could not ask for more.'

That evening feeling, warm and content, Mursi idly flicked through the various television channels. He paused at a documentary of World War Two in black and white. The names Lidice and Oradour sur Glane were being discussed. These were only two of many villages and towns subjected to the worst of the Nazi atrocities.

Both these villages were practically razed to the ground. Dead villages. Only one soul left alive. Lidice is preserved as a national shrine to the192 men women and children butchered on the smallest of pretences. Oradour sur Glane remains untouched since the 10th of June 1944 and is also preserved as a memorial to one of the most horrific massacres of the war.

A retreating Waffen SS Panzer regiment rounded up 190 men and shot them in small groups. Old men, women and children were herded into the church, which was boarded up and then set on fire. The entire 452 were roasted alive.

Only one lady managed to escape to tell the story. Even to this day no one has any idea what prompted this heartrending and vicious act of unmitigated violence.

Mursi, deep in thought sat and gazed at the screen until long after the programme had ended. An idea was forming in his brain. His initial thoughts, in agreement with the Al Qaeda hierarchy was to detonate his device in England's capital. However, what if the bomb was used to wipe an entire village or small town off the map?

It would most probably have more impact and be remembered longer than the comparatively easy task of killing a few thousand Londoners. The death toll would only be counted in hundreds but he just KNEW it would prove to be more effective.

What is more Mursi knew of a place. Had he not only just returned from such a place! England's very own Oradour or Lidice to be?

A lovely Market town that is full of character and life. Situated in one of England's areas of outstanding natural beauty. A thriving tourist attraction. Wensleydale's very own Hawes!

Driving home from work Tom stopped outside Jeb's small cottage. The door was unlocked but in these small villages very few ever bothered to lock their doors. Tom went in and called out but no sign of Jeb. Someone had mentioned that, oddly enough Jeb's van had turned up parked and locked just off the market place. This was Mursi's idea to sow more seeds of confusion.

By the Monday evening Tom began to feel more than a little anxious. It simply was not Jeb's style to miss out on a night at the pub. At this stage he never gave the slightest thought that the murder victim could possibly be his missing friend. Things like that just did not happen to people you knew. With still no sight or sign of Jeb Tom decided to mention it to one of the policemen. Since the discovery of the corpse the area was swarming with them. 'I'd like to report a friend of mine missing. His van is parked up and locked and he is not at home. I have just been and checked. In fact I've not seen him for a few days now.'

'Really? You should phone in on the non emergency number.'

'Why? I have just reported it to you so what is to stop you making some enquiries?'

'It is not my job to go looking for missing persons. If he drives a van he must be old enough and free to do as he wishes. I have more important things to do.'

'You're a pompous, lazy, bastard. I'll take your number and complain to the police Headquarters. You lot are lost if you aren't victimising some poor motorist. I've never heard anything like it in my life. I am reporting it because it just is not in the man's nature to piss off and not say anything to anyone.'

Tom was more than a little hot under the collar at the policeman's attitude.

'There is no need to use language like that sir. We happen to be busy dealing with a murder enquiry. However, give me the man's details and I will pass them on. I expect he has gone off for a dirty weekend somewhere.'

'Oh yes Sherlock. So why is his bloody van still parked in the street? I have already told you, it just isn't his style at all. His name is Jeb Metcalfe,' offered Tom.

'Just a moment sir.' The Constable spoke quietly into his radio.

'I have a gentleman with me enquiring about a Jeb Metcalfe. Yes, that is what I thought.'

'Mr Prescott would you mind waiting here a moment. My Inspector is sending a car and would like to speak with you.'

'That sounds better. Let's get some big guns on the job.' Tom said triumphantly.

All of a sudden a terrible feeling of dread came over Tom. 'Here, this chap that has been found! It isn't Jeb is it?'

'The car won't be a moment sir.'

'Tell me. He is my best mate. Is it Jeb?'

With a deep sense of horror and dismay Tom knew, inside, that it was, indeed, his mate. Within minutes an unmarked police car pulled up alongside the two men. 'You are Mr Prescott?' demanded a pretty young policewoman. Without waiting for an answer, 'Get in, my boss wants to talk with you.'

The car tore up the road towards the Druid's Wood car park. The policewoman was concentrating on her driving and ignoring Tom's frantic questioning. A portacabin had been sited in the car park and was obviously the Control Unit.

Jeb was ushered inside. Tom saw a battery of computers and telephones being used by a small army of police personnel.

'Mr Prescott, I am Inspector Deptford. Good of you to come. Can I get you a coffee or something?'

'No you can't Inspector, I want to know what is going on.'

'It is a wise decision not to try our coffee. Please sit down and tell me about Mr Metcalfe.'

'I'm not saying a bloody thing unless you tell me whether it was Jeb or not.' Tom truculently announced.

'Were you close to Mr Metcalfe.'

'No fucking comment.'

'Please bear with me Mr Prescott.'

'Very well! We were/are the best mates for years, Jeb and I. It was him wasn't it?'

Inside Tom was dreading the answer but had to know.

'I am afraid to inform you that it was. We identified him from his fingerprints. A couple of years back we had him in on suspicion of theft but could not prove anything. He was fingerprinted at the time. This allowed us to identify him quickly. His name is not to be mentioned until his relatives have been informed.'

'I could have identified him if you'd let me see him,' protested Tom.

'In any case he only has one sister living. She is in Leyburn and they have not spoken for donkeys. Never got on with each other.'

'Mr Prescott. Despite your long friendship you would not have been able to identify your friend. Whoever killed him made certain his face was unrecognisable. I really am sorry to be the bearer of such distressing news.'

'Good God not Jeb. Why? Who would have reason to do that? Jeb could be a pain at times but he was harmless.'

'Mr Prescott! Do you know if Jeb had anything to do with any religious or pagan groups?'

'Jeb? Not in a million years,' exclaimed Tom.

'He thought they were all nutter's but why do you ask?'

With a sigh the Inspector began to explain to Tom where and how Jeb had been found and that the body had the appearance of a ritual sacrifice.

'His body has been terribly mutilated and his private parts pushed inside his mouth. The arms were placed to give the body a cruciform appearance. Whoever did it intended it to look like some sort of ritual killing.'

'Those fucking Russians,' exploded Tom.

'I told him to stay away. I had intended to report it to the police on Monday but forgot with all the goings on.'

'Russians?' The Inspector's eyebrows were raised quizzically.

'Russians? What do you mean?' asked the surprised Inspector.

'Look, can we go up to the Temple? I want to check on something,' pleaded Tom.

'It is a sterile SOC area, we should not go there without their say so. Mind you, I imagine they have all the information the place had to reveal by now. Why not tell me here and I can have whatever it is checked,' pointed out the Inspector.

'I bet I know one thing they will not have checked out. No. I want to check on something myself and we need two good torches.'

Realising how badly the news had affected Tom and accepting he was adamant he would not say another word, the Inspector stood.

'Get me two SOC coveralls. We are going to the Temple.'

Two pairs of white coveralls were produced and Tom told to put one on. The Inspector following suit, so to speak!! No pun intended. Once kitted out they set off towards the Temple where a further portacabin was located.

'OK here we are,' stated the policeman as they neared the Temple and stepped over Police Crime barrier tape.

'Sergeant, is it OK if I have a look at something?' the policeman called out to a white clad SOC investigator.

'Help yourself. We won't get anymore and we will be winding up shortly.'

'I don't mean here in the Temple but up this bank. Follow me.' Tom interjected as he set off up the slope with the now curious Inspector in tow. Kneeling down at the bunker Tom hastily scraped the leaves and grass away to expose the metal lid.

'Well now. What do we have here?' questioned the astonished

Inspector as Tom raised the lid and made to descend the metal ladder. 'I can't understand why my people never discovered this. They were supposed to have searched the area for any likely clues. Anyway what has this to do with anything?'

'If my guess is right it has everything to do with Jeb's murder,' added a grim-faced Tom.

'Wait whilst I get some of our people up here. Don't go down there in case you obliterate any fingerprints or anything else that might help us with this case.'

Bugger waiting, thought Tom as the Inspector radioed his Chief, Tom was already disappearing through the opening. He felt even more certain Jeb,s death was somehow linked to this bunker.

'Gone! I knew it. I told him to stay away,' came Tom's anguished voice from below.

At that the Inspector, overcome with curiosity, decided not to wait for his men and clambered down to join Tom. 'What has gone and what on earth is this place and how did you find it?'

Tom quickly put the policeman in the picture about how Jeb had literally stumbled onto the site by tripping over the metal cover. Tom also explained about the supply of Russian tins of food, cigarettes and chocolate, adding that Jeb would smoke, eat or drink anything. Particularly if it was free gratis.

'There were two heavy metal cases on the floor. They have gone.' Tom pointed out the obvious. And more chocolate and all the cigarettes have gone.

'What sort of cases?' enquired the Inspector.

'Oi, you down there,' called out a voice from above.

'What's going on?'

'Sir, you had better come down here and look at this.'

'I just hope it is not too mucky and shitty down there.' Someone cursed as his feet slipped on the metal rungs announcing the arrival of the senior officer as he stumbled into the dim interior.

'Well, Inspector, and what do we have here?'

'Tom, tell the Chief Inspector what you told me.'

With that Tom ran through the story for the second time in as many minutes.

'Mr Prescott! What do you think was in those metal boxes and what did they look like?'

'They looked a bit like machinery of some sort, or fancy electrical equipment. I thought they might have been some type of radios as there was a small light on one of the units to show it was switched on. There was quite a lot of electric wiring. I lifted one up and it was fairly heavy but nothing difficult. These are some of the boxes Jeb opened. See, the writing is in Russian.'

'Well, Mr Prescott! I don't think you will be very popular with my SOC people. They were in the process of winding down. Thanks to you it looks as if they are about to start all over again,' muttered the Chief Inspector.

'OK, everyone out now! I don't know what you have come across but I do not like the looks of it. As you pointed out Mr Prescott, the writing is, indeed, Russian. It is also pretty old as well. I would appreciate it if you did not say a word about this to anyone Mr Prescott. In fact, I go as far as to insist you do not tell a soul.'

The men climbed back up out of the bunker and headed towards the SOC portacabin. 'I will find a driver to take you back to Masham. Leave a number where we can contact you at any time. Someone will be in touch very soon.'

'Right. I'll leave my works number as well. Some of us have to work for a living,' Tom said as he stepped out of the white SOC suit and shoes.

'Did you spot how clean and tidy the place was and how brightly the bulb shone. Someone has been keeping this place in good fettle.'

'Now you mention it, Mr Prescott, yes it was pretty well maintained for its age,' stated the Chief Inspector.

'My people will give the place an extra good going over. You can be sure we shall need to speak with you again very soon. You say there was a small light on one of the units. What sort of light do you mean?'

'Like the little light you see when your TV is left on standby. Come to think of it there were two identical lights, except one was green and the other red.'

'Thank you! We will be in touch very shortly Mr Prescott. We shall also need your finger prints to identify you in case we discover any others.'

'Don't worry about that squire. If I don't hear from you soon you will be hearing from me. I want the buggers who murdered Jeb caught.'

Tom's parting words as he strode back to the waiting police car.

CHAPTER 30

Wednesday 6th February 0715 hours

After an almost sleepless night Mursi had finalised, in his mind, how he would carry out the task of eradicating Hawes from the map. He had drafted a coded message to be sent to Al Qaeda's ruling body proffering his radical idea and seeking their approval. In effect it was merely a formality. He knew they would go with his amended suggestion. This outrage would go down in history as one of Al Qaeda's greatest achievements, if not its greatest ever.

He donned a plain grey suit and placed a *keffiyeh* carefully round his head. He walked slowly along St Thomas's road and into the mosque, where he knew Karim Mahasheer would be.

'Karim, this message must be sent with all haste. I have coded it so send it exactly as I have written it out. Bring the answer to me the moment it arrives.'

'Certainly Midhat! Is there anything else you wish of me?'

'No thank you Karim! Just you get back to me the minute the reply is in your hands.'

With that out of the way there was little more Mursi could do. He returned to his flat, settled down and tried to catch up on his lost sleep.

Only an hour or so later a rap at the door roused Mursi. It was Mahasheer. 'Midhat you did say you wanted this as soon as it arrived. It does not make sense to me but you will know what it means.'

'Thank you Karim, give it me quickly,' ordered Mursi. Taking the note to a small table he had soon decoded the short message. As anticipated, an emergency quorum of Al Qaeda's ruling council had authorised Mursi to go ahead with his amended proposal.

Before Mahasheer returned to the mosque Mursi ordered him to contact the technician. Mursi now had a real need for the man's knowledge and expertise. The only irritating thing was when he realised that he had instructed the device to be brought from the Yorkshire Dales and it now had to do the return journey.

Although one section would be in the boot the second part had to travel on the rear seats. Perhaps a car with a larger boot was called for. So many things could go wrong. A breakdown. A minor accident. It just needed one inquisitive policeman for Mursi's outstandingly grand scheme to turn to dust. So be it. It would just be the policeman's bad luck. Nothing, but nothing was going to hold Mursi back now.

CHAPTER 31

Wednesday 6th February 0850 hours

'Tom, a bird on the phone for you.' Called out Tom's boss.

'Tell her not to phone you at work another time.'

'Tom Prescott.' Into the mouthpiece.

'Mr Prescott this is DC Caroline Tuckley. We have someone here who wishes to meet you and speak with you rather urgently.'

'OK put him on.'

'No, Mr Prescott, not on the phone but here at the Incident Room. We will have a car collect you in a few minutes.'

'Hold your horses, I need to ask my boss if it is OK.'

'We need you with or without your boss's approval. Let me speak to him please.'

'Boss, she wants you.' Handing the phone over.

'I have a business to run here. Do I get some sort of compensation? Mr Prescott is a key man. Very well, but don't make it too often.' Tom was grudgingly given the OK.

'Key man am I? I'll remember that next time I am due for a rise. A key man should be worth a few extra quid,' Grinned Tom at his boss.

'Bugger off and don't take all day,' Grumbled his boss.

A car pulled into the parking area and he noted the same policewoman as before.

'People will talk if you keep meeting me like this.'

'So long as my husband doesn't find out,' Joked DC Tuckley.

They were soon drawing to a halt at the Temple car park where the dishy policewoman directed Tom to the Portacabin. A tall thin man, in civvies, strode over to Tom and shook hands with a firmer grip that belied his appearance.

'Please join me over here, my name is Stewart. I have some

photographs I want you to look at. Please tell me if you see anything vaguely resembling those metal containers. If you find any put them to one side and we will talk about them later.'

Tom wondered if Stewart was his Christian or surname, or in fact any part of his real name. There was just something spooky altogether about his manner.

Slowly flicking through the photos Tom began putting certain ones aside as instructed. Some were photo's of radios from the forties, and fifties. Why on earth were they included. There was even a photo of an old twin-tub washing machine.

Tom looked inquisitively at Stewart who merely nodded for Tom to continue. After scanning almost eighty a pile of nine or ten had been placed to one side.

'Finished? asked Stewart. 'Now let's see what we have here.'

'What is the purpose of some of the pictures? Radios? Washing machines? Just wasting my time,' grumbled Tom.

'They are to make certain you are not confused and only select pictures of items that are similar to those you found.'

Carefully examining the small pile, Stewart began questioning Tom about the pictures he had placed to one side.

'Right. This one, are you positive it looked like this?'

'Near as I can remember,' nodded Tom. 'Those bits there looked exactly the same but the fitting on top was bigger than the one here.'

'Good, leave that for now. What about these others?'

Tom shortlisted another four that jogged his mind. 'Almost finished. Now how many out of ten for accuracy of the photos you selected?'

'The top one ten out of ten. Apart from the cover which I told you about. The others at least eight or nine out of ten. Remember I only saw them under a small light and a torch. As near as I can recall these are what I saw.' Tom sat back and looked at Stewart, 'so what was in those boxes to cause all this fuss, or is it some sort of secret?'

'Mr Prescott, listen carefully. I know the Chief Inspector told you not to say anything about those missing containers or the bunker itself. I am now telling you that if the merest whisper gets out about the bunker or the containers you will find yourself in very deep water. Everyone here is sworn to secrecy. That includes you, especially.'

'I said I would not say anything and I won't, but can't you give me some idea?' requested Tom.

'I am not permitted to discuss them but I will tell you this. If your memory of those boxes is correct, the British Government may be faced with a catastrophe too immense for you to comprehend.'

The manner in which Stewart said this sent a chill down Tom's spine but he was not sure why exactly. 'No point in you signing a copy of the Official Secrets Act. I do hope, however, that you appreciate the gravity of the situation. The Chief Inspector wishes to speak with you now. He wants anything you can tell him about Mr Metcalfe. It is vital that we find out who Jeb was dealing with. More importantly, who has taken those containers and where have they taken them?'

With that Stewart strode over to one of the telephones ignoring Tom completely and not even saying thank you or goodbye!

'Ungrateful bastard,' Tom commented towards Stewart's disappearing back.

As Tom rose to leave DC Tuckley told him to follow her to the Mobile Control Unit near the Temple. Arriving there he was questioned about every aspect of Jeb's life and other friends or acquaintances. As Jeb tended to keep himself to himself even Tom could not help much. Jeb was Jeb and never did anything that wasn't typically Jeb.

Nothing mysterious or sinister would even occur to him. The DCI thanked Tom and told him they would need him again. If he remembered anything that would help, to give them a call immediately. He handed Tom a card with the mobile number shown. As Prescott walked out he turned to the DCI.

'There is one thing. It might not be important but I did ask Jeb why he was so flush. Usually he never had a penny to scratch his arse.'

'The smallest detail may be helpful. What was it'? asked the DCI.

'He said something about thanks to the oil sheikhs he was only getting his own money back from what he had paid them for petrol. I never took him up on it because Jeb was always going off at a tangent. Looking back now it did seem an odd thing to say, even for Jeb.'

'Just a moment Mr Prescott. Stewart would you join us please?'

Stewart had finished his call and was playing Russian roulette by risking a cup of police coffee. He approached the DCI and Prescott, still carrying the sludge, looking coffee.

'Mr Prescott. Please repeat to Stewart what you just told me.'

'Shit. Are you absolutely positive that is what Mr Metcalfe said?'

'Near enough word for word. It did not seem to mean anything. Jeb was always saying dopey things at times. Why should mentioning oil sheikhs be so important?'

'Mr Prescott. It is even more important now that none of this is discussed out of this hut. Do you understand?'

'I told you. I won't say a word. I can't see why all the fuss over Jeb's rambling.'

'Mr Prescott, while you are here we will take your fingerprints. Luckily we wore gloves when you took me into the bunker,' ordered Inspector Deptford.

'Why mine? You don't think I killed Jeb, do you?' snorted Tom.

'It is merely to try to identify all prints and eliminate ones we are sure of, as I told you previously. As regards those containers, did you or Mr Metcalfe touch them?'

'I lifted the nearest one by the handle but did not touch it otherwise. Jeb didn't, he was too busy stuffing his pockets.'

'Thank you Mr Prescott. We will most certainly need to see you again.' With that the Inspector nodded to DC Tuckley, indicating she should take Tom back to his work.

CHAPTER 32

Wednesday 6th February 1800 hours

After sitting patiently behind the curtained window Mursi, once again, noticed his technician ally approaching. No one appeared to be following and on reaching Mursi's flat, found the door already open for him.

'Welcome my brother,' as Mursi embraced his visitor.

'Come in, come in. I will take your coat for you.'

'What can I do for you now my friend?' enquired the technician.

'A target has been identified. I need you to go through once again how to operate the bomb. I appreciate you showed me previously and that it is simple but I wish to be certain. Obviously I also want to ensure I am well clear from the area before detonation. I want you to give me full details of everything I need to know to use the device successfully.'

With that the technician began pointing out the relevant components. He explained that Mursi would find it more convenient to have someone help him assemble the two devices. He demonstrated the timing unit and also the remote control.

'To remind you, the remote control unit will override any settings on the timer. Should you use the remote, for any reason, you must ensure you are at least three miles from the weapon. Even then you must exercise caution as I am not completely satisfied as to the bomb's yield. Ideally, even at that distance, you should be sheltering behind something solid.'

Mursi asked question after question with a plethora of 'what ifs' and 'how's'. He made notes which were to be committed to memory and the note later destroyed.

It was close to midnight when, fully satisfied, Mursi bade his visitor goodnight. He seated himself and perused the copious details on his note pad. Again and again he checked and rechecked. Eventually deciding that he was totally au fait with operating the device he put a match to the sheets of paper. They burnt to ashes and he carefully flushed them down the kitchen sink.

Thursday 0730 hours

A visit to the mosque was called for. Mahasheer was instructed to get a message to Anas Al Liby. He would be ideal as Mursi's aide. He had already proved himself to be ruthless and calm under pressure, his handling of Jeb Metcalfe being ample evidence of his devotion to the cause. Always the cause.

By 0830 Al Liby had contacted Mursi on his mobile, when they arranged to meet in one of the many cafes frequented by Muslims. This time both mobiles were disposed of. From now onwards any mobiles would be one-call units only. An expensive choice but vitally important. It was all too easy to trace a mobile's location and eavesdrop messages. If the GCHQ at Cheltenham did not intercept the message you could be sure that Menwith Hill outside Harrogate would.

When Hawes was wiped off the map Mursi also hoped his bomb would provide collateral damage, the largest army camp in Europe, Catterick Garrison, being only a few miles away as the crow flies. If the wind was in the right direction Catterick was sure to be enveloped in a curtain of deadly radiation from the fallout.

Mursi's tame technician felt certain that Menwith Hill would lose some of its communications intercepting ability. These days, however, everyone in the comms business was fully aware of what EMP meant and took appropriate precautions to shield sensitive equipment. Oh well, Mursi could but hope. In any case his real interest lay in the town of Hawes being obliterated.

Few people appreciate the fact that GCHQ and Menwith Hill intercept millions of emails, mobile, radio and even landline messages each working day. These communications stations were programmed to search for and pick out pertinent words. Examples probably would be names of known terrorist strongholds such as Iraq and Afghanistan. The mention of Al Qaeda was sure to set alarm bells ringing.

Together with a multitude of names and other details programmed into the system. These messages originated from every corner of the globe, hence terrorists were compelled to use mobiles on a one shot basis or risk being located and arrested, or worse. In this technological age any message sent by any electronic means was liable to be picked up. Even machines with 'scramblers' could be intercepted with the right equipment.

CHAPTER 33

Thursday 7th February 0807 hours

'This is Inspector Deptford, will you ask Stewart to contact me with the greatest urgency. He knows where I am.'

With that Deptford replaced the phone and looked at the details of the fingerprints for the hundredth time. Since the possible Russian involvement the case had been pursued with far more vigour than was usual for a murder investigation. The bunker, checked for fingerprints as well as many of the stones on the altars of the Temple. A bloody palm print was visible next to where the mutilated corpse had been discovered. Unfortunately it was too smudged to give any details. Stewart had insisted the prints were to be given priority in case they yielded anything of interest. What they did have was a number of different and clear prints from inside the bunker. Jeb Metcalfes had been taken from his lifeless fingers and identified. Tom Prescott's were also clearly visible.

Just then the warbling of the phone brought the Inspector out of his reverie. 'Deptford.'

'Inspector, it is Stewart. What do you have for me?'

'I think you should come and see for yourself. It seems unbelievable what has turned up. It makes no sense to me unless...' He absentmindedly replaced the receiver.

'I will be with you in a few minutes,' said Stewart not realising the Inspector had already hung up. With that Stewart hurried out of the King's Head hotel in Masham. He had booked in there to be on hand for any sudden developments and to push things along. The Russian connection had demanded a spook of Stewart's grade.

'What is so important Inspector?' asked Stewart as he entered the Portacabin.

'Tell me what you think to these,' indicating copies of fingerprints taken from inside the bunker.

'I did some telephoning to confirm they are the real McCoy. I also learned something else that is even more interesting. The Americans claim to have already killed this man. Twice! When we sent the ones from the bunker to be identified the computer threw these up.'

One of their experts had done a comparison and pencilled circles round prominent features. Written below were the words 'Match confirmed,' together with a name and a pair of aliases.

'So how did a dead man manage to put his dabs inside this bunker?' mused Stewart.

Picking up the phone Stewart dialled a London number. It terminated in an office in Thames House. home of Britain's Security Service, better known as MI5.

'Good morning. Stewart here. Put me through to the DG please.'

The DG or Director General, head of the organisation being Jonathan Edwards was well known for his anti-Al Qaeda activities.

'I'm sorry sir but the DG is very busy. May I put you on to someone else.'

'No you bloody can't. This is urgent. I need to speak with him. Now!'

'I will try his number and see if he can speak with you. Please hold a moment.'

Some moments later the Director General was on the line. 'Stewart, what do you mean by bullying my secretary. She feels rather put out that you swore at her.'

'Sorry sir, I'll put her on my Christmas Card list' replied Stewart.

'What's the problem Stewart? You only have a couple of minutes. I really am up to my ears. A meeting with the PM later, he is a little concerned about the Soviet equipment that was in that underground bunker.'

'Sir, you can now really make the PM's day. In addition to the Russians you can include an Arab involvement. Knowing how you love Al Qaeda what would you say if I told you they had got their hands on an atom bomb.'

Stewart held the phone from his ear waiting for the explosion from Jonathan Edwards. 'I wish you were joking but something tells me you are not, hold all my calls Helen, he yelled to his secretary, and this time I mean all calls.'

Stewart explained clearly and concisely the events that had unfolded in North Yorkshire.

'There is one thing I would be grateful if you would do for me sir.'

'Yes Stewart, what?'

'One set of the prints was left by Mursi and a further set identified as Anas al Liby. Both inside the bunker and both, obviously, very recent. The police computer churned them out. Inspector Deptford gave me the good news five minutes ago. Would you contact our friends at Grosvenor Square and ask them what the bloody hell prompted them to 'greatly exaggerate' the report of Mursi's death in January of this year?' Taking a leaf from Winston Churchill's erroneous obituary report many years earlier.

'If you recall sir, the Americans also claimed to have killed Mursi some years previously. Apparently these AQ guys need to be killed at least twice.' The 'friends', supposingly attaches of one kind or another were, in reality, members of America's CIA. Quite often referred to as Clowns In Action after a number of very embarrassing home goals.

'Will do. I do not think the Americans will be very happy to know Mursi is still alive and kicking You stay there and see what you can come up with. Our Muslim friends must have stayed in the area. I will send Newman and Franklin to help you.'

'Thanks boss. Please let me know what the Yanks come up with. I'm sure you will enjoy rubbing their noses in it over Mursi's resurrection. We might be able to milk it for a little more co-operation from them, I have plenty here to keep Butch Cassidy and The Sundance Kid busy, Newman's first name being Paul so it followed that he and Franklin, who usually worked together, were known as Butch and Sundance.

'One more thing before you go? I will tell Helen that when you call, in future, you are to be put through straight away. I will also have her go through the files to see who else I can send up there. This is now a major situation. I don't relish the thought that I am going to have to tell the PM that it very much looks as if Al Qaeda are now the proud owners of a bonny bouncing bloody A Bomb.'

'Thank you sir. I will be in touch. Speak soon, cheers.'

A click indicated the DG had hung up.

'Hmmm interesting,' said Inspector Deptford looking up at Stewart.

'What is?'

'Me thinking you were Special Branch, but you aren't are you? You are a genuine real live spook,' smiled the Inspector.

'You mentioned The DG. The only one that comes to my mind is Jonathan Edwards.'

'There are lots of DG's out there,' countered Stewart.

'Yes, but not with the clout to have contacts in Grosvenor Square which just happens to be where the American Embassy is located.'

'I must be slipping in my old age, but merely supposition on your part Inspector. Might I suggest you keep your ideas to yourself. Shall we get on with the business in hand. This has now upped from a murder enquiry to a major terrorist situation.'

Stewart picked up the copies of Mursi's prints and studied them, deep in thought.

CHAPTER 34

'Jonathan Edwards here, I phoned earlier asking to speak to Mr Turner. Is he clear yet?'

A smooth and seductive sounding American lady purred,

'He was about to call your office now sir. Just one moment please.'

'Jonathan, great to hear from you,' boomed Robert Holmes Turner, the US Ambassador to the Court of St James, I'm sure it is not a social call, what can I do you for?'

'Good day Mr Ambassador. I believe we may have a very serious problem on our hands. Even calling it very serious massively understates the situation.'

He then gave a brief outline to the Ambassador stating, what he knew. Adding what help he needed and expected from his counterparts with the American Government.

'Jonathan. Indeed, I am sure we all have one helluva big problem. I'll send a guy round to see you right now. Anything you need just ask, anything.'

Tuttle had grasped the enormity of the situation immediately.

'Thank you Mr Ambassador. We will be pleased to work closely with your men on this. We need all the input we can get. There is one other thing I can think of.'

'Ask away Jonathan.'

'The lady that put me through to you. I don't suppose she fancies working for me.'

A hearty laugh came down the phone.

'Jonathan, you old dog. You are welcome to her. I should warn you the voice is nothing like the rest of the package. Her voice is the best bit by a long shot. Have a nice day.'

Still laughing, the Ambassador replaced his phone on its cradle.

CHAPTER 35

Thursday 7th February

Butch and Sundance barged into the portacabin around teatime. 'Hello, you must be Inspector Deptford, I am Paul Newman and this is Malcolm Franklin. Before you make any wisecracks about my name – I've heard them all. Any idea where Stewart is?'

'Yep, he is going round the hotels, guest houses and boarding houses showing photos of this man and asking if him or anyone like him has been staying there recently. This is his mobile, if you can get a signal.'

With that Stewart walked in. 'Hi guys. Good journey?'

Without waiting for a reply he picked up a copy of Yellow Pages and dumped it on the desk in front of Butch and Sundance.

'Start by phoning every sort of accommodation within 25 miles asking if an Arab looking person or persons has stayed there this past week. Work closely with the Inspector as his men are working on the same line of enquiry.'

A groan went up from the pair.

'Right, we will start first thing in the morning. We need to book in somewhere.'

'You will start now and you are booked in to the same hotel as me, in Masham. Fear not, I shall be helping you.'

'A question.' This time from Newman. 'Do we KNOW for certain those things are Russian RA 115s?'

'We have to assume that is what they were until we know differently. We cannot afford to take the slightest chance. Photographs were shown to Prescott and he not only picked the correct photographs out but he sketched differences. The boffins are convinced they are modified 115s.'

Stewart slumped into a chair as if he had the world on his

shoulders. 'The DG had a meeting with the PM today. Arranged before he knew about our possible bomb. You can be sure what the main topic of conversation turned out to be. He also contacted the US Embassy seeking their help, but I would not count on them being too helpful. Particularly as he asked them why a couple of high ranking AQ men are still alive and kicking after the Yanks reported them dead some weeks back. Oh bollocks, forget those phone calls for now. You've had a long drive and I'm knackered. Let's call it a day and resume in the morning bright and early.'

Leading the way out, Stewart turned to Butch and Sundance. 'By the way. That doesn't mean you don't have to bring the Yellow Pages. A little bedtime reading for you.'

'Geez, boss. I just glanced at the accommodation, there are dozen's. groused Butch.

'Not quite correct Butch my boy. There are, in fact, many hundreds,' offered Stewart, a smile on his lips for the first time that day.

'We can also expect more as the Inspector has been in touch with the Yorkshire Tourist Board.'

CHAPTER 36

Friday 8th February

Having had extra telephones installed in the Police Control Unit, early morning found the three spooks busily ringing hotels and so on. They had liaised with the Inspector and began checking to the west of Masham. Deptford's men were checking hotels to the east, including Ripon and Northallerton. Stewart had already visited every accommodation facility of any size in the immediate Masham area. At Stewart's suggestion they were to start with hotels and gradually work down to B & Bs. This was something of a relief after seeing the Yorkshire Tourist Board's list of various types of accommodation.

'You are certain?' enquired Franklin.

'OK, I will be there shortly and thank you for your help.'

Already one of Franklin's calls had led to a hotel owner saying he had had Arab looking people stay with them. Things were looking promising.

'An hotel in Middleham had two Arabs stay there for a few days. It may be nothing but we will go and speak with the owner.'

'Don't hold out too much hope and keep me informed.' Stewart wished them luck as Butch and Sundance left together for the ten mile or so drive to Middleham.

'Hello, someone called us about some Arab looking men staying here, recently.'

'That will have been the boss. Can I get you anything to drink while I fetch him?'

'That sounds good. Two white coffees would go down very well, thank you.'

Ten minutes later they were sitting in the comfortable lounge in front of a blazing log fire, talking earnestly with the owner. A middl aged man and woman sat in the corner drinking coffee and both reading their own newspapers. A typical married couple and well out of earshot.

'You described the two men well. Will you please look at these mug shots and see if you recognise anyone?'

The landlord pointed to one. 'I am pretty certain this bloke was one but he looks different as neither of the men here had a beard.'

The landlady wandered through asking if anyone wanted more tea or coffee, idly glancing at the photographs. Seeing her interest Franklin asked, 'Do you recognise anyone?'

'You bet. This one.'

'You seem positive, why do you remember him?' queried Franklin.

'Easy. He looked a bit of alright. Real go-to-bed eyes. I recognise him even with the beard in the photo.'

'You don't recognise anyone else. How about this one?' Sundance pointed to a photo of Mursi.

'No, I would have told you if I had seen the other one's picture. Some look a bit like the other but I can't really say. This one is the only one I can definitely identify. Anyway why don't you check the tapes. Then you can see for yourselves. It cost enough having the CCTV system installed. We may as well use it?' she suggested.

'Tapes, what tapes?'

'Bloody hell, yes I forgot them,' replied the landlord. We have CCTV cameras installed. The tapes will still have them on it. We had a power failure and I forgot to reset the system so it has been off for a few days.'

'I don't know! We spend a fortune on having CCTV and you forget to switch the bloody thing back on. You useless lump,' grumbled the landlady.

'Well, you forgot as well. I can't do everything damn thing round here.'

'Hang on. We did not mean to start a family fallout. Can you get them now and have you a player where we can look at them?' enquired Butch.

'No problem. Come upstairs you can watch them on our telly.'

'Do you think we should phone Stewart?' asked Sundance.

'No point until we have something concrete for him Butch.'

Twenty minutes later with Butch operating the remote control the two of them fast forwarded until they saw two darker-skinned people in the dining area. They made notes of places on the tape where the apparent Arabs could be seen. Then two head-and-shoulders shots of both men appeared on the screen.

'Hold it there,' yelled Franklin.

'That must be them. Just a mo. Landlady, can you join us please?' Newman called downstairs.

Looking at the rewound tape the landlady confirmed they had been the two guests. The two spooks looked at more tape but decided the two head and shoulder shots were the best. Leaving the image paused on the TV screen the two men began scanning their books of mugshots.

'Fucking bingo man. See who this is?' exclaimed Franklin.

'Anas fucking Al Liby. NOW I'll give Stewart a call.' So saying Newman put through a call to Stewart.

'Right. I will be with you directly,' Stewart had said after the call.

Meanwhile they were struggling to put a name to the second Arab, looking man. They used their mugshot books and a laptop but so far nothing on the second one. Eventually the sound of heavy footsteps heralded the arrival of Stewart, breathing hard from rushing up the stairs.

'Show me.' ordered Stewart No good day, kiss my arse, or preamble.

'By God, give the man a coconut. Anas Al Liby himself. Where has he been hiding? You know what the Yanks are offering for that bugger.' Without waiting for a response he added, 'Five fucking mill.'

'I'd better give the boss the good news.'

With that Stewart pushed a speed dial number on his mobile to call Thames House.

'You can give the man a second coconut now. I've just clocked this bastard. Add another five mill. Usually known as Mohammed Jamal

Khalifa. It says here he is the main financier for AQ,' called out Butch, sitting back with a smug look on his face.

Stewart cancelled his call, which had started ringing, and looked over Newman's shoulder. 'Butch, you can have a bloody bag full of coconuts. Bulls eye!'

The face on the video tape matched one staring at them from the laptop. It was not a good likeness but it was enough to clock the guy. A warbling and vibration alerted Stewart to an incoming call. He recognised the number.

'Hello, you just called. Did you want the DG?' asked Helen, Edwards, PA.

'You bet I do. How would you like a coconut to get your lips round? A big fat, juicy, hairy coconut?'

'Pardon? Stewart, are you making obscene telephone calls to my PA?'

Chalk one up to Helen. Hearing Stewart going on about coconuts she had deliberately put his call direct to the DG, momentarily catching Stewart out.

'That will teach him to swear at me,' she muttered under her breath.

'Sorry sir but I have been dishing out coconuts as prizes. Butch and Sundance have confirmed two Arabs. It is pretty certain they are top players in the bomb game. Both are on America's Ten Most Wanted. A cool ten mill for the pair.'

Stewart quickly explained.

'Well done to all three of you. At least it is a start. We do not know if they are involved but I'd bet my boots they are in some way mixed up in it. Are you still OK up there or is there anything else I can do for you?'

'We are fine thank you sir, but there is at least one big Muslim fly in the ointment.'

'What bad news are you going to hand me now Stewart?'

'Two Arabs but neither of them Mursi. So what the hell is he up to and where is he now? It is dead certain he was in that bunker with

Al Liby as both their prints were all over the place. If they were together, where was Khalifa. It doesn't add up yet.'

'I see what you mean. You have made progress so stick at it. It will come together eventually. I damn well hope so.'

The DG cut in. 'Before you go, something you might be interested to know. The PM summoned the Soviet Ambassador to Number 10. He demanded to know what the Russians were doing leaving fucking A bombs littering the British countryside. Phrased in more diplomatic terms, of course.'

'What came of it?' interrupted Stewart.

'The Russkie denied any knowledge of it. The PM told him that to prevent the spread of panic in the UK and to defuse a potentially major diplomatic incident he wanted maximum co-operation from them. The Ambassador left, tail between his legs, saying he would consult with Moscow. We are waiting for him to come back to us but the PM laid it on the line. Immediate action or fuck off out of the UK. The problem being, if word got out the public would go ape.'

'It might help if we had the Russkies on our side in this. Anything on the Yanks?' enquired Stewart.

'Yes, they are pulling all the stops out. It seems that several Al Qaeda high rankers were definitely in Derunta camp. The Yanks bombed and wiped it out. The body count, and local intelligence led them to believe they had got Jamal Khalifa and Midhat Mursi, or whatever they call themselves. The Americans also found papers and documentation proving that the two men had definitely been in the camp only hours before the raid. It now turns out that they appear to have left the camp only hours prior to the bombardment. Bodies were obviously smashed up beyond recognition. It was wishful thinking on the part of the Americans. I do not know if you were aware of it but the Americans also claimed to have killed Mursi some months earlier. We now know, beyond all doubt, that Khalifa is alive as is Mursi. Until we prove otherwise. One final thing Stewart!'

'Sir?'

'Direct from the PM. We do not want to be left with any martyrs once we locate these people. Do I make myself clear? No martyrs at all!'

'Message understood sir. It will be a pleasure to comply!'

CHAPTER 38

Monday 11th February Mid afternoon

After lunching in Hawes the two spooks were weary from almost a week of non-stop work. Asking questions. Visiting hotels, B and Bs, caravan sites, holiday lets. Any and every place that offered some sort of accommodation. The Dales being a popular venue, almost every other house provided some sort of accommodation.

'I've had enough, I don't think the family at the Stone House hotel are worth asking about. I can't see dad saying, 'bye family, I'm off to nick an atom bomb', let's toss whether we go there or not', suggested Butch.

'Aye, go on then. Heads we return to Masham. Tails one last hotel visit for the day.'

Butch's 50p coin spun in the air and landed on the floor, spinning on its edge before clattering to a stop. Showing tails. Stone House was on.

'Best of three', said Butch, retrieving the coin to toss it a second time.

'I don't fancy another visit today and all this fresh air is not good for my chest.'

'No, tails it is. We go to the hotel', insisted Sundance.

'Just my luck to get landed with another slave driver like Stewart', moaned Butch.

It seemed fate had destined they should check this hotel out after all. Their car turned into the hotel car park and they walked to reception.

Showing his ID card, briefly, Newman said, 'the Manager is expecting us.'

'Certainly Mr Newman, walk this way please', invited the trim young lady.

Butch quietly whispered into Franklins' ear, 'if I could walk that way I'd be worried about you walking behind me!'

Following the delightful looking bottom, the two were shown into a small room. 'The Manager will be here directly. Can I get you tea or coffee?' enquired the sweet young thing.

Answering for both, Franklin said, 'no thank you we are fine.' Thinking, if I have another coffee today I'll drown.

A pleasant looking man strode in, shook hands with both and introduced himself. 'Hello, I am the Manager, barman, handyman, whatever is needed. I am the owner actually. You said on the phone you were interested in any foreign looking gentlemen staying here over the past couple of weeks or thereabouts.' He was holding the hotel register. 'You are welcome to look at this. However, to save you time I have listed every foreigner on this sheet of paper. It would help if I knew what you were looking for.'

'At this stage we are merely trying to locate a couple of persons.' Passing the list across to them the owner went on, 'I have my copy here and I can vouch for most of them.' Starting at the top they worked down the list of a dozen names.

'The first three arrived, together, for the shooting. They are regulars and stay with us every year,' explained the man. 'The next, a Dutchman and his wife. Both well into their seventies. I am sure I could be more helpful if I knew who you were looking for.'

'We believe one or two of them may be able to help us with some enquiries into a local murder,' stated Newman.

'I assume you have pictures of the men you are looking for. May I see them please?' asked the owner without showing the remotest interest in having a possible murderer stay with him.

'These are photos of three men but they may have altered their appearances by now.' Newman passed the small bundle of photos across.

'Would you please carry on with your list. Then, with your permission, we would like to check the register for ourselves.'

'Most mysterious I must say. Anyhow, next. A very delightful family from Kuwait. Father, mother and son. The father works in the Kuwaiti Embassy in London, they speak very good English. Just a moment. This photo. It is the man from Kuwait!'

'You are certain?' asked Butch.

'Of course. No doubt whatsoever. Both the husband and wife were so nice and polite. Even their little boy was very well behaved. I only wish all my guests were as nice. Do you know I have had some guests...?'

'Just a moment sir,' Butch butted in.

'May I see your register please to check their details? Oh, one other thing,' remembering the CCTV from the Middleham hotel.

'Do you use CCTV cameras?' Asked Newman.

'Well we do have CCTV and until some days ago all was well, then I noticed the tape was not turning. It appeared to have jammed. I had to replace the tape with a new one to make sure the machine is not damaged.'

'Does that mean you do not have these people on any of your tapes?'

'Oh, no. I am sure they will be on the old tape but it is no use now. It has jammed and will not play.'

'May we see the tape please? Perhaps we can do something with it.'

'By all means. I will fetch it. You are welcome to keep it. I won't be using it again in case it damages the recorder.' With that the man disappeared, to return seconds later with a video tape. It had a few feet of tape hanging loosely from it looking, for all the world, like a ribbon of dried intestines.

'See, I told you it was useless,' said the owner.

Just then the receptionist called through saying there was a Miss Metcalfe on the phone to speak to the owner.

'If you will excuse me please. It is someone wishing to book a wedding reception. Please call if you need anything else. I will only be in my office.'

As soon as he had gone, 'Bloody hell. Am I pleased we decided on this last one for today. We would have lost twenty-four hours. Just imagine if I had followed your advice and called it a day.'

'Stop moaning you old sod. You go through the register and I'll check the tape to see if I can fix it.'

With that Sundance took a Swiss Army knife from his pocket, with every gadget you could imagine. Even the extremely useful tool for taking stones out of a horse's hoof.

Not that anyone has ever heard of it being used for such purpose. Newman busily listed various names. He discovered that car registration numbers were also listed next to where the person had signed in.

Some minutes later, after having dismantled and reassembled the tape Sundance proudly announced it was working OK. At least the cogs turned when he inserted his finger.

'We can try this back at the ranch,' said Sundance.

'Have you done yet?' he enquired of Newman.

'Almost. One odd thing about this family. The woman has signed the register. I know they are supposed to live in the UK and have Western ways but as a rule the Arab man deals with that sort of thing. It looks as if Mursi slipped up letting her sign the register. I have the car make, registration number and a London address. Assuming they are genuine,' explained Newman.

'Good job our fifty piece fell the right way up. Stewart would have skinned us alive.'

'Would you like to pass this on to Thames House. As Mursi, supposedly, works in the Kuwaiti Embassy, ask them just to make a few covert enquiries so as not to upset the Kuwaitis. Perhaps Mursi has some connection with Kuwait. If so they may know his present whereabouts.'

Little did the duo realise that fate and the 50p coin were beginning to work in their favour.

'You can also ask Thames to do a quick check on the car and number. I expect they are false but it is worth a try. Not forgetting the London address, but that surely is too much to hope for.'

'Will do. I will also suggest they discreetly visit the street to see if anyone can clock the man or woman. Just on the off chance it might be a genuine address.'

'Great, I'll ask the receptionist if she can photo copy a few pages of the register.'

Stepping outside Franklin, standing on an outdoor table for a signal, passed the details onto Thames House. Within seconds the car was confirmed as belonging to a car hire firm. In addition, a street of the name the woman had given did exist.

Before leaving he also contacted Stewart who was over the moon at hearing such splendid news.

'By God, it would be too much to hope to find Mursi staying at that address.'

Having done as much as possible at Stone House the pair thanked the owner and said they would be in touch later, handing over a business card in case the owner managed to remember any other details. Butch used the journey time to continue fiddling with the jammed tape. Both of them were extremely anxious to look at the tape and hopefully gain much, much more information from it. If it worked!

CHAPTER 39

That evening, in the bar of the King's Head they quietly filled Stewart in with the day's apparent wasted efforts.

'So where is the tape and have you tried it yet?' asked Stewart.

'In my room. Why, do you want to run through it now?'

'Well anything is better than watching a noisy football match on TV. Bring it to my room and we will see if your handiwork did any good.' The three carried their pints to Stewart's room where he slid the tape into the hotel's VTR. It was useful as the tape had the day and time overprinted on it. For the second time they scanned through a hotel's CCTV tape.

'Stop it!' commanded Stewart. Two adults of Eastern origin and a young child were seen walking up to reception. Adjusting it frame by frame they soon found a good image of them and particularly the man.

'They look OK,' said Franklin.

'Yes, I am afraid so. I can't see them being involved in murdering someone or nicking an A-bomb,' agreed Stewart, and noted the date and time of those frames.

'Go on play a bit more. Then I will treat you to a nightcap in the bar.' The film played on showing various comings and goings but nothing of any import.

'Now what have we?' queried Newman. The Kuwaiti had walked into the lounge and within minutes was joined by two other Arab looking men. They greeted each other like old friends, ordered coffee and biscuits and sat quietly chatting. The two newcomer's faces were not very clear. After a time one of them stood, looked round and headed for the toilets, staring into the camera as he walked towards the 'gents'. As if electrified, all three men called out in unison 'Al Liby'. There was a connection.

'Boss, I have a confession,' stated Newman.

'What's that?'

'I thought this hotel was going to be another waste of time. The day was almost over and I told Sundance to toss a coin. If it had not been for him, I dread to think.'

'I can't see you making that mistake again. It is getting on but I'd better call the DG. at his home.' Minutes later, 'Sorry to disturb you sir but we have a break and need your help.' Stewart stated what he needed. A check on the Arab woman who had signed the Register, and the car registration number, verifying if all or none was genuine.

'Fingers crossed, excellent progress. I'm buying the coconuts this time. I'll let you know what I discover about the woman.' A click indicated the DG had gone.

'Do I get a pat on the back as well as another coconut?' asked Franklin.

'And why would I want to pat your back?' responded Stewart.

'Because this is the biggie. The 'doting fucking father'. None other than Midhat Mursi the AQ bomb master.' Franklin had been sifting through the mugshots, not really expecting anything when suddenly staring at him from one of the pages was Mursi. Stewart punched a number into his secure mobile once again.

'Now what can I do for you?' demanded the DG.

'It is what we can do for you sir. Franklin has just matched a mug shot with the man from Stone House Hotel. A chap going by a number of aliases but we know him as Mr Midhat Mursi.'

'Confirmed?' the DG. asked tersely.

'No doubt sir. That really puts the cat amongst the fucking dicky birds.'

'My guess is they HAVE the device. Once again, first class work all three of you. Our job now is to locate them and it and bloody fast. You can bet they won't want to hang on to it for long. The phone went dead.

CHAPTER 40

Tuesday 12th February 0820 hours

Stewart sat reading some of the statements when the phone close to his elbow rang.

'Stewart!'

'Hold the line please I have the DG,' came Helen's voice, still a touch frosty over Stewart swearing on the phone.

'Stewart, things have moved apace here. Firstly, I can confirm Mursi has nothing whatsoever to do with the Kuwaiti Embassy. Mind you we were both pretty sure about that. So no surprises there. Secondly. The woman. Amazingly, not realising the significance she very carelessly signed her correct name and address. That would upset Mursi if he found out. There is still more. She is a teacher on compassionate leave. Guess why?' Without waiting for an answer he went on.

'Her REAL husband died after a car accident a month or so back. Obviously she was part of Mursi's cover. Being efficient and helpful by writing down the car number. We confirm it was hired from a legit hire company. We are still chasing that up. A most helpful lady. For her sake let's hope Mursi does not discover her stupidity.'

'Are you going to pick her up and question her?' asked Stewart.

'No. We will let her run but she will be under discreet and intense surveillance. She is small fry and not really part of this, otherwise she would have provided false details. There is not much chance but Mursi MAY just contact her again. It is Mursi and his crowd we want. And that bloody bomb of course. The PM is meeting the Russians today so we may get something out of that.'

'It would help if the Russkies played ball. You never know how many more of these bloody things they managed to plant on our doorstep.'

'I can practically guarantee they will. Otherwise the PM will declare a bunch of their people undesirables and boot them out. He is considering closing down the Russian Embassy but does not want to. It would take too long to patch things up. These days Russia is a major importer of UK goods so we do not want to needle them too much. The PM is taking this bomb threat VERY seriously. I have been invited to join them as has the Head of 6.' Meaning MI6 – the crowd responsible for security external to the UK. The Secret Intelligence Service.

'Sir, I don't wish to teach granny to suck eggs but I have been researching these possible suitcase bombs. In 1997 Alexander Lebel, the Russian National Security Advisor claimed that a hundred of the two hundred and fifty were 'not under the control of the Russian armed forces'. I read that to mean the buggers have lost, sold or had about a hundred stolen. Obviously the Russian Government rejected the claims at first then issued contradictory statements. Thought you'd like to know,' offered Stewart.

'It may surprise you to know but we do manage to struggle through a spot of work up here, between luncheons and golf,' added the DG frostily.

'Of course sir. Put it down to me thinking aloud.'

Jonathan Edwards continued. 'We have been looking into them at this end. They are not large and have a yield of about one to one and a half kilotons. Still powerful enough to give a lot of people a very bad hair day. Apparently they were developed to increase their EMP footprint and at the time Menwith Hill was pretty new. Back in the sixties the Reds probably thought the bunker was close enough to Menwith to have some significant effect on its comms abilities. We want EVERYTHING from them so they had better give.' With that Edwards had gone.

CHAPTER 41

Tuesday 12th February 0826 hours

A policeman was speaking on a phone. 'I think it best if someone comes to the office right now if that is convenient?'

'Sir.' To his Inspector.

'That was the Estate Office, they have come up with details of people that worked for them up to forty years ago. Would you like me to go and see them?' queried the constable.

'Yes, nip along but don't take all day about it. We are clutching at straws after all this time but something may come of it.'

Tuesday 0925

'Got them sir.' The constable had just returned from the local estate office and placed the list of former estate employees in front of the Inspector.

'Just give me the nitty gritty. Are any still alive, if so did you obtain their last known addresses?'

'The secretary dug the info out but suggested I had a word with the lady who cleans the offices. The cleaner has been there since Noah was a lad. She was there this morning. A lively old dear who was very helpful.'

'Will you get on with it man?' said the exasperated Inspector.

'Of course sir. The cleaning lady gave me the name of a retired gamekeeper a chap known as 'Fluff' Maltby. He still lives in the area in a cottage in Fearby. It is only a few miles from here. The most promising seems to be an Edwin Stanton. He was the Estate Manager for years. He is still alive and lives in Masham. I have his address. None of the other names are much use and quite a few have died since the sixties. Oh, the land owner at the time is also deceased.'

'Thank you Pearson, well done.'

'Would you like me to go see these two? I do have their phone numbers.'

'We will both go. I fancy some fresh air. You'd better phone first and make sure they are at home and able to see us.'

Having contacted both men and confirmed their availability the two policemen decided to visit Fluff Maltby first.

A small wiry man, alerted by their knocking, came round the corner of the cottage. 'Good morning Mr Maltby, I am Inspector Deptford and this is Constable Pearson.'

'You'd best come inside. Mother get the pot on.' Fluff called out.

Once indoors they were offered seats at the living room table. The room was stifling due to a blazing log fire.

'Mek yer sens comfy in front o' the fire. As I used to work on the estate ah gits free logs. This weather we allus have the fire up t' chimney.'

'Milk and sugar both?' called Mrs Maltby from the kitchen.

'Yes, for both of us please. Thank you very much.' The Inspector raised his eyebrows enquiringly to Pearson who nodded in agreement.

'Nice lovely place you have here Mr Maltby. I've never seen such a well kept garden and neatly manicured lawn' added the inspector.

'Nay lad. Not Mr Maltby. You will have me thinking I am somebody important. Did y'ear that mother. The gentleman called me Mr. Call me Fluff, every other bugger does. Never user ter but I fon out after I retired.'

'Fluff!' yelled his wife from the kitchen.

'Mind your language in front of the gentlemen.'

Before he could go on his wife entered with a small tray with cups and biscuits on it.

'He got that nickname years ago. I am partly to blame. He used to swear like a trooper. I got on to him so much that instead of using rude swear words he said fluffing this and that instead. It just stuck with him,' explained the wife.

'Mr Maltby, Fluff, we are wondering if you can cast your mind back to the sixties. An underground bunker was built on the Estate. Being a keeper you would know the place as well as anyone. Do you remember it?'

'Aye, I do remember it. By, I'm jiggered that is going back a bit. What a kerfuffle over nowt.'

'How do you mean?' queried the Inspector.

'Well, Stanton ordered us to stay clear of the area as it was supposed to be secret. It made our job as keepers extra hard with all the comings and goings. See, with it being part of the Ministry of Defence there wasn't much we could do about it. As for Walt Wiseman, the big headed sod.'

'Fluff. Language,' chided his wife.

'Well, you'd have thought he was building Buck House the way he went on. He allus thought he was somebody.'

'Who is Walter Wiseman?' asked Deptford.

'He was given the contract to build it. As it was MOD it used to go to his head. Full of himself in them days, he was. Mind you, he hasn't changed much even today.'

'So you do not really know a lot more about it. Will this Wiseman know much more?'

'Well, he built it so he will know as much as anyone. He lives near Theakston's Brewery in Masham. The old Theakston's, not the Black Sheep brewery. Anyway we stayed clear of it but we never saw anyone much up there. Not a lot more I can tell you. Oh, Arthur Patience was always up there. Said he liked to walk and was into bird watching. Bloody nuisance, we kept warning him about scaring the game. He might have seen summat's. Sorry I can't help you much.'

'On the contrary Mr Maltby, er, Fluff, you have given us another two names. Do these two still live in the area?'

'Ay, they are both easy to find. Anybody in Masham will see you right.'

Well thank you for your time.' The two policeman thanked Mrs Maltby for the tea and biscuits and made their way outside.

'You made a note of those names didn't you Pearson? We will go and see this Stanton now. He managed the estate office.'

Ten minutes saw them drawing up outside Stanton's bungalow in Masham. A man was leaning on the front gate. He straightened up as they approached him.

'Inspector Deptford, I presume. I am Edwin Stanton. Please come inside.' So saying he led them into a room, every chair and much of the floor covered in books, magazines and papers. He hastily cleared a space.

'Here have a seat. Sorry about the mess but I'm getting rid of a load of clutter. Some of this stuff goes back over thirty years. An antique shop in Harrogate is interested in some of it. Look at this.' He held out a battered old Beano Annual.

'These old annuals belonged to my only son. He died of cancer some ten years back. You never expect your kids to go before you. Olive, my wife died two years back after a series of strokes,' added Stanton. His eyes moistening over.

'Anyhow you don't want to hear my history.'

'I am sorry to hear about your family sir. But in fact part of your history may be of great interest to us.'

'You said on the phone it was something to do with the nineteen-sixties. I will help if I can but it is a very long time ago now.'

'It relates to an underground bunker that was constructed on estate property. Up above the Druid's Temple. What can you tell me about it.'

'Well, I am not sure I should tell you anything Inspector.'

'Why on earth not sir?'

'Well the chap that arranged it asked me to sign the Official Secrets Act.'

'That was almost fifty years ago!' exclaimed the Inspector in amazement.

'Yes, but you know what it is like with these things. I do not want to get into trouble with the authorities.'

'Firstly Mr Stanton, it was constructed a very long time ago.

Secondly it is concerning the recent murder which I am sure you know about. So we are hoping you can throw some light on it.'

'Well, I am not happy but what is it you wish to know?'

'Please tell me everything from start to finish.'

"I will do my best but as I said, fifty years is a long time. This gentleman came from the government asking permission to build an underground bunker for the Royal Observer Corps. As it was secret he offered to pay cash for everything in order to have it all off the record. I informed my employer who said he would be delighted to help. Particularly as it was cash on the nail, so no need for the taxman to know.'

'What made you think the man was from the government?'

'You only had to see him to realise he was a senior official. His card was very impressive too, printed with gold lettering and an official looking design on it. His briefcase had the royal seal embossed on it. He was some high up in the government. I got the impression he worked for some hush-hush department.

He was definitely important. No doubt about that.'

'Mm, OK carry on please,' interrupted the Inspector.

'He turned up one day with a briefcase full of money and handed me the fee for the right to build it on our land. He also handed over a year's rental in advance. £3,600 altogether and £50 for my help. Mind you I did not really earn it.'

'You remember that clearly enough Mr Stanton.'

'I should, because I counted it myself. It was a lot of money in those days. The boss also gave me £25 for myself. Not a bad backhander at that time.'

'Yes, I imagine it was worth having. Can you think of anything else?'

'No, I never even went to look at the place. It was restricted MOD property and I left it at that. I never actually heard of it being used though. They did keep paying the annual rental for some time afterwards. A large registered envelope with £100 in it arrived regular as clockwork each January. It was sent up to the Big House. I imagine they still pay every January to this very day.'

'Thank you Mr Stanton, you have been most helpful. I wish you well with those annuals. I imagine some of them will be very valuable.'

Leaving Stanton they eventually found Walter Wiseman winter digging his allotment.

'Mr Wiseman, I believe. I am Inspector Deptford and this is Constable Pearson. We are making enquiries about an underground chamber you built back in the sixties.'

'Oh I don't remember. In any case I always pay my income tax,' Protested Wiseman.

'Rest assured Mr Wiseman, I am not in the least concerned about your income tax. I want to know as much as you can tell me about the work and who you dealt with.'

When the Inspector made it clear he was not interested in his tax fiddle's Wiseman opened up.

'The bloke was some big noise from a government department. He insisted in paying me in cash so that no record was kept as it was top secret.'

'Once the job was complete did you hear from the man again?'

'No, he more or less promised me more work but nothing came of it. That is as much as I can tell you, and it was a long time ago. The last time I met him was when he settled up and checked to make sure I had done a good job.'

'Did he identify himself in any way.'

'Come to think of it I don't think he did but he had a swanky car and a briefcase with official writing on it. I was more interested in the work and being paid cash in the hand. Could have been the Queen of Sheba for all I cared.'

'Thank you Mr Wiseman, if you come up with anything else this is my card. I don't expect we will need to see you again.'

The two policemen returned to their car.

'Well, Constable, it looks like another waste of our time. We will try this Patience bloke another time. Back to the grind.'

CHAPTER 42

Tuesday 12th February 1120 hours, London

'Good morning madam, sorry to bother you but we suspect a gas leak in this street. Would you please remain inside with your windows closed and do not have an open fire if you can avoid it. We will let you know when all is clear.'

It is amazing the skills that employees from Thames House possess. Gas Board workers now!

Looking across the street Hanan could see a couple of Gas Board vans and a small red and white striped canvas cover over one of the manholes. Two men were walking along the street operating 'gas sniffers'.

'Thank you for letting me know. I hope everything will be safe for us. I do hope my gas cooker and pipe work is in order.' The thought of a gas leak alarmed Hanan.

'No problem ma'am, we believe it is in an underground pipe. It is pretty ancient but usually they last for years. We should not be long. If we have time I can ask one of my men to give your gas fittings the once over. Shouldn't take a minute.'

'Would you really? I would feel much happier but how much will I have to pay?'

'Don't you worry about that. I am sure I can spare one of the men to put your mind at ease. After all we are practically on your doorstep and we like our customers not only to be customers but satisfied customers. I'll have him here as soon as we are done. Shouldn't be a jiffy now.'

With that the 'gas board' man returned to one of the vans, thinking he liked the bit about the satisfied customer as opposed to just a customer. Nice touch that. He decided to pass it on to the Gas

Board. They could use it as a slogan. He picked up a walkie talkie and spoke into the mouthpiece.

'Wake up you lot! A piece of piss. Mark – get your gear ready. Give it ten minutes or so then and go do your kind gasman bit for the lady. The rest of you give it an hour and pack in. A couple of you keep wandering around with your 'sniffers' just to make it look good.'

'Guv?'

'What Mark?'

'I suggest planting one in the lounge, one in the kitchen and a third in the bedroom if you think that will be sufficient. I'll take Andy with me to keep her occupied.'

'Fine, I don't think they will be a lot of use, but we have been ordered to pull all the stops out so we cover our arses. What with the Home Secretary authorising phone taps left and right, we should pick something up from somewhere and her phone has an intercept on it. I really can't see that Mursi bloke calling to see her.'

'OK Guv, me and Andy will get our gear sorted now and go over in a few minutes.'

'See you lot back at the ranch. Remember, about an hour and pack in, all of you.'

With that the 'foreman' drove off to return the borrowed van to the Gas Depot.

'Morning lady. Our guvnor says you are worried about your gas installation. We can give it the once over if you want us to. He must be in a good mood today as we usually charge for this. I expect it is because we found the leak straight off and soon had it repaired' explained Mark.

'Please come in. You are so kind and to do it for nothing as well. It will put my mind at ease. I do worry about gas leaks. You hear of so many accidents and explosions.'

So saying Hanan invited the two 'gasmen' into her home. Mark glanced at Andy and read his mind thinking 'You, of all people to worry about explosions, when that bastard boyfriend of yours is walking round with a bloody A Bomb in his back pocket.'

'The cooker is here. It is not very old.' Hanan pointed it out to the gas board workers.

'Andy you check the cooker and fittings. Would you show me where the main gas tap is please, best turn it off. Better safe than sorry?' said Mark.

'I find it difficult to re-light the pilot. I hope I can manage to do it,' pleaded Hanan.

'Don't you worry your pretty little head about that. It is all part of the service.'

With that Hanan led Mark to the hallway and pointed out a cupboard under the stairs.

'I believe the main tap is in there but I am not sure,' explained Hanan.

With that Mark dived into the cupboard and yelled to Andy, 'I am turning off the main now. Check to make sure no gas is coming through.'

Mark showed Hanan where the gas main tap was located.

'Cheers mate,' called back Andy, thinking how the fuck can gas come through if the mains are off. However, he fiddled with the gas taps whilst Hanan, who had returned to the kitchen, gazed in awe and wonderment at the man's expertise. Well, not everyone can turn a gas tap on and off with the same amount of enthusiasm Andy was putting into it.

Minutes later Mark strolled into the kitchen.

'OK mate?' he enquired of Andy.

'Perfect. You can turn on again when you are ready. Did you finish checking the mains?' What was there to check. They are either ON or Off but it all looked good in Hanan's eyes. As for the almost brand-new oven you would not expect a lot to go wrong there. Mind you a good twiddle wouldn't do any harm. And his twiddling seemed to satisfy the lady. After the umpteenth time of turning all the taps on and off, Andy proudly announced that they were working OK.

'If you are satisfied I will go and open the main valve again.' Mark gave an imperceptible nod to Andy, staring at the electric torch – gas proof, of course.

Ah, as they were expert gas technicians NOT gas proof BUT intrinsically safe, the words made all the difference!

Catching on, Andy said, 'excuse me ma'am would you please hold this torch whilst I just have a quick look inside the oven?'

With that Andy plunged his head inside the oven with Hanan holding the light for him. He made tapping sounds with a small screwdriver whilst enjoying gazing at Hanan's shapely legs.

'A little to the left please.' Hanan kindly obliged by moving the beam to the other side of the oven.

'Nearly done,' Andy said to Hanan, thinking, come on Mark my fucking neck is killing me and this oven honks of curry.

'All done now,' reported Mark.

Getting to his feet Andy took the torch from Hanan, thanking her for her help.

'Everything OK mate?' Andy asked Mark.

Turning to Hanan Mark told her, 'The installation is in very good working order. You can rest assured that it is as safe as houses. Your gleaming cooker does you great credit ma'am.' Soft soap works every time on most women!

'Thank you gentlemen, I do like to keep it like new, it is only a few months old. Can I offer you tea or anything? You have been so kind.'

'No thank you ma'am, the pleasure is all ours and I have lit your pilot light again. Nice to know we have a satisfied customer. We have quite a lot on today.' Thinking to himself, all due to that fucking terrorist friend of yours with his bastard atom bomb.

Back outside Mark confirmed the three bugs were in place and working. Miraculously The 'gas leak' had been repaired and the canvas tent, vans and other equipment were soon on the way back to the local Gas board depot.

'One thing Mark?'

'What's that mate?'

'What if the bloody cooker really gets a leak and blows up?'

CHAPTER 43
Tuesday 12th February noon, North Yorkshire

'It's for youuuuuuuu. Mimicking the well known BT slogan Inspector Deptford handed the phone to Stewart.

'Stewart. How are things going? Down here we have phone taps on the woman's House, the mosque, and a half dozen other likely targets. The Home Secretary has come up trumps. Requests for taps are being given top priority. I suppose the promise of the PM's size nines up one's backside provides more than a little incentive.' 'Not much more we can do here, sir, I was going to suggest we return to the smoke. Butch and Sundance are trying to get hold of a chap called Arthur Patience. He is the retired teacher bloke who did a lot of bird watching in the area. Otherwise things have dried up.'

'Very well. Leave those two there a little longer and you come back as soon as you have wound up.' Click. With that the DG had hung up.

'Time for our ways to part Inspector. I'm leaving today to go back to civilisation. No more 'Ay oops', no more 'tha's 'reet' or 'sithees.'

'Ah you know you will miss us. I do not envy you being in London one little bit. Give me the dales and moors every time. A good walk over Ingleborough would do you the world of good. In any case, that accent sounds more Cornish than Yorkshire. You could do with more time here to improve the local patois.'

Standing up, Stewart reached out to shake hands with the Inspector. 'To be honest I must admit the efficiency of you and your lot did impress me. It was a pleasure meeting you. Perhaps one day I might even try Ingleborough.'

'You weren't so bad yourself for a spook. Good luck down there. We will try to do our little bit here but as you said yourself, the trail has not just gone cold, it has bloody well frozen over. We have covered every possibility we can think of. We will close our operation down pretty soon but keep a few men looking for our murderer. Like yourself, I am inclined to believe he may be hiding out in London. I bet my boots he has no idea of the major effort we are making to find him. That may work in our favour. He certainly will realise that as an Al Qaeda operative we would be looking for him but he probably thinks we have no idea he is even in the UK.'

'It might be to our advantage, as you say. What we do want is to find the bugger and that damned bomb. And fast.'

With that Stewart left to go and brief Butch and Sundance. He found them in their Masham hotel poring over a pile of statements and other documents. Both looking totally dejected.

'Hi boss. We have gone through these so many times I do not think there is anything else we can glean from them.'

'I have just spoken with the DG. I am returning to London forthwith. You will be delighted to know you two will be enjoying the crisp Yorkshire air for a bit longer.'

'Why do we need to stay up here in the sticks?' groaned Butch.

'Sundance is OK, he has got a thing going with the receptionist here, but I miss the crowded streets, traffic jams and fume-filled air. This fresh air is doing for me.'

'A phone call for a Mr Stewart,' called one of the bar staff.

'That's me, thank you.'

'Yes sir, I will pass it on to these two. It isn't much but at least the Russkies have come up with something. Nothing else though apart from that? OK sir, thank you. I will be leaving directly.'

'This should brighten your day. According to the Russians their 'sleeper' here is none other than a gentleman called?' Stewart let the question hang in the air.

'Go on then Butch, any ideas?'

'No, not a single solitary Masham sausage.'

'Try this name, Arthur Patience!'

'Fucking hell, that is the bloke the police and myself have been trying to locate for a week. The neighbours have not seen him for a few days but he often goes off on bird watching holidays. We assumed that was why we could not find him. The curtains are open and the house locked. Why has it taken the bloody Reds so long to let us know? Mind you, I can't see him being able, or willing, to throw any more light on what we already have,' added Butch.

'Something for you to chase up whilst I am in the smoke. Keep in touch and try to find our twitcher. Cheers.' With that Stewart walked to Reception to settle his bill before driving towards the A1 and London.

'Move yourself Sundance. Time we paid another visit to Patience's place and also further chats with his neighbours. Let's get out of here into that fresh air you don't like in your lungs.'

Drawing up outside Patience's bungalow the pair walked to the front door. No response to the bell but there was a fair amount of mail on the hallway floor.

'No sign of life yet. Let's try next door, see if they can help any further.'

No, the neighbours could not shed any more light on his absence but they all confirmed that Mr Patience was away quite regularly. He often gave interesting talks on birds found in that part of the world and was a very keen ornithologist.The duo decided to have one more nose round Patience's bungalow. The garage window had a curtain across it but a small gap showed something shining inside. A car?

'How about this? A car. If so, has Mr Patience travelled with friends, gone on a train or a coach or what?' said Sundance.

'I think we should take a look in here first and then the house,' suggested Sundance.

With that a hearty, and totally unlawful, kick soon dislodged the small lock on the hasp of the door. The odour of engine fumes was still heavy in the air. A small figure could be seen slumped across the steering wheel, very clearly dead.

'A fiver says this is him and I don't think he feels like talking right now,' said Butch as he took out his mobile and busied himself dialling Stewart's number.

CHAPTER 44
Tuesday 12th Feb 1630 hours, Thames House

'Sir, with respect, the Russians are just pissing us about.' Stewart to the DG.

'I think we should recall our two men from North Yorkshire back to liaise with Legoland.'

'Stewart, whenever someone says to me 'with respect' I know bloody well that it is being said without respect and that person takes me for a cretin. Also, may I remind you, I resent you and others here referring to that edifice as Legoland simply because of its futuristic design. We do not want to upset 6 by being discourteous about their new office block, even if it is an eyesore. We need all the help we can get.'

'Sorry sir, but because of the Russians we have spent hours on visits and phone calls in an effort to locate Patience. They could have said a week ago he was their sleeper. We were simply trying to locate a bird watcher that frequents the area of the murder. We certainly did not have him pegged as a possible sleeper.'

'For once I agree, Stewart, but I suspect they wanted to forewarn their man. In any case I really do not think he would have been much help after all this time. I suggest the two up there dig around a little longer, you never know what might turn up.'

'With respect sir.'

'Stewart!'

'Sorry sir but I do not feel Newman and Franklin will be any use stuck up there.'

'They stay until further notice, is that clear. Now, I have contacted the PM's Office regarding the Russian's lack of co-operation. I do agree we wasted precious time. A lot of people are wound up very tightly at present. One: We have no idea where our Arabs have gone to ground. Two: Likewise the explosive device. I would imagine that they have it hidden well away from wherever they are. They would not want to be found anywhere near it. Three: Lastly we have no idea of the intended target but it seems pretty certain it will be used somewhere in the UK. My guess is London or another large city. It is highly unlikely that they will try to ship it abroad. The Americans half believe it will be sent to New York but I do not buy that. I am positive it is in Britain. That would be the obvious and safest place for them to detonate it. The more they move it about the more risk they take of it being discovered.'

'Yes, it looks as if a large number of Britons will soon be vapourised or glowing in the dark. I only wish we had some idea of where. Despite pressurising our Muslim grasses not one has come up with anything so far. Al Qaeda is keeping the lid firmly closed shut. If that is all, sir, I would like to get back to my office and maintain the pressure on my people, but I just do not know what more we can do.'

'Rest assured the Americans are squeezing their sources. They won't share names with us but they are moving heaven and earth. Surely something will turn up, we desperately need a breakthrough. OK Stewart, keep me informed and good luck. We certainly could do with some. I very much fear time is running out!'

CHAPTER 45
Wednesday 13th February, North London Central Mosque

Mahasheer was sitting in his small office when Midhat Mursi strode in, clothed in his full Arab outfit, only his eyes showing.

'Salaam aleikum Karim. Are you keeping well?'

'Wa aleikum es salaam Midhat, it is good to see you. Tell me, how did you injure your leg? You are limping badly.'

'Ha ha Karim. I assure you my leg is perfect. This is just a little subterfuge.'

'If you say so Midhat. So, what can I do for you?'

'Karim, I will need another five thousand English pounds and a car for Friday morning. Contact Al Liby and instruct him to meet me on Friday morning nine o'clcok at my flat. He will need to pack an overnight bag as we will be away for a few nights.'

'It shall be done Midhat. Is there anything else you wish of me?' Mahasheer knew better than to ask Mursi where he would be going.

'Yes, one more thing. I will need another six or eight mobile phones. Make sure they are new and can not be traced. I will collect the money and phones on Thursday afternoon.'

'If there is any way I can help you further I would be greatly honoured. I wish you well with your vengeance on these Christian pigs.'

'You have done well Karim and if I ever need anything more you are the one person I would come to.'

Leaving the mosque Mursi headed back towards his flat, doing his best to be the grey man and lessen the chances of him being noticed. He did not think anyone would be following him or watching him but he was very aware that he was a wanted man worldwide. Although forewarned about the MI5 van permanently parked there, he was totally unaware that in an empty, fire-damaged property across the road from the mosque he and anyone else entering or leaving the mosque was being filmed.

'Did you get that one?' asked one of the Special Branch men.

'Yeah but not a lot of good. The bugger has his face well hidden behind that dish cloth. With that limp I don't think he is going to run very far.'

Mursi had been well trained in disguising not only his body but also his walk and stance. The small hard pebble taped to the sole of his foot was painful enough to ensure he had a pronounced limp without even having to think about it to maintain it. This allowed him to concentrate on other matters. His hunched shoulders added to his bent and aged outline and disguised his true stature. He was not overly concerned about the Intelligence Service van, which was common knowledge. It seemed to be more of a deterrent than anything as they made no great attempts to conceal their cameras.

These not-so-discreet observations had been maintained ever since the terrorist links with the mosque years earlier. It had been going on for so long that many of the Muslims joked that the cameras probably had not even got any film. Mursi felt satisfied and pretty confident with himself.

'Marvin, just follow that little bastard and see where he goes. I don't think he is anything to write home about but I don't remember seeing him around here before.'

A council street cleaner of West Indian origin slowly pushed his cart along brushing the pavement as he set off after Mursi, picking up the occasional fag end and other sundry items of litter. Obviously listening to reggae music to help his day along through his cheap, looking headphones. Only they just happened to be hi-tech radio phones. The best on the market.

'OK I have him. One thing though. I do not think he is as old as he seems. As he passed he stared directly at me. His eyes were bright. Not the eyes of an old man.'

'Cheers mate, that bloke is as old as the hills. Maybe been trying a little hash out or something. More likely looking at mucky books to bring a twinkle to his eye.' With a laugh the watcher closed the connection.

Mursi limped slowly along in the confidence he was not being observed. The only person anywhere near to him was that scruffy looking street cleaner listening to his music. He looked so stupid Mursi suspected he would have difficulty even finding his way back to the council depot. Arriving outside his flat Mursi glanced carefully round. All clear! Turning his key in the Yale lock he entered his flat.

'Marvin. Leave that guy and get back here. We have another target. Smartly dressed, grey suit, specs and grey hair combed straight back. Arab –looking, coming in your direction. See if he gets into a car or where he goes?'

'OK, in any case this old bloke has gone into a flat. Either seventeen or nineteen but it has a maroon, coloured door.'

Turning his hand cart Marvin had only gone a handful of steps when he clocked the next target. He was walking briskly in Marvin's direction when he suddenly disappeared into a doorway.

Ambling slowly but purposefully towards the doorway Marvin saw it was a shop. The target had removed his jacket and was donning a white coverall. Not unusual when Marvin realised he was the owner of the shop! He had returned to work after prayer!!

'Returning to the mosque area. This target is Hassan, the owner of Hassan's Delicacies. Just gone back to work by the look of things. I will return along the other side of the road.'

'Thanks Marv. You may as well knock off. No point being out now it is getting dark. Get shut of the gear at the depot.'

Marvin acknowledged by two pushes of the pressel on his transceiver.

CHAPTER 46
Wednesday 13th February 1135 hours, Thames House

'Thank you for coming gentlemen. I am here merely as an observer. The Home Secretary will speak for me. Quite obviously, like yourselves, we too have burnt a lot of midnight oil discussing our current problem. Our friend Putin is continuing to flex his muscles. However, with pressure from the US of A and the British Government he has begun to be more helpful. The Home Secretary now has the blueprints, together with the operating instructions for the nuclear device. And before you ask, yes, they are in English.'

So saying the Prime Minister sat back wearing his usual sour, dour face. Easing himself into the very expensive leather armchair, resting his feet in the ankle-deep pile of the royal blue axminster. Behind him was a panoramic view across the Thames and London clearly visible from the Director General's office, located on the fifth floor. That, office, folks, took a chunk and a half of your tax.

'Thank you PM and also the DG for the use of his office. We opted to meet here as the PM and myself will be attending a luncheon close by. I do have something that may or may not be of use. The Russians have, with much arm twisting, provided these plans of the device. The relevant information relating to its power, size and operating procedures. As I say, they may or may not be helpful.' The Home Secretary placed the documents before the DG before continuing. 'As the PM said, on this occasion, I will be speaking for him.' The PM nodded slowly to indicate his approval.

'So far you have not made one iota of progress for days now. Nothing further about the bomb or the suspected terrorists. It is a well known fact that there is long established friction between 5 and 6 and a reluctance to share information.'

169

'Home Secretary...' protested the DG.

'Jonathan, deny it all you will but it is and has been a way of life for your two services for many years. Consequently, the present gravity of the situation DEMANDS that henceforth you work and share everything relevant to the case at issue. For the duration of our present crisis you WILL work hand in glove. Is that perfectly clear? Forget your past animosities, the country is above your petty squabbles. This situation is probably the most critical this country has faced since World War Two.' Quite a speech from the Home Secretary!

'Home Secretary, I insist on being heard!'

'You have two minutes Director,' stated the Home Secretary.

'Firstly the Russians delayed our investigation by at least a week when they could have helped. One thing, now, that is hampering our investigation is the fact that the Government has tied our hands. If we could bring in the Arab woman for questioning we might glean something from her, however insignificant, it might fit the puzzle somewhere.'

'I concur completely with the DG,' agreed the Police Commissioner. 'That woman could be the missing link to give us the leads we desperately need. Home Secretary, you yourself said we had to work together as a team. Why don't you join the team and help us by allowing us to question this woman.'

'That was totally uncalled for Commissioner. The woman's house is bugged and her phone is being monitored. The PM and myself feel that if she is approached she is likely to warn Mursi and Al Liby off. At this stage you tell me that you firmly believe these two men are totally unaware that we are covertly carrying out the biggest manhunt this country has ever known to locate both them and the device. You assure me they have no idea that we suspect they are in possession of a nuclear device. OK, let's keep it that way. Right now they will be maintaining their usual low profile when they play away from home and not going to greater lengths. If they have the slightest suspicion that we know about them obtaining the bomb two things could happen. They could both flee the country and destroy any hopes of us finding them until they have wreaked further atrocities elsewhere. Secondly, they may panic and detonate the device. At this stage we are harbouring the forlorn hope that someone will eventually contact us demanding a massive ransom for the recovery of the device. As it is Al Qaeda we are dealing with that scenario is most improbable but it is a straw to grasp at.'

'If I may?' interrupted the Prime Minister.

'You certainly do not need me to indicate the extreme gravity of the situation. I accept that President Vladimir Petrovsky could have been far more cooperative, but he is a separate problem at present. The recovery of the device is paramount, the capture of the two terrorists secondary. Consequently I have decided that if no further progress is made within forty-eight hours you have my permission to detain the lady for questioning. That should satisfy all concerned and put us all on the same team. As the Commissioner so ably suggested.'

For the first time in many days, smiles appeared on faces that had registered only frustration, desperation, tiredness and hopelessness.

'Prime Minister, may I thank you on behalf of all of us seated at this table. We do appear to have reached an impasse. Bringing in this woman has been one of our major concerns from the very beginning,' stated a beaming Director General.

Standing, looking haggard and worn, the Prime Minister announced, 'time is running out gentlemen. You must lean harder, much harder on your informants. I wish to emphasise what the Home Secretary said we must ALL work together. A break through must be found. I did not consider it necessary to invite the Foreign Secretary today but he is being kept fully in the picture. Come Josie, we have a luncheon appointment. Good luck to us all.'

As the Prime Minister and Home Secretary approached the door it opened silently as if by magic to allow their egress.

'Well, they don't call him U Turn Gaunt for nothing. That was a welcome bit of News,' Added John Scofield, head of the Secret Intelligence Service, more commonly known as MI6.

'Let's hope it leads somewhere. Pity, though, about the two day wait. That time could be vital to our enquiries. So where do we go from here gentlemen? Jonathan, as it is your office how about taking the chair and also being 'mother' to rustle up some coffee and biscuits.'

The D.G's finger reached for the intercom.

'Helen would you be good enough to send coffee – any of you for tea?' They all agreed coffee would do fine.

'Coffee for four and biscuits please my dear.'

Two minutes later Helen herself entered carrying a tray which she placed on the large, oak desk.

'Is it the legs sir?' she asked in her gentle West Coast of Scotland accent.

'Is what the legs?' enquired a bemused DG.

'Did you no notice your own coffee pot and cups on yon side table? Together with a supply of ginger nuts and chocolate digestives. I just thought perhaps you were having trouble with those varicose veins and had difficulty in walking sir.' At that his Scots PA beat a hasty but grinning retreat.

'Jonathan, how do you put up with that cheek?' asked John Scofield.

'Very easily John. Helen knows how far she can go. However, in all my years I have never met anyone as hard working and conscientious as she. Her memory is phenomenal, names, telephone numbers, personal details. I tell you that lass is better than a whole desk full of computers. Last September I had some work that I wanted completing that night. Without a word of protest she sat down and worked at it until gone nine. The next morning one of the secretaries mentioned to me that the previous day had been Helen's twenty-eighth wedding anniversary and they had booked a special meal. Imagine how I felt. Anyhow, I made up for it. I knew her husband was on holiday for a week but Helen was working. I used my prerogative as the Big Cheese to award her three days leave and treated the two of them to two nights in Paris via Eurostar. I bought the tickets and had them delivered, to her door by courier before Helen set off for work so as to ward off any protests.'

'You are just a big softie at heart DG,' put in Stewart.

'That is how much that lady means to me. I will hear not a single word against her. That reminds me, Stewart, get your backside off that seat and go and investigate.'

'OK boss, any suggestions as to what I should investigate?'

'Have you anything back from the two reprobates in Yorkshire?'

'No, the body was confirmed to be our Russian sleeper-cum-birdwatcher but they are still working on his background.' Rising to his feet as he spoke, Stewart departed to 'investigate', at the same time wishing to hell he could think of what and where to investigate next, all apparent stones having been overturned countless times. Hopefully hauling that Arab woman in would help. It MUST help. At this precise moment it seemed to be the only thing going for them.

CHAPTER 47

Wednesday 13th February 1607 hours, North Yorkshire

'Highly irregular gentlemen but your credentials leave me little choice. I have also been instructed by Head Office to help you in any way I can, bar filling your pockets from the safe.' Chuckling at his mild attempt at humour the bank manager gazed expectantly at Butch and Sundance.

'Thank you Mr Mainwaring,' said Sundance.

'Matteson, Matteson,' pointed out the Manager.

'Oh yes, so sorry about that.' Sundance smiled blandly at his deliberate gaffe.

Newman and Franklin had given Matteson the nickname of Mainwaring of Dad's Army fame due to his pompous manner and also because he even looked like Mainwaring, right down to his moustache and shiny bald head.

'These are the printouts of Mr Patience's account over the past five years. It meant quite a lot of extra work for a member of my staff and we are only a small branch you know.' Realising he had referred to his branch as small he hurriedly continued.

'When I say small I mean that we are not quite as large as some of our other branches. We are more??'

'Compact?' offered Butch.

'That is it, precisely, but of course we provide a vitally important service to our customers. They depend on our guidance and expertise. Yes, indeed.'

'We appreciate your cooperation. If only everyone was as efficient and helpful as yourself. As soon as we entered the bank we realised that we were encountering a well managed and well run establishment, Mr Mainwaring,' said Sundance, buttering the man up.

'Matteson, Matteson.'

Butch glanced at Sundance, amused at the buttering up treatment and then had to look down at his folder so as not to burst out laughing.

'One does one's best. I say, would either of you gentlemen care for tea and biscuits.'

'That is most generous of you but we must press on,' explained Butch.

'Looking at these printouts, I see that every three months the Black and Red Knight General Insurance Company have paid in £500,' noted Franklin.

'Regular as clockwork fifth of every month. No doubt an annuity prudently taken out by the late Mr Patience,' proffered Matteson.

'His pension is also paid into his account which, as you see, has a tidy sum in it. On several occasion I have advised him to invest much of it but he was not interested.'

'Twenty-four thousand pounds is worth having but it is his money so it is his decision. Or was. Did you know him at all?' asked Franklin.

'No, no one really knew him well. He kept himself to himself. He did enjoy his bird watching though. Always dashing off somewhere with his camera and binoculars. He was a most courteous and well-mannered gentleman and highly thought of as a teacher.'

Newman was thinking. Yes, I bet he was quite busy with his camera. Especially bird watching around Menwith Hill, RAF Leeming and Catterick Garrison.

'Well thank you for sparing us a few minutes of your valuable time. Please thank your staff member who printed this out for us. We may need to return but in the meantime we will hang on to these printouts. Good day Mr Mainwaring,' said Franklin standing up. Newman quickly followed Franklin's lead.

'Bye Mr Mainwaring, you have been a great help. It is so refreshing to have a busy person like yourself putting yourself out to help us with our enquiries.'

'Matteson, Matteson. Think nothing of it. Just doing my job

y'know. Good afternoon gentlemen,' said the manager as he showed the grinning Butch and Sundance from his office.

'Happy to help the police any time,' he called out as the pair were about to step outside. Butch and Sundance exchanged pained glances, both thinking. Fucking police. Do you mind.

As they looked back both had noticed a twinkling in his eyes. It struck them that the wily old devil been getting his own back for giving him the Mainwaring tag.

CHAPTER 48

Thursday 14th February noon, The Mosque

Once again in his lame old man guise Mursi limped in Mahasheer's office.

'Greetings, Midhat, my brother,' called out Mahasheer looking up from some paperwork on his desk and standing respectfully.

'I have everything you requested. Money, a car and six mobile phones. Anas al Liby has been contacted. He will be at your flat as ordered by nine o'clcok tomorrow.'

'Thank you Karim. As ever you have excelled yourself. Wish us well next week. I promise that in a few days the name Al Qaeda will be on everyone's lips.'

Mursi's eyes were burning with the fire of fanaticism. Or, more probably, the fire of a madman!

'If only I could know a little more Midhat?' whined Mahasheer.

'Karim, my friend, it is better that you do not know now. Watch the television over the next few days and then all will be clear. Not only the news programmes but also be on the look out for special news flashes.'

'I shall do as you say Midhat and pray for your success.'

'My faithful friend. It will make even the Twin Towers seem insignificant. That merely devastated a comparatively small area. Just imagine what if it had been an entire town? But I have already said too much. I will be on my way now. Thank you again. You have done well.' With that Mursi secreted the items, Mahasheer had obtained beneath his thobe, bade Mahasheer a final farewell and limped out of the mosque, being photographed by the known van camera and also the unknown camera in the fire-damaged building.

'That old bugger is getting to be a regular these days,' commented one of the Special Branch watchers, at the same time jotting down the details of Mursi's and others comings and goings.

Marvin, still carrying out his road-sweeper act, radioed in.

'You don't want me to follow him again do you?'

'No, Marv we know where the old sod lives. I can't imagine him being up to much.'

Had Marvin followed 'the old sod' he might have wondered why he had suddenly darted into a side street. He might also have wondered how it was the old man had suddenly recovered from his limp, walking much more purposefully. He would most definitely have wondered why the old sod was now entering the passageway leading to the rear of Hanan's house.

CHAPTER 49

Thursday 14th February 1317 hours

Mursi's gentle knocking brought Hanan to open her rear door. 'Why what a pleasant surprise. Please do come in.' Hanan was clearly delighted to see Mursi again and had recognised him instantly.

'Would you care for tea or coffee?'

'That would be marvellous my Hanan. I don't suppose you have any *ghahwa Arabia*?' The delicious Arabic coffee spiced with cardamon seeds.

'I will be honoured to make you some Midhat.' Walking into the kitchen Hanan placed the kettle on her shiny gas cooker, her radio playing Arabic music in the background from a tape.

'My, what a magnificent cooker. It looks new,' Mursi commented.

'It is almost new. I prefer gas but I worry about it. Yesterday we had a gas leak in the road. The man came to warn me to keep my windows closed and not light any fires.'

'I expect they soon had it repaired,' said Mursi.

'Oh yes. No time at all and because I was concerned about the pipe work in the house two men came in and checked it over. Would you believe? They did not charge me at all,' added Hanan switching off the radio as she walked past it.

An alarmed Mursi raised a finger to his lips to hush Hanan. Grasping her arm he savagely pulled her to the back door and out into the small rear garden. Hanan, wearing a shocked expression, stared open mouthed at Mursi.

Meanwhile, sitting in a parked car, two hundred yards away, one of the occupants said 'I thought I heard a man's voice, but what with that weird Arab music and that bloody dustbin lorry crunching up the rubbish. Ah, the radio has gone off.'

'Tell me about these gas men who came into your house.'

Once again Hanan explained about the gas leak and how the men had kindly given her gas installation a good check over.

'Do not speak but show me where the men were. Were they both together all the time and were you with both of them at all times?'

'More or less. Except whilst one turned the mains tap off in the cupboard, the other one was checking my cooker in the kitchen. They were very thorough indeed.'

Entering the kitchen Mursi switched on the tape player once again. He mouthed the words, 'show me where they worked'.

Hanan opened the cupboard door, under the stairs, and pointed out the gas meter. She then returned to the kitchen, pointing at the cooker.

'Anywhere else?' Mursi whispered, his mouth touching Hanan's ear.

'No, this is all' answered Hanan shaking her head vigorously.

In the car one of the men was about to say it was quiet again in Hanan's house.

'Bugger. The music is back on but other than that I can't hear a thing.'

'You probably heard a man's voice on the radio and she has not had a single visitor all day. She has not even used her phone either.'

'I expect you are right but just for a moment I thought I heard a snatch of conversation.'

Leaning back in his seat he adjusted his earpiece and settled himself comfortably for the remaining couple of hours of his shift, straining to hear some indication that he had heard another voice, courtesy of the three hidden bugs in Hanan's house.

In the house Mursi began to feel under the table and ledges, searching likely places where a bug could be quickly concealed. His fingers touched something small and round under the lip of the kitchen cupboard. Bending down he was rewarded by the sight of a small object. Clearly a bug. He beckoned Hanan to bend down and see for herself. Her mouth opened, wordlessly, in total surprise as she shook her head, unable to comprehend what the gas men had done. Mursi indicated Hanan should go outside into the garden where they could talk.

'Why should they suspect you, do you have any idea? We must also assume they have planted at least a further one or more bugs, most likely in your lounge.'

'They cannot possibly suspect me of anything. Only Mahasheer knew, in addition to yourself, that I would be going away with you. I did not say a word to a soul and I know my little boy has not mentioned it to anyone.' Hanan just knew she had not done anything to justify her home being bugged.

'We must also assume your phone has been tapped. Are you positive you did not mention our going away together to anyone?' enquired an agitated Mursi.

Tears appeared in Hanan's eyes.

'Please, Midhat, you must believe me. I told no one. I am on compassionate leave from the school so had no reason to even mention it to them. Only you, Mahasheer and your friends that met you in the hotel know I was with you.'

'Hanan, there is something you have forgotten. Something you have done has alerted the authorities. Think, think!!!'

'I do not have to think. I KNOW I never mentioned a word. No one has any reason to suspect me of anything. If they had then surely someone would have been to question me.'

'Hanan, this bug proves someone is very curious about you. Have you noticed any people watching or following you. Have you noticed any cars or vans parked with people just sitting in them for longer than a few minutes?'

'No. I promise you, but I would not know if I was being watched or followed anyhow. I live on a fairly busy road and there are always lots of people about.'

'Show me your front room.'

In the lounge Mursi cautiously peered around the curtains. Quite a few cars were parked but he could not see if any had occupants or not.

'Hanan, walk to the shop to buy milk or something. Walk steadily and do not appear to be looking for anyone but let me know if you see any cars parked with maybe a couple of people just sitting there. If you do, make a mental note and tell on your return. Be very careful not to appear nervous or inquisitive. Simply walk to the shop. Buy things and walk back.'

Slipping a coat over her shoulders Hanan did as Mursi had commanded. Near to the shop she observed a stationary vehicle with two men sitting inside. The windows were partly steamed up indicating it had been there for some time. Returning with her shopping she noticed the men had lowered their heads as if not wishing to be seen. The passenger seemed to be listening to some music as he had headphones on. How very rude to listen to music and not speak to the driver. Hanan took all this in as she walked back to her home.

Unlocking her door and entering, she saw Mursi, standing behind the door, once again He signalled for her to be quiet. He guided her into the bathroom, flushed the toilet and opened a tap to cover any noise from their whisperings.

'Well?' quizzed Mursi

'Did you see anything unusual?'

'Two men are sitting in a car. I do not think they are watching my house as the car is facing away. Also one of them is listening to music or something as he has headphones on and the other man is reading a newspaper. The car is slightly steamed up so it has been there for some time. I do not think they are anything to do with me or those bugs as you call them. We have nothing to fear from them.'

'Hanan, my guess is that the man with the earpiece is monitoring every sound that comes from your house. These bugs have a range of several hundred metres. They can not have heard my voice as you can be sure the house would have been surrounded by now. However, I must leave quickly. Here, this mobile has one of my numbers programmed in. If you can think of any reason at all why they should suspect you please phone the number immediately. Use it only once then break it and throw it away. Do you understand?'

Nodding that she did, Hanan flung her arms round Mursi.

'Midhat, I know I did nothing to cast suspicion on myself or put you in any danger.'

'It is too late now but I must hurry. We will repay the infidels a thousandfold for all the wrongs they have done. Just keep looking at the news programmes. You will know. The world will know.'

With that Mursi carefully opened the back door to the house. He could not see or hear anything except the occasional dog barking and traffic in the nearby streets. He kissed Hanan on the lips and hurried off to disappear into the maze of alleyways. His mind was in turmoil. It must have been something Hanan did inadvertently but he believed she was not aware of what she had done. Mursi fervently mouthed a quiet prayer to Allah as he walked hurriedly back to the safety of his flat.

'Allah, I implore you. Please, a few more hours is all I need. A day or so and my mission will be completed. That will be the end of Hawes!'

CHAPTER 50

Friday 15th February 1130 hours, Thames House

Stewart's phone warbled.

'Stewart!'

'My office. Now. Today is Christmas.' The DG had phoned Stewart directly.

On his way up in the lift Stewart racked his brain. What does he mean Christmas in the middle of bloody February?

As Stewart entered Helen's office she waved him to go straight in, 'the DG is expecting you.'

As he crossed her office Stewart thought he detected a glimmer of a welcoming smile. Perhaps frosty pants was thawing. Had she forgiven him for swearing at her some time earlier. No, on second thoughts, knowing her, she just had a touch of wind.

'Morning boss,' as he entered and prepared to sit himself in one of the chairs.

'Don't bother sitting. Get to New Scotland Yard. Two policemen will be waiting for you. The PM's 48 hours have just expired. Pick the woman up!'

'Great, we have waited long enough, now perhaps we will get somewhere. Now I know what you meant by Christmas, this could be the break we need. How do I play it? Do I go in hard, soft or play it by ear?'

'Let the police do the questioning. They have already been primed. You will merely tag along to see what you feel about the woman. Whatever happens phone me directly you have anything. Well? Why aren't you at the Yard?'

'On my way.' Rushing out of the office Stewart even blew a hurried kiss to Helen, beaming his nicest smile at her!

Arriving at the Yard Stewart skidded to a halt on double yellows, ignoring the frantic cries of a patrolling bobby. Striding rapidly towards the reception desk he was suddenly confronted by a uniformed Inspector and a stunning blonde in a neat and well-fitting business outfit.

'You must be Stewart. This is detective sergeant Kate Holloway and I am Inspector Bailey.' Stewart shook hands with both in turn.

'So what now?'

I presume we will travel in one of your cars. Mine is out front. Get someone to shift it please so as not to waste time?' Tossing the keys to the DS.

'Correct, our car is out back. Perhaps you can fill us in with more detail on the way. We have the outlines but anything will help.'

DS Holloway re-joined them after handing the keys to the Desk Sergeant. She was looking none too pleased at Stewart's cavalier manner. Pointing to an unmarked car the DS climbed into the driving seat with Stewart beside her, the Inspector relegated to the rear seat. In addition to admiring her obvious driving skills Stewart also admired her trim-looking legs encased in a sheath-like skirt of expensive-looking material.

'So, what can you tell us?' queried Bailey from the rear of the car.

'We have been given the background. It does seem a lot of fuss over a couple of missing men.'

'Quite clearly you have NOT been put fully in the picture. All I can tell you is that this is the most important case either of you have or will ever be involved in. You will have to play it by ear and see if the woman cooperates or is obstructive. I have here a list of questions that we need answers to. I cannot stress the importance of your task this morning. I prefer you did not arrest her but invite her to the station for questioning. Try not to come across heavy in order to put her at her ease.'

Opening a small briefcase Stewart handed over a sheet with a number of questions on.

'Read them out loud please so the DS knows what is going on.'

Glancing at the list the Inspector began reading out the questions handed to him by Stewart.

'OK, question one, 'what can you tell us about Hamid al Fadhil, or you may know him as Abu Khabab al Masri? Two, what do you know of his present whereabouts? Three, can you tell us anything about these two men (photographs provided). One being Mohammed Jamal Khalifa, the second none other that Anas al Liby, alias Mansour al Bakry. DO NOT PROMPT HER WITH THESE NAMES. Four, are you or do you know of anyone storing containers like these, again more photographs, this time of the nuclear device. Five, what was your purpose in staying at The Stone House hotel, near Hawes in North Yorkshire? Then tell her, 'If we find you have withheld any information or not co-operated fully you and your son will be deported from the United Kingdom, with no right of appeal. Do you fully understand the seriousness of helping us find answers to our questions?'

'You can't just deport people these days like that.' stated the Inspector.

'Oh but you are so very wrong in this instance Inspector. I told you earlier, this case is of such vital importance that we virtually have carte blanche, we can write our own rules – direct from the Prime Minister himself. So you make damned sure you do your job properly. This woman may hold information so vital to this country you just would not believe it. My boss spoke to the Assistant Commissioner who seems to feel you two work well together and will get the answers we need. Don't let any of us down.'

'Here we are sir,' chirped the lovely Holloway.

'Very well. It is all yours from now on. I shall intercede only if I think of something you missed. With your glowing recommendations I have every faith in you.'

186

CHAPTER 51
Friday 15th February, The Mosque

'Karim, Karim.' An alarmed Yusef burst into Mahasheer's office in the North London Central Mosque.

'Steady my brother, steady. What is the matter?'

'I was passing Hanan's house when I saw her taken away in a car by three people. Two men and one woman.' The words tumbling from Yusef's mouth.

'What do you mean taken away?'

'Hanan was crying. A woman was leading her to the car by her arm. One of the men was a senior police officer. I saw his uniform.'

'Did you hear any of them speak to her? Was she arrested or merely taken away. Do you know where they have taken her. Do you have any other information at all?'

'No Karim. Nothing. I was walking past as they led her from the house to the car. I did not stare as I did not wish them to notice me.'

'Thank you Yusef, you have done well. If you learn anything further you are to let me know immediately. You may go now but do not mention a word of this to anyone. Anyone, do you understand?'

'You may rely on me Karim. I will not say a word to anyone. If I learn anything else I shall tell you straightaway.'

'Please do that Yusef. It could be most important. You may go now.'

Unlocking a drawer of his desk Mahasheer took out a mobile phone. Once it was powered up he pushed the speed dial button of the only number entered.

About a hundred miles north Mursi and Al Liby were walking towards their car after stopping for coffee at a Little Chef. At the second ring Mursi answered. 'Yes,' knowing full well it was Mahasheer.

'Midhat, it is about Hanan.'

'No names you fool,' snarled Mursi.

'I am sorry. The police have arrested the person you recently took on holiday. It was just reported to me. At present I have no further information,' whined Mahasheer, abashed at having used the two names.

'Call me when you have more details. Now destroy the phone.' A click indicated the connection was broken.

Mursi and Mahasheer simultaneously ground their heels into the two mobiles.

'What was that about?' enquired Al Liby.

'It would appear the police have arrested Hanan for some reason. I can only assume it is somehow connected with me. She swears she has not mentioned the holiday, or myself, to a living soul and I believe her. I should have expected this and warned her to be prepared. I found her house had been bugged.'

As if thinking aloud, Mursi asked himself again and again. 'How? What did she do to attract the attention of the police?' Knowing he, himself, had not put a foot wrong. Sitting in the car in the big car park he continued to mull it over in his mind but could not come up with a thing. It now meant that, even more so, they had to be increasingly vigilant.

'What do we do now Midhat?' asked Al Liby.

'We carry on as planned but we must remain fully alert at all times. I know Hanan will not say anything to incriminate me but I am concerned as to how the police got onto her?'

Having refuelled Mursi drove thoughtfully up the A1 to the B2627 where he turned off towards Masham and subsequently Hawes. Approaching Middleham, Al Liby pointed out the hotel he had stayed in.

'This is a very nice place. I stayed here the last time I was here. Perhaps we could dine and stay the night here?'

'We will eat there if you recommend it but I do not think it would be wise for us to stay there. We will look for one of those anonymous bed and breakfast places closer to Hawes. Accommodation will be no problem, many of the houses in that part of the world provide holiday accommodation. Driving into the town it is a veritable forest of B and B signs. Then tomorrow we can search for a suitable location to place our two friends.' The two friends being the two parts comprising the nuclear device.

Having dined well at the hotel the two enjoyed a leisurely drive to the town of Hawes, selected by Mursi, to be the ground zero for his beloved bomb. No thought, whatsoever, given to the many men, women and children who would surely perish when the device was detonated. In a very short time the quaint market town of Hawes would become Yorkshire's very own Lidice!

CHAPTER 52
Friday 15th 1253 hours, a North Loindon Police Station

At the police station Inspector Bailey led the way along a corridor to a door marked Interview Room No2. The four of them entered.

'Why have you arrested me and brought me here?' pleaded a tearful Hanan.

'You have not been arrested Mrs Khaled, we would just like you to assist us in our enquiries by answering a few questions' explained the Inspector.

'But what questions, how can I help you?'

'DS Holloway has a short list of questions which we feel you may be able to help us with. Would you care for tea or coffee before we begin?'

'No thank you. How long will it take? I have to pick up my son from school at half past three.'

'It should not take too long, you will be clear in plenty of time to collect young Eid,' responded the Inspector.

'How do you know my son's name?'

'Oh we know quite a lot about you Hanan, if I may call you that?' Continuing, the DS said, 'I would like you to answer the questions as fully as you are able. What can you tell us about Hamid al Fadhil also known as Abu Khabab al Masri or Midhat Mursi?'

'I do not know anyone by those names,' blurted Hanan.

'They are aliases of the same man Mrs Khaled. I was about to ask you if you knew of his whereabouts.'

'If I do not know the man I cannot possibly know of his whereabouts.'

BANG, Stewart smashed his hand on the table startling not only Hanan but also the two police officers.

'Stop this shit and start answering the Sergeant's questions,' he thundered.

'I have my rights, you cannot keep me here like this. I want a solicitor,' stammered Hanan.

'In here you have no rights. Answer the Sergeant or by God you and your brat will be on this evening's flight back to Iran. You can also tell her why you signed in to the Stone House hotel as Mr and Mrs al Fadhil, considering that a minute ago you said you did not know him,' stormed Stewart.

The Inspector and Sergeant could only stare, open mouthed, at Stewart's outburst.

'Detective Sergeant, begin the questions again and this time Hanan Khaled or Hanan al Fadhil will cooperate fully.'

Still a little shaken the DS cleared her throat. 'Mrs Khaled, you heard the gentleman so we will try again. We are well aware that you know this man in the photograph.'

With her lower lip trembling and looking as if she was about to burst into tears again, Hanan realised that she would have to answer the questions as truthfully as she dare. Returning to Iraq with young Eid was unthinkable.

'Very well. My husband was killed a few weeks back in a motoring accident. I have been on compassionate leave ever since. Mr Fadhil offered to take us to Yorkshire with him for a few days break as he had business there.'

'Your husband has been dead a matter of weeks and you go off on holiday with a strange man. Do you consider that right and proper for a grieving widow. So why did you book in as Mr and Mrs al Fadhil? Surely a recently widowed lady would never dream of using a strange man's name and posing as his wife. I could, perhaps, give your tale more credence if you had registered in your own name.'

That was a good point I missed. Well done Sergeant, thought Stewart to himself.

'Mr Fadhil said it would look better if we appeared to be man and wife but he is a real gentleman and he slept on the bedroom floor.'

In a blinding flash Hanan suddenly realised how the police had got on to her so quickly. Quite innocently she had completed the details in the hotel register. She had remembered to sign in as Mr and Mrs Al Fadhil to maintain the façade that they were married. Thoughtlessly and automatically she had written down her home address.

Further columns asked for details of the car make and registration number. On top of that, Hanan remembered the CCTV camera because Eid had been excited seeing himself on the TV monitor. He always made a point of standing directly in front of the camera and waving his hand. There would be a video tape showing the three of them together on several occasions.

'You expect us to believe that after you have already lied to us. Where is he now?'

'I do not know. I swear it,' replied Hanan glancing nervously at Stewart and feeling her cheeks burning at the thought of having slept with Mursi.

'Look at these photographs.' The Sergeant passed across a photograph of Anas al Liby and Mohammed Jamal Khalifa.

'Can you tell us anything about either of these men?'

Hanan looked up with a puzzled expression. 'I have never seen either of them in my life before. I have no idea who they are.'

Making no comment about the first two photographs the Sergeant passed over several more photographs. 'Have you ever seen these containers or anything like them or heard al Fadhil talk about them with anyone?'

'No, no. I know nothing about them. Why are you asking all these questions?'

Ignoring her the Sergeant went on. 'What was Al Fadhil's reason for staying at The Stone House?'

'I have told you. He had business there and kindly offered to take Eid and myself for a short break. He had heard about my husband's death and thought it would take my mind off things for a time. I told you, he is a very kind and generous man.'

'How did you know him?'

'I didn't. We both use the same mosque and someone must have mentioned to him that I was upset over my husband's death and that a few days away might help.'

'It did not worry you that you would be staying overnight with a man you claim you had never heard of before that day?'

'If he had not been a gentleman no one would have suggested that I should go away with him, and I did have little Eid with me.'

'Did he not discuss his business with you?'

'Of course not. Arab men do not usually discuss their business with a woman.'

'What did you think his business was?'

'I tell you. I do not know. He would go off alone by car, sometimes at night and I assumed he was attending business meetings.'

'Who arranged the car? It was hired was it not? We discovered the details from the hotel register.'

'I do not know. I assumed it was his own car.'

'One last question. Are you certain there were no large containers in the boot of the car or on the back seat?'

'Definitely not, apart from my suitcases. Hamid had commented on my taking so much luggage for such a short stay.'

Holloway looked up at Stewart leaning against the wall.

'Anything else sir?'

'Mrs Khaled, we will arrange for you to be taken home now but we shall certainly want to see you again. If I suspect you have not been entirely honest with us I guarantee your deportation will follow so fast it will make your head spin.'

After Hanan had been fixed up with a lift home, Stewart thanked the two police officers.

'I will almost certainly want to see her again. I don't know if you noticed but when you mentioned the car she seemed quite agitated but for the life of me I can't think why. Oh yes, and a brownie point Sergeant regarding the comment about the grieving widow signing in and not using her own name. That aspect had not occurred to me. Well done.'

In actual fact it had not been the car causing concern, but that was the point when Hanan realised her blunder with the register.

'Thank you sir. It was the woman's point of view.' His words of thanks partly made up for his previous cavalier attitude, thought DS Holloway.

The Inspector chipped in. 'Yes sir, I did notice that the fact we knew about the car seemed to rattle her somewhat. I don't know what caused it because we know the car was legit so it beats me.'

'DS, sort my car out for me would you? Bring it round to the front.'

Holloway smiled sweetly, 'Of course sir. Anything to please.' Inwardly seething over the fact that bloody Franz Hals was back with his Laughing Cavalier.

CHAPTER 53

Friday 15th February 1407 hours, Hanan's Home

Drawing to a halt outside her home a policeman, driving an unmarked car, dropped Hanan off at her front door. She frantically rummaged through her handbag for her front door key. In her haste she dropped it onto the pavement. Retrieving it she hurriedly unlocked her front door and raced into her kitchen. Opening the cutlery drawer she grabbed the half-hidden mobile that Mursi had given her the previous day. Pressing the 'on' button she impatiently mouthed 'come on, come on' as she waited the few seconds needed to bring it into operation. Once it was up and running she stabbed the speed dial button to call up the only number entered into the phone. Very quickly she recognised Mursi's voice.

'Yes?'

'Midhat, Midhat it is Hanan. I now know how the police got onto me so fast!' Racing on she continued, 'I wrote my address in the hotel register with details of the hire car.'

Mursi struggled to interrupt. 'Stop, stop this now, and calm yourself. I hear and understand what you say. Now, smash the phone and never ever use names again.' Cursing to himself, first that fool Mahasheer and now Hanan. Do they not realise that people can listen in to mobiles?

'I am so sorry. I just wanted you to know how it had come about. I did not appreciate the fact that I was writing my own address.' Then, realising she was speaking into a dead phone Hanan closed the connection. For some seconds she stared at the mobile as if it was some malignant creature she held in her hand. Gathering her wits she hurried over to her work surface. The only heavy object close to hand was a tin of beans. With tears streaming down her cheeks at her foolishness she picked up the can of beans. Again and again she brought the heavy can down onto the phone until it was smashed into small pieces. Still shaking from the day's events Hanan decided that a cup of strong sweet tea would help settle her shattered nerves. Sipping the hot beverage she very soon convinced herself that, this time, no damage had been done.

After all, she had only been on the phone for a matter of seconds. There was no possibility whatsoever that anyone could have overheard the call, was there? Surely not in such a short time. Feeling decidedly reassured Hanan put her coat on and set off to collect Eid from his school.

Some distance along the road, one of the two Special Branch men suddenly sat up, pressing his earpiece tighter to his ear. Once it had gone quiet again.

'Bloody hell, listen to this.' Rewinding the last section of the tape he played it back so his colleague could hear the one-sided conversation. At the same time his mobile was also connecting with one of the phones on his superior's desk.

'Sir, it's me. The woman has just called the man Midhat. I clearly heard her use his name twice. She sounded to be in a right old tizzy. Midhat Mursi is one of the names I have in front of me.'

'Excellent, let me hear it.'

Less than half a minute later, 'I am relaying this to 'Five' now. Keep an ear out for anything more and don't take your eyes off that house. It looks as if our bugs have earned their keep at last. The boy did good! Stay in touch.'

CHAPTER 54

Friday 15th February 1411 hours, Hawes

'What was that Midhat? Trouble?' enquired Al Liby.

'It was Hanan. She now realises how the police got onto her. What I do not like is that she used my name, as well as her own. That is the second serious slip in about an hour. The British have a saying that things happen in threes. I am now wondering what our third slip up will be. It is so incredibly unbelievable that both Mahasheer and Hanan call me and stupidly use names over their mobiles in such a short time.'

'Both calls were quickly cut off by you, Midhat, so no harm done. In any case no one has the slightest idea where we are. Relax my brother. Tomorrow is your big day. From tomorrow your deed and your name will be praised for many years to come. Your followers of today will pass it on round the camp fires to their children and their grandchildren.'

'Yes, I expect you are correct. Both calls were very short. In addition my nerves are a little on edge at the magnitude of what you and I are about to achieve for Al Qaeda. Mahasheer and Hanan have no knowledge of my plans and as you say, no one has any idea of our whereabouts. The authorities do not even know we are in the UK.'

The men decided to rest in their rooms for a few hours. Sometime after seven thirty Mursi invited Al Liby to join him for a drink in a cosy little pub he had used a few weeks earlier. The third piece of 'things happen in threes' was about to occur.

Walking into the Board hotel they were met by a noisy crowd of smiling faces. A darts match was taking place between the Board and the Bruce Arms, Masham. Squeezing through the throng at the bar Mursi ordered two pints of best. With no spare seats they had to stand

and position themselves clear of the darts throwers as well as the occasional rebounding dart that had struck the wire. The match was a close run thing with the final game deciding the eventual winner. Since the entrance of the two swarthy looking men, Tom Prescott had had great difficulty in studying the two men without them noticing his interest. Ever since learning of his friend's gruesome death, almost certainly at the hands of an Arab, he suspected every Arab-looking person to be somehow involved. He knew it was ridiculous, as they would not return to the area so soon had they been mixed up in it. All the same, to Tom an Arab was an Arab. Mursi's sixth sense had alerted him to the feeling of being watched but he could not see who the watcher was if, indeed, there was one. His eyes flicked over to Tom Prescott, the last thrower. He was staring directly at Mursi. Mursi quickly looked away with a distinctly uneasy feeling. Prescott had a grim look on his face but no doubt due to the fact that the outcome of the match rested on him. Thirty-two remained for the game. A dartsman's dream. Double sixteen was the most liked and easy double on the board. Tom threw his dart. Sod, a single sixteen. Groans of dismay from his team mates.

'Tom what are you playing at? That is your favourite shot.' Another coarsely suggested that he might do better if it had some hair round it. Anyway, double eight was a dead certainty. This was a double he had seldom missed.

There is a first time for everything and this time his second dart clipped the double wire to slide into the single eight. Again more groans but the Board supporters yelled with joy. It looked as if the game was not in the bag after all. The Bruce supporters called out words of encouragement for Tom amid threats as to what fate would befall him if he missed the double four. Shuffling nervously he toed the oche preparing to fling the final and most vital dart of the evening. The dart sped through the air to plant itself dead centre of the double four. The room erupted with victory shouts from the Bruce Arms people. Tom was the most surprised and the most relieved person in the room. He had felt inside that he was going to miss this double as well. All down to that bloody coloured bloke. Looking round he realised the pair had left. As Tom had prepared to throw his final arrow Mursi nudged Al Liby.

'I think it is time we left.' With that both drained their glasses and walked from the crowded bar.

'What was that in aid of Midhat?'

'No reason, I just had a feeling of unease. That last dart player looked at me in a strange manner.'

'Have you ever met him before?' asked Al Liby.

'No but there was something in the way he kept staring at me when he thought I was not looking. Forget it, tomorrow is our big day. Nothing must mar its success. An early evening will do neither of us any harm. I shall feel much happier when we have positioned the device and left this area for good. I do not feel happy with it still being in our possession.'

Letting themselves into their B&B they silently climbed the stairs to their rooms.

'Goodnight my brother, and Allah willing tomorrow will be a glorious day for Al Qaeda. Sleep well my friend,' Al Liby murmured quietly to Mursi.

'You also Anas, and thank you for all your support.'

Before falling into his bed Mursi gazed for a few minutes at his car resting quietly in the rear car park of their B&B. It looked so ordinary and innocuous, just a parked car. Yet he knew full well the misery, mayhem and destruction it held in its cavernous boot. Just waiting for him to bring the device to life and wreak a dreadful vengeance on this lovely Dales town the following day. He mouthed a silent prayer to Allah asking for his blessings on the morrow.

CHAPTER 55
February 15th 1429 hours, North London Central Mosque

'Thank you Hanan but do not call me to discuss this sort of business, ever again, on the phone. Come in person, to the mosque, if it is something of this nature.' Hanan had decided to tell Mahasheer that she had spoken to Midhat to explain how the police had managed to trace her. Mahasheer was still smarting from Mursi's angry response from a couple of hours earlier. Mahasheer killed Hanan's call and after a few moments thought used his own mobile to call a friend in Bradford.

'Salaam my brother, we have not spoken for some time.' Mahasheer hurried on before his friend could say a word.

'Do not use any names, just in case.'

'As you wish my friend but it all seems very mysterious. I assume that this is not entirely a social call. What can I do for you my brother?'

'You recall I told you about having a very important visitor?'

'You mean the one from a much warmer location?'

'Yes that is the one. I just had to call you with exciting news. This man did not tell me precisely what he intends to do but he says he has plans for something more dramatic than 9/11.'

'Surely this cannot be. 9/11 was our greatest triumph over the Americans. It was so shockingly brilliant that the entire world knew of it within minutes.' This was spoken with great pride as Al Qaeda's greatest coup.

'He assures me it will be much more spectacular. All he would tell me was listen to the news or keep the TV on. He says that, without any doubt, newsflashes will be sent worldwide!'

'Have you and idea when this will be? I expect it will happen in London if it is to have such a dramatic outcome.'

'No, I have told you all I know of it. Oh, there is one other thing. He told me that much as he wanted it to be on film it would not be possible. He claimed it would be far too dangerous to remain in the area.'

'My dear friend, do you really believe this man? Surely what he says cannot be correct. Too dangerous to be in the area? I think he is merely trying to inflate his own importance.'

'No, in all seriousness I truly believe that he will do what he says. He is a man of his word. He is highly honoured and respected in the movement and the elders have given him their blessings to go ahead. If he says it will be sensational then you must believe it will be so.'

'Very well my brother. I will make a point of paying special attention to the news bulletins. I will also warn some of my friends, here, to do the same. May Allah bless you with a long and prosperous life.'

With that the two men closed their call and both sat back, deep in their own thoughts, both men wondering just what Mursi had planned, Mahasheer totally believing and trusting in Mursi. His colleague, in Bradford, was not quite so convinced. All the same he would be heeding the news reports. Just on the offchance that Mursi could pull off a momentous operation against the West.

CHAPTER 56
Friday 15th February 1430 hours, GCHQ

About one hundred miles to the north west of the capital banks of computers were busily working away. They were housed in a building known to its inmates as the Doughnut. Otherwise GCHQ or Government Communications Headquarters based in Cheltenham.

The raison d'etre for these premises? To monitor millions of electronically initiated messages every single minute of every day. Emails, mobile phones, faxes, radios. The lot! The recent email that you sent to your Aunt Nellie wishing her well, after her recent illness! It could as quickly have been seen by the staff here as when it had arrived at poor Aunt Nellie's. To filter out straightforward and innocent messages such as Aunt Nellie's and the millions of other routine messages certain words, phrases, names and places have been programmed into the system.

Any one of these preprogrammed words would trigger an alert causing the screen to flash a signal and an audible high-pitched bleep would sound. In fact, at this precise moment one of the multitude of operators sat bolt upright. Such an alert had just been picked up by his unit.

Identifying the precise message, he had a printout copied. Grabbing the message he tore it off and sped away to place it on the desk of his immediate supervisor.

'This just came through. I have alerted our people to check which transmitters were used.' The transmitter would give an accurate fix as to the location of the mobiles at that particular time.'

'Good work Simon. I think the director should see this right now. Come with me.'

The two men hurried along to Sir David Peglar's office. Seeing them expectantly peering in through his open door, he waved them to enter. 'You two look pleased with yourselves, so what is it?'

'This sir.' Placing the sheet in front of Sir David. 'It just popped up on Simon's screen. The name of one of the men Five warned us to listen out for. He seems to have surfaced!'

Scanning the document, 'This will please Jonathan no end. Do you know which transmitting masts were used?'

'Not yet sir but we will any minute now.'

'Let me know soonest. Ruth, get me the DG at Thames,' called out the Director to his PA. Seconds later one of his phones trilled.

'Thank you both.' Signalling for the two men to leave he picked up the phone.

'Jonathan, how are things in the big smoky city?'

'Not so smoky these days but busy as always Sir David. Am I correct in assuming your call is to tell me your electronic ears have some good news for us?'

'Sharp as ever Jonathan. Let me read you this short passage we picked up just now.'

After a couple of seconds. 'Well, Jonathan what do you have to say to that?'

'How about SNAP?'

'Go on tell me,' sighed the director.

'We have the woman's house bugged and two SB listeners overheard her speaking. I don't know Sir David. With your multi-million pound set up we obtained the same information from a couple of our 50p bugs. However, what you will have which I don't, is which transmitters were used to give us a location.'

'Cheeky young fella Jonathan, but it is nice to know that both our systems work. There is one thing, however, my boys picked up BOTH sides of the conversation. What I'm wondering is why the lapse in their security. These people are usually very wary and the use of names strictly taboo. No news yet on the masts, however, but I will have it in a moment.'

'The lapse in their security is most likely down to us. We finally managed to haul the woman in for questioning. I think she realised how we had got on to her and her companion, the chap Mursi. In her haste to warn him we believe she panicked and let his name slip out. We are sure she is not a hardened player but simply chosen to fulfil a particular role. This seems to be confirmed by your team when they picked up both conversations.'

'Happy to know we are earning our crust over here. Are you able to tell me what all this fuss is in aid of'?'

'I am sorry Sir David, not yet. I appreciate that our phones are secure but...'

'Not another word Jonathan. I understand. Need to know and all that. Possibly big enough to earn you your KT.'

'If it works out for us it should be enough to sit me on the throne, never mind a KT.'

'Oh, Jonathan I'd no idea. I apologise for even thinking of asking you.'

'Not a problem Sir David. Just one other thing. The relaying masts. One in north London and the other alongside the A1 near Ripon, North Yorkshire.'

'You certainly have been quick off the mark. It is my turn now to say SNAP. The same information has just arrived on my desk. Keep in touch and good luck. If this is as big as you suggest, it seems as if you may well need it.'

CHAPTER 57

Saturday 16th February 0805 hours, Hawes

Having had a restless night Mursi rose early to wash and dress. Looking through the window at his car he noticed that the day was quite foggy. Probably all the better for what they had in mind! Less people to see what they were up to. Although neither felt like eating, the two Arabs decided to go down for breakfast. Six other guests were there. Four at one table were obviously a family and two men were seated at a second table quietly eating their bowls of cereal. Two other places were laid at their table. The two men nodded politely at Mursi and Al Liby one saying, 'help yourselves to juice and cereals. The landlady will be back in a mo.'

The Arabs did so and ordered a cheese and mushroom omelette each from their hostess when she came through for their order.

'Staying long?' asked one of their fellow guests.

'No, just passing through. How about yourselves?'

'A working holiday. My mate is a chopper jockey.' Seeing the puzzled look on Mursi's face he went on, 'he is a helicopter pilot.'

'Ah I see now,' replied Mursi.

Without being prompted, the breakfast companion went on. 'I am his crewman. We are here to ferry stone and rocks along Stags Fell. You know, the big hill behind Hawes.'

'Why would you do that?' queried Al Liby.

'It is to repair the path across the fell. We have a small landing area for refuelling and basic maintenance alongside the road to Thwaite.'

'Surely this must be very expensive?' questioned Mursi.

The pilot sat quietly through all the chatter, eating his fry-up with some enthusiasm. 'It does not work out too badly when you consider how quickly we can do the job compared to lorries. On top of that we deliver the cargo right to the precise spot on top of the fell, to the worker's feet.'

'Yes, I can see the advantage,' murmured Mursi.

When the omelettes arrived. Mursi ate automatically and slowly, hardly tasting his fluffy and delicious meal. Thanks to his two breakfast companions an idea was forming in his head. Perhaps it might be possible to film the explosion after all.

CHAPTER 58
Saturday 16th February 0805hours, Midedleham

About twenty miles away from Hawes another two men were sitting down to breakfast in the Middleham hotel, having moved from their Masham hotel so as to be more centrally located. The real reason being it was cheaper and they could make more on their expense allowance. A file containing photos of Britain's Ten Most Wanted lay open between the toast and the coffee. Mary, their bright and cheery waitress bounced past.

'Any more toast?'

'No thanks Mary we are fine,' replied Butch.

'That bloke was in here yesterday for lunch,' announced Mary pointing a chubby finger at Al Liby's photograph.

'Bugger off Mary. Go and poison some other guests with your toast,' growled Butch. Mary was the original wind-up merchant and they were already well used to her ways.

'OK, bye. Hope you choke on your toast. Don't say I didn't tell you.' Laughing, she flounced away to take orders from some of the other guests. On her way back from the kitchen she leaned towards Butch and Sundance.

'If you don't believe me I will tell your boss now he is here. He will believe me.'

'Mary love, not today please, we had a heavy night.'

She was a treasure, but after a session of serious drinking it needed a stout constitution to handle her lively disposition and sense of humour at this hour of the morning.

'Morning, boys,' announced Stewart, causing Butch and Sundance to almost follow Mary's advice and choke on their toast.

'Boss, to what do we owe this honour?'

Stewart, knowing Mary from previous visit's called her over.

'Any chance of a black coffee and some toast?'

'Certainly sir. I will fetch it straight away. I was just telling these two that this man,' indicating Al Libys' photograph.

'Had lunch here yesterday with another foreign bloke, but these two were not interested.'

'Mary, are you sure? Really sure?' demanded Stewart.

'Course I'm sure. Him and another bloke. I should remember because he left me a five pound tip.'

'Come here Mary, sit down. Shift your backside for the lady Butch.'

'I can't sit down, I'm working.'

'Not now you're not. Sit. Look at the rest of these photos. Tell me if you recognise the other man.'

'OK but I need to tell them in the kitchen so someone can serve for a minute or two.'

Returning after about half a minute she took her seat and flipped the pages of the mugshot book over. She pointed once more at Al Liby. Two pages later she triumphantly announced, 'this was the other man.'

'Mary, this is really important. Are you positive?' demanded Stewart again.

'You are as bad as these two. I told you already. A fiver tip for lunch! Anyone would remember. If they ever came in again I'd make sure I served them.'

CHAPTER 59

Saturday 16th February, 0811 hrs, Middleham

'Come on you two, up to your room and I will explain there.'

Once upstairs he called Thames on his mobile, managing to reach the DG direct.

'Sir, Stewart. It is confirmed that Mursi, or whatever he calls himself, and Al Liby were in this very hotel yesterday. They stopped in Middleham for lunch. A waitress positively identified them both. It seems clear that the Arab woman knows much more. I'd like her lifted immediately and this time given the works!'

'Will do Stewart.'

'Sir, I'd prefer the same two police officers to question her as they have met her already. They are not aware of how big the problem is. I think they should be told. It might just give them the edge to come down heavier.'

'Helen, get me the Commissioner. OK I am on with that now. I presume you will need more back up.'

'If they arrived yesterday they must be well advanced in their plans. I can't see them hanging around here too long, after all they do stand out quite a lot in this neck of the woods. So, yes, I need more men but fast!'

'Agreed. I'll sort out a dozen or so and fly them from the City Airport to RAF Leeming. I will arrange for Leeming to lay on three cars and have them waiting.'

'Thank you sir. These bastards certainly wrong footed us. We anticipated London or Birmingham. It now seems curtains for somewhere around here.'

'Mm, I think you may be right. The one good thing, if they do detonate that bloody device up there, loss of life will be less severe than it going off in the Capital. Thank you, Helen. OK Stewart I'll get things moving this end.' Picking up another phone, 'Morning Commissioner. Yesterday two of your people picked up an Arab woman for questioning. We need her again and urgently and we must have answers.'

'Very well Jonathan. This relates to our present major headache I imagine.'

'Yes, it seems London is off the hook after all. We now believe the target is to be in the North Yorkshire area.'

'Your two officers were called Bailey and Holloway. I'd like them again as they already know the woman!'

'I will get them Jonathan. I don't think I will reduce our threat level just in case. The Royals have refused to leave Buck House. You can imagine what Philip said when it was suggested they go to Sandringham for a few days. Given the reason why, his reply was typical of him. Her Majesty said the same but far more politely. Good for them! However, some MP's decided to leg it to their constituencies, again typical of the calibre of some of our less worthy Dishonourable Members. I have just sent for one of my people to chase up Bailey and Holloway. Anything else I can do to help?'

'Thank you Commissioner. There is one thing. Would you, personally, put your two officers fully in the picture. We feel it will give them the necessary incentive when questioning the woman. She may hold the key, even if unknowingly, to the two terrorist's whereabouts. We do need her knowledge very urgently.'

'Do you think it wise to tell the two officers. After all this is Cosmic Top Secret.'

'I feel they need to appreciate the gravity of the situation. You can do it on my authority or I can get the PM's office to contact you if that will make you feel any easier Commissioner.'

'No, it is fine by me. In any case I expect that the whole country will know about it within twenty-four hours or so. Bye Jonathan.'

'Helen. My office please.'

Walking in with her shorthand notebook at the ready she plumped herself down into a seat opposite her boss. Her experience told her that this was going to be important.

'Yes sir?' She looked questioningly at the Director.

'Take a seat, why don't you?' He smiled across at her. Adopting his manner she smiled back sweetly.

'Aye, I think I will at that. Thank you very much sir.'

'Right. ONE, I need about a dozen operatives up to North Yorkshire. Contact any that we know are handy and available. I want them at the City Airport but fast. TWO, Contact the City Airport and get them to organise a charter large enough to fly the men to RAF Leeming. Make sure they understand I want it within the hour. Righto, take these personnel files and get phoning. I will come through to help you in a minute or two. Any questions?'

'No sir, I am on it now.' With that Helen hurried back to her own desk and began rapidly sorting through the files to find the men Stewart needed.

'I had better let the Home Secretary know we are hot on the trail of our two baddies. No I won't, dammit. I will tell the PM himself and brighten his day. Oh Helen, get someone to phone RAF Leeming and tell them to expect a civvy plane later this morning AND make sure they have three cars ready and waiting. I will contact Stewart and put him in the frame.'

Dialling Stewart himself, the DG spoke the moment he heard Stewart's voice. 'Stewart. I am arranging to fly a dozen or so men to RAF Leeming. They should be with you in two to two and a half hours from now. Cars will be waiting for them. Anything else you can think of?'

'Not at the moment sir, apart from information from that damned woman.' This time Stewart closed the call on his boss.

Stewart suddenly remembered one other thing. He telephoned the headquarter's of the North Yorkshire Constabulary at Newby Wiske near Northallerton.

'Police, can I help?'

'Yes, I need your most senior duty officer.'

'He is busy right now. Can I give him a message.'

'No you bloody can't. Get him on the phone this second!'

Something told the policeman that he was dealing with a man with far more authority than he wanted to handle. Seconds later.

'This is Inspector Davies. Who are you please?'

'My name is Stewart. During a recent murder enquiry one of your Inspectors, Deptford, led your team. I want him and half a dozen men that worked on the case with him in Middleham in an hour.'

'Just a moment sir. I do not know you from Adam and in any case some of the officers may be off duty.' That would tell the jumped-up prick on the phone.

'Inspector. Stay by that phone. In five minutes the Home Secretary will be calling you. Is that high enough authority? In the meantime move it and get those people to me and bloody quickly.'

Like the policeman on the switchboard, something told the Inspector that he should start to locate the officers. Phoning a Superintendent he recited Stewart's call to him. Whilst he was explaining another phone on his desk trilled.

'Excuse me sir, I won't be a second,' to his Super.

'Inspector Davies here.'

'Inspector, you very recently had a man on the phone called Stewart. Do you recognise my voice?'

'It sounds familiar madam, but I can't quite place it.'

'It should. I am the Home Secretary. Now be a good man and do as Stewart asked, and quickly, if you value your pension. Confirmation will come down from the Chief Constable in minutes. Remember, I want SPEED. Good day Inspector.'

'Er, goodbye ma'am.' But he was wasting his breath, she had gone.

He resumed his conversation with the Super with a touch of incredulity in his voice.

'Sir, that was the Home Secretary. Authorisation will be here in minutes from the Chief Constable. The other bloke must have been kosher.'

'Ah well, that's made your day. Thank you Inspector, I'll take it from here. Give me the name of the Inspector he asked for, before you go.'

CHAPTER 60

Saturday 16th Feb, 0827 hours, Hawes

Finishing their breakfasts Mursi and Al Liby excused themselves and made to leave the table.

'I do not think you will be flying today. It is very foggy.'

'Do you want to take any bets on it? I spoke to the Met Office at RAF Leeming and they forecast it will burn off within a couple of hours.'

'So you plan on flying after all? If you do I would like to watch you at work.'

'No problem. Follow the road over Stags towards Thwaite. You will see our spot taped off on the left side of the road. I look forward to seeing you later.'

Al Liby was looking curiously at Mursi. 'Surely we won't have time to watch these people transporting rocks. We have our own business to attend to?'

'Let's go up and pack. We can discuss the situation upstairs.'

Once in his room Mursi proceeded to outline his recently amended plan. 'When 9/11 happened there was very dramatic filming actually showing the aircraft crashing into the Twin Towers. Those images will remain etched in the minds of everyone who saw them until the day they die.'

'Yes but we cannot film your masterpiece. We have to be well clear of the area by the time the bomb explodes. This is not merely an aircraft smashing into a building. This is an atomic bomb!'

'Precisely, and that is why I must film it. I also have a plan for us to be well clear of the blast.'

'Mursi, my brother, it is not possible to have it on film and escape with our lives. You must realise that.'

'Anas. Have I ever let you down before?' Without waiting for an answer he went on. 'We shall use the helicopter to film the explosion from a safe distance. I shall order the pilot to fly a couple of metres above Dodd Fell so as to drop quickly behind the hill to escape any blast. Do not forget this bomb is of low yield and I assure you we will not be blasted out of the sky in a huge fireball. I shall detonate the weapon by remote control. You will make certain the camera is on and pointing towards Stags Fell. None of us will actually look in that direction once I have pressed the button so it is vital you aim the camera exactly. With wide angle it will not matter if you are a little off target. Quite obviously, we will close our eyes in addition to wearing very dark sun glasses. I will also brief the pilot to avert his eyes and also use the darkest sunglasses we can obtain.'

'I must confess to being more that a little anxious Midhat. When I have seen films of nuclear weapons the flash and explosion is huge.'

'Yes, but this device is only one kiloton or less. You saw films of devices of at least ten or more kilotons. We will be perfectly safe flying near Dodd Fell. I checked on the Ordnance Survey map for a safe filming location. From there we can see the creamery car park quite clearly. Once I press the button the pilot will descend rapidly behind the top of the hill. I promise we will be safe.

This device was designed, initially, to generate a huge electromagnetic pulse to fry electrical equipment, particularly radios and other electronic communications equipment. Certainly the blast will flatten much of Hawes and kill many hundreds. However, the initial and residual radiation will be the real killers. People will be dying years after the bomb goes off and it will render the entire area uninhabitable for years to come. Hawes will cease to exist.'

Chapter 61
Saturday 16th February 0818ours, Middleham

'OK any questions?' asked Stewart.

'No boss, except what do we do now?'

'We can make a start by checking on B&B's again. See if we can locate our two Arab friends. With luck they may be staying a few nights but if not the proprietor might have some idea of where they are headed if they only stayed the one night.' Loud groans came from Butch and Sundance.

'You remember how many accommodation places there are in this area, Boss.'

'Yes, so the sooner we get started the better. Holloway and his officers will be here before our own troops fly into Leeming. So we will have more help shortly.' Donning coats and gathering up pens and notebooks, the three left the Middleham hotel. It had been decided they would begin, on foot, checking local accommodation.

'Hey!' Looking round, Stewart spotted Tom Prescott striding towards him.

'Good morning Mr Prescott. Carry on you two, I'll catch you up.'

'Just the man. Anything on the blokes that killed Jeb?'

'Actually you may be able to help. Let's go inside for a few minutes.'

'OK but I can't stop long, I've a job on in Hawes.'

'Very well, it won't take long.' Sitting in the bar Stewart explained that they suspected the men involved in Jeb's death were in the area.

'Here, have a look at these two photos. If you happen to spot them give me a call. Here is my card with my number on it.' Jumping to his feet Prescott demanded.

'Are these the bastards that murdered Jeb...?' Looking a little shocked Stewart stated they were the prime suspects.

'Why, what is it?'

'These sods were in the Board last night.'

'Where? What board?'

'The Board Hotel, Hawes. We had a darts match there last night.'

'You seem quite certain.'

'No doubt at all. That little bastard,' indicating Mursi, 'was staring at me. Look, I have to go. I am picking up two other volunteers. We are working on Stags Fell near Hawes. I will take them and come back to help in any way I can.'

'Thank you Mr Prescott but I have quite a few people of my own arriving shortly. However, should you spot them do not approach them, they are very dangerous men. You have my card, phone me on any of those numbers. You can hang onto those two photographs.'

'Not much chance of coming across them on Stags Fell, more's the pity. I owe them, the bastards.'

'Just one more question. If you were a terrorist what would you choose to blow up in this area that would be spectacular?'

'There isn't a lot here unless you want to kill a string of racehorses,' nodding towards the window as a dozen or so valuable horses, from one of the many local stables, trotted past, heading for the 'Gallops' for their morning run.

'Something certainly brought them back here. What about Catterick Garrison?' Well, they say it is the largest army camp in Europe but there won't be so many people over the weekend and it is also well spread out.'

'We thought of Catterick. In fact the more I think about it the more certain I am that it could well be the target. Even with the personnel dispersed there would be a large number of fatalties.'

'But they would need a massive bomb to do much damage there. No, in my opinion it can't be Catterick.'

'And what if they did have a massively powerful bomb? What then?' asked Stewart.

'No, the camp is too big. You would need a bloody atom bomb to do any good.' Looking at Stewart, Tom saw a grim look on his face. The idea began to dawn on him.

'My God. Those boxes, they were atom bombs.' Amazement and disbelief showed in Tom's face.

'We believe so. Quite obviously you do not breathe a word of this. If I thought you were likely to I'd have you in custody so fast your head would spin.'

'You know you can rely on me, but bloody hell, an atom bomb in North Yorkshire. No, it just can't be.'

'I trust your discretion but keep an eye out all the same. Now you know why you must not approach them. Phone me. My men will take care of them. It is absolutely vital that we find them and prevent them using that device.'

'You can count on me, but as I said, I don't expect to come across them on Stags.' As Tom walked thoughtfully away, Stewart phoned Butch.

'You two! Back here and look sharp about it.'

CHAPTER 62
Saturday 16th February 0834 hours, Hawes

'Hello, is my laundry ready?' Mursi to his contact in Bradford.

'Do you have your ticket number sir?'

'It is 2411 and I am calling from 01969...Get back to me quickly.'

'I will check and call you back sir.' Having replaced the receiver he once again lifted it to his ear when it rang shortly afterwards.

'Hello, is that my dry cleaners?' enquired Mursi.

'Yes sir, your laundry is ready.' Having gone through his security procedure Mursi then asked.

'Please get me a top quality camcorder with a wide angle lens, fully charged batteries and a new cassette. I also need three pairs of the strongest sunglasses you can find. Welders goggles will be ideal. Deliver them to the usual place. I will be waiting there. Speed is essential.' To Al Liby, 'well, my brother that is the camera arranged. I will drive across to collect these few items. There is no need to rush, the helicopter cannot fly as it is still too foggy.' With that the two Arabs climbed into Mursi's car.

'By usual place I assume you mean the White Scar Caves car park?' offered Al Liby.

'Yes but first we will check out the improvised helipad. It should be quiet with this fog about.' They drove up Stags Fell on the Thwaite Road. As Mursi crested a steep section he passed over a cattle grid and made out a parking area on the left. Half a mile further on he could just make out the taped landing area through the thinning fog.

'This looks ideal Anas. We will hi-jack their helicopter with no difficulty whatsoever. Your *khanjar* will ensure the pilot's cooperation.' Turning the car round, Mursi drove back onto the small parking area and climbed out to be joined by Al Liby.

'The fog prevents you from seeing but Hawes is more or less directly in front of us. Allah seems to be blessing our work.' They stood there for a minute or so, trying to imagine what it would be like in a few hour's time. Someone standing where they were now would see an area of utter devastation. Driving past the Wensleydale Creamery, Mursi drove in through the open gateway on to the upper car park. It was thanks to little Eid, who had asked if they could visit the place, that Mursi knew of this smaller, quieter, car park.

'Come with me Anas.' Walking up to a stone wall he peered over and pointed out a small clump of bushes, still leafless so early in the year.

'That is where I intend to place our device. If the car park is quiet that will be the ideal place. It is only yards short of Hawes market place. We can easily lift the boxes over the wall and then cover them with small twigs. It is most unlikely that anyone would spot them.' At that moment Allah's smile lessened somewhat. A car drove in disgorging three noisy and lively children, the largest of which proceeded to clamber over the wall directly where Mursi had intended placing the device. The two Arabs looked at each other.

'I had another spot in mind, a small industrial estate where the Fire Station is located, but this place is in just the right location.'

'Midhat. Could your contact obtain another vehicle for us? After all, this is a car park and it is where a car would not look out of place. It would also save us the trouble of handling our cargo to locate it where we need it.'

'Anas, you are brilliant. Of course. I had not considered leaving the car but we will do so and I will arrange a replacement.' Taking another mobile from his small haversack Mursi called the Laundry direct. Not wanting to waste time he spoke as soon as the contact answered.

'I called just now to order a camera and other things. Forget the security rigmarole, time is of the essence. I now need another car. Something reliable but one that won't stand out. Is that clear? It should also have a nice large boot.'

'It shall be as you wish sir. We may need an extra half hour to arrange it.' A ray of weak sunlight swept across Mursi's face. It would soon be clear enough for the helicopter to start flying.

'Very well, but as fast as you can please.'

The Police Commissioner had certainly pulled out all the stops. An unmarked police car lurched to a halt outside Hanan's house. Looking pale after learning of the nuclear device. Inspector Bailey and Detective Sergeant Holloway hurried to the front door. Sitting in the rear of their car was a woman from Social Services. Her job, to babysit little Eid. The officers knew that Hanan was home, courtesy of the two Special Branch listeners sitting in their car along the road. A quick rap brought Hanan to her door.

'Mrs Khaled, get your coat. We need you to assist in our enquiries again.'

'But I can not help you further and I have my son to look after.' Bailey beckoned the Social Services lady to join them.

'This lady will care for your son. Get your coat and look quick about it.' Gone were the niceties of their first meeting with this woman. The threat of mass murder tends to concentrate the mind considerably. Her mind in a whirl, Hanan found herself speeding to the same police station. Once inside she was quickly escorted to the same interview room. Bailey was about to take a leaf from Stewart's book. No sooner was Hanan seated when the Inspector slammed two airline tickets on the desk in front of her. A startled Hanan looked up.

'These two tickets are for you and that brat of yours to fly to Iraq on this evening's flight!' Even the DS looked a little surprised.

'But you can't do this,' stammered a tearful Hanan.

'We warned you before what would happen and you lied to us. You have one choice. Help us locate this man,' Mursi's photo was placed in front of her, 'or you leave the United Kingdom tonight. For good.'

'How can I help you. I have not seen or heard from him for over two weeks.'

'You are a liar and a fool to yourself. Sergeant, if you please?' DS Holloway lifted a dictaphone from her pocket and pressed the play button.

'Midhat, Midhat it is Hanan.'

'Need I play more Mrs Khaled? This was you, yesterday afternoon, warning the man.' At that Hanan's shoulders shook as she collapsed with her head on the desk, sobs racking her body.

'That, Mrs Khaled, has just guaranteed you and your son a flight to Iraq. You leave tonight. I will hold your tickets for you and gladly see you aboard the aircraft, we will give to five minutes to reconsider.' With that the Inspector picked up the airline tickets and marched from the room with the Sergeant. Outside, the Sergeant said, 'I had not realised you were serious about flying her out this evening. You already have their tickets as well.' The Inspector handed the tickets over to the Sergeant. A smile began to form on her face. But these are in your name and your wife's to fly to Tenerife on Friday.'

The Inspector, with a mischievous grin on his face, asked, 'Are they really? Well, if they fooled you they should do the same for her.'

CHAPTER 64

Saturday 16th February 0937 hours, London

'Well Mrs Khaled. What is your decision? Remain here with your teaching job or use these airline tickets to start a new life full of misery in Iraq for you and your boy?' the Inspector asked whilst waving the fake tickets in front of her face. The Detective Sergeant struggled to hide her grin since being put in the picture about the tickets.

'I cannot tell you much but Midhat did visit me on Thursday. I do not know what he has planned but he said he would repay the infidels a thousandfold. It must be something very big.'

'Mrs Khaled, we know he is in the Hawes area at this very moment. Why would he return there?'

'Hawes, but why Hawes?'

'That is what we want to know. Did he mention anything that might be a target? Do you know where he went and whom he visited?'

'I just do not know. You must believe me now. I swear to Allah that this is the truth. Sometimes he went out on business during the day and sometimes during the evening.'

'And you have no idea what he was up to? Remember, if we consider you are lying to us again or hiding things from us you will soon be living in Iraq. Or perhaps dying.'

'I remember one thing. One night he came in very late with blood on his clothes.'

'What night was this, do you remember and where did you say the blood came from?' demanded Inspector Bailey.

'It was our last night there, the Friday, but he did not say what had happened and I dare not ask. I rinsed the blood from some of his clothes. It was then he told me that we would be leaving the following morning.'

'This is not helping us very much. I think you can do better. The blood came from a man that your friend either killed or helped in to kill.'

'No, he could never do anything like that. He was kind and a gentleman all the time. There must be some other reason for the blood.'

'Mrs Khaled, any normal person would enquire about another being bloodstained. You really expect us to believe your story. Do you know what car he is driving?'

'I have told you as much as I know. Perhaps Karim might know more.'

'Karim, who is this Karim.'

'He can be found at the mosque. I do know that Midhat visited the mosque quite often to meet Karim.'

'Excuse me one moment. The Sergeant here will ask you further questions.' Leaving the room the Inspector walked into the open office of the Superintendent.

'Sir, this woman has mentioned a man who may be able to help us. A chap called Karim at the mosque. Would you please have him picked up quickly?'

'Why all the rush Inspector, can't this wait until Monday?'

'Sir, I assumed you knew what the cause of the urgency was. It is obvious you do not and I cannot tell you.'

'What do you mean you can't tell me? Out with it man.'

'Sir, may I use your phone?' Without waiting for approval the Inspector dialled.

'Inspector, you are pissing me off. Don't be so bloody impertinent.'

'Sir, if I may be allowed to make a phone call I am sure It will be explained. In the meantime will you please order a car to bring this Karim in as soon as possible?' A voice confirmed the connection had been made.

'This is Inspector Bailey, would it be possible to speak with the Commissioner?' A moment later.

'Sir, Bailey here. Would it be possible for you to have a word with my Super? I need an Arab to be brought in quickly for questioning and my Super is doubting me.'

'Put him on, I assume you are in his office.' Bailey handed the phone over and the Superintendent's face slowly reddened with him saying 'yes sir' a few times and then laying the phone back in its cradle.

'Inspector, I am not happy that one of my junior officers knows more about what is happening than I do. Your man will be on his way here in minutes.'

'Thank you sir.' As he left the Inspector thought, that is my promotion chances shot to shit.

'Well, did you get anything further Sergeant?'

'Only that Mrs Khaled has the impression that our man will be leaving the country very soon. Whatever he has planned is big because he told her the whole world would hear about it.'

'Mrs Khaled. We would like you to volunteer to remain here overnight. Your son will be brought to you.'

'Does this mean you will not send me back to Iraq?'

'Not necessarily but I am now going to give you some information that is still top secret. Think about what I am going to tell you and then see if you can come up with any further information on this man,' the Detective Sergeant interrupted, 'but sir.'

Disregarding the interruption the Inspector went on, 'We are confident that this man you were with has in his possession a small nuclear device.'

'NO, no I would have known. He is not like that. He is a good man.

'It is for that reason that I have give you this information. So, if you can think of anything it is vitally important you tell me. This madman is planning to slaughter hundreds if not thousands of innocent men, women and children. Because of what you now know you will not be allowed to leave our custody until he and the device are located and dealt with.'

'I cannot think of anything else. He never discussed anything with me. I know he obtained money and his car through Karim. Oh, he is very good at disguises. I did not recognise him until he spoke when he visited me. He looked like a stooped old man with a very bad limp. Please believe me Inspector, if I could tell you more I would. I will try to remember if there is something I have missed. Eid and myself will willingly remain here until this business is finished. You must have the wrong man though. Midhat is kind and gentle.'

Opening his briefcase the Inspector took out the photograph of Jeb's mutilated body. 'Mrs. Khaled. We firmly believe your 'kind and gentle' man, working with another terrorist, was responsible for this atrocious act of murder.'

Hanan had nothing to say. She was lying on the floor in a dead faint!

CHAPTER 65
Saturday 16th February, 0953 hours, Hawes

Knowing that the two terrorists had been seen in Hawes, Stewart had moved the search directly to the small Dales town. Inspector Deptford had turned up with five of his officers. Photocopies of Mursi and Al Liby were handed to them and they began a systematic check of all types of accommodation within a ten mile radius. Stewart felt his phone vibrate.

'Stewart.'

'Stewart. The woman has told us that our man arrived at their hotel late on the Friday evening with quite a lot of blood on his clothes.' the DG informed Stewart.

'So, it looks as if those two did kill this man up here. Anything else?'

'Two things. She gave us a name of one of their contacts and I am sorry to pass this on to you. It is a case of I'm alright Jack. I am well away if they do manage to detonate the weapon but you are right in the firing line. He did tell her to watch the news as it would be sufficiently important to be broadcast worldwide.'

'The CO has put Catterick Garrison on Red Alert, but quietly, so as not to create a panic. He has done it under the guise of a major exercise. It still seems that is the probable target. If we get anything from this other chap I will let you know soonest. We managed to scrape up ten from our section and they will be leaving the City Airport about now. I will have them contact you when they arrive at Leeming.'

'Sir, I assume they have photographs of our two men. I'd like them to go to Catterick as soon as they arrive. Still no news on what car he is using?'

'Nothing yet. Bye.' Butch and Sundance opted to check on The

Stone House hotel in the hopes of seeing the trim receptionist again. Their luck was out. A teenage boy was manning the desk.

'Hello, I wonder if you could help. Did either of these men stay here last night?' enquired Sundance.

'No, I was on duty last night. We had a wedding party so there were no available rooms.'

'Good morning Mr Franklin, is Tim looking after you?' It was the owner of the hotel.

'Yes thank you sir. We were asking if these two men stayed here last night,' explained Sundance passing photos of the two Arabs across.

'No, we only had white guests with us. Oh that reminds me, just a moment please.' The man disappeared into his office only to return a moment later with a slip of paper in his hand.

'When the police came, following that horrible murder, they searched the two rooms the Arab had for his wife and their son. They took bags away containing possible evidence, they said. Well, as it happens we were using a quiet period to redecorate whilst we had the chance. When we cleared the room the man and woman were using I happened to pick this up from behind the washstand. It was this bloodstain that made me hang on to it. I am afraid it slipped my mind until I saw you two just now. It might be nothing but you never know.' He held out a Morrison's till receipt dated a few days before Jeb's murder took place. Not only did it have a bloodstain but scribbled on the reverse was what looked like a mobile telephone number.

'You found this in the room the man was using? Had anyone been in the room after they left?'

'No, it just happened that that was the first room we started to work on.'

'Thank you sir, I do not imagine we will obtain any useful prints off it but the lab boys may well come up with some DNA traces. If they can obtain positive results it would tie that man into the murder. The other thing being that this is obviously a mobile phone number. We will find out who it belongs to. I can't get a signal here on my mobile so may I please use your landline?'

'By all means. I am only sorry it slipped my mind earlier.' Smiling nicely, Butch thanked the man for being so thoughtful in saving the slip of Paper, at the same time thinking you great stupid twit this could be important. Picking up the phone, Butch dialled the duty desk at Thames House.

'Morning mate, Butch here. I'd like a check doing on this number. I feel certain it is a mobile number. I'd like this yesterday please. Once you have it call Stewart as he has a sat phone. Thanks, bye.' Meanwhile reports from the police were all coming up negative. A good number of customers and staff from the Board Hotel remembered the two Arabs but no one had seen if they left by car or on foot. Quite a few of the B& B owners were out, either shopping or doing other things. It would be necessary to follow up with further visits. All taking time and doubling the already huge work load. All this when everyone felt that time was running out, and running out very quickly.

CHAPTER 66
Saturday 16th February 1039 hours, White Scar Caves Car Park

Mursi and Al Liby had only been waiting about twenty minutes when two cars pulled up alongside them. Al Liby recognised the man he had met previously so got out of his car to greet him.

'Sabah el khayr my brother. It is good to see you again.'

'Sabah el nurr to you my friend. May Allah's blessings be upon you.' By then Mursi had joined them and after exchanging similar greetings he asked.

'Did you obtain everything I asked of you?'

'Yes my friend and we also included a further thousand pounds of English money in case you were in need of more funds. This also arrived from London. I was told you know what it is for. It is some sort of radio transmitter.'

'Thank you for the money and yes, indeed I do know what the transmitter is for. I am delighted that I now have it but whether I will be able to use it or not is a different matter.' Leading Mursi to one of the cars the man opened the boot, pointing out the box containing the camcorder. The car park was not yet busy at this time of the day so their contact removed the camcorder from its box and proceeded to give Mursi the rundown. It proved to be quite straightforward and Mursi expressed his satisfaction.

'This is the other car you requested so the camera and sun glasses can remain in here until you need them. I fear there may be a mistake. These goggles are for use by welders and are too dark for normal use.'

'They are precisely what I asked for. You have done well.' Pulling Al Liby to one side Mursi asked him if he wished to remain in the UK after their coup or if he preferred to travel to the Middle East until things quietened down. Al Liby opted to remain in the UK, in the Bradford area, where he had numerous friends and acquaintances.Mursi then waved one of their contacts to join him. They walked away from the others and began an earnest conversation. At one stage the man looked at Mursi with astonishment on his face and then burst out laughing.

'Midhat, it will give me the greatest pleasure to carry out your wishes. I look forward to meeting you later.' Still laughing, the man walked to his car. Bidding the other two Arabs farewell, Mursi and Al Liby drove from the car park back towards Hawes.Their contacts, driving back to Bradford.

'What was so funny Midhat?' asked Al Liby.

'Merely making arrangements to leave the country.' answered Mursi, not wishing to enlarge on his plans. Al Liby did not question him further, but did wonder what was so funny. At the lay by close to the Ribblehead viaduct Mursi pulled off the road, Al Liby drawing to a halt behind him. The fog had still not cleared sufficiently for the helicopter to fly so there was no particular reason to hurry. He took the opportunity to show Al Liby how to operate the camcorder. Three smaller boxes contained new and very dark sunglasses. Al Liby was soon quite au fait with the camcorder and he also pocketed a pair of the sunglasses. Mursi took the other two, one for himself and a pair for the pilot. The two men then transferred their cases and other personal items from the car which was to be parked in the Creamery car park.

'It is time we took the car to the car park. It is unfortunate that the boxes will not fit in this car. I quite enjoy driving this BMW. Mind you, after we park the BMW, we shall only need the other car for a few miles.' The pair drove both cars to the upper car park, ensuring the BMW was securely locked and that there was no trace showing of the threatening menace resting in its boot.

'This cursed fog is still not good for flying. I will drive you past the helicopter landing site to a delightful hotel for coffee and a bite to eat. We have time to kill and I prefer not to drive into Hawes.' As they drove past the taped-off landing area they had to slow for a group of people manhandling a quad bike off a trailer. Just as the quad bike came down the last couple of feet it seemed to take on a life of its own. It partly ran onto the road causing Mursi to swerve violently to avoid colliding with it and one of the men trying to control it.

'Fucking wog nearly had my leg off,' the man exclaimed as Mursi drove on disappearing slowly into the fog.

'You can't blame him. He was going slowly enough. It was the bike that caused the problem,' pointed out one of the other volunteers. The quad bike had a small trailer which was soon heaped with tools and some of the Worker's lunch bags. A small party had already set off on foot to begin preparing the ground ready for stone and rock to be flown in by helicopter. Starting the bike the two men mounted it and set off bumping and bouncing steadily up the steep slope to the summit of Stags Fell. It reached the top as Mursi and Al Liby pulled into the car park of Kearton Guest House in Thwaite.

CHAPTER 67

Saturday 16th February 1049hours, London

Ten minutes after Mursi had met his contacts at The White Scar Caves a shocked and extremely nervous Karim Mahasheer was shown into the same interview Rrom used for Hanan earlier.

'No one will tell me why I have been brought here. I want my solicitor,' blustered Mahasheer.

'We would like you to help us with our enquiries. And why would you need a solicitor Mr Mahahseer. What have you done to justify needing one?' asked the Inspector, smiling blandly at Mahasheer.

'Nothing, I know nothing. I do not know what you want.'

'Well, for a start we need to know where these two men are.' Once again placing photos of Mursi and Al Liby on the desk.

'I do not know either of these men. I cannot help you.'

'Here we go again. Why must you people insist on lying when asked a simple question? That is, unless you have something to hide?'

'I tell you I know nothing of these men. I would help you if I could.' The Inspector nodded to the Sergeant. The Detective Sergeant once again took the dictaphone from her pocket. Once again she pressed the play button.

'You recall I told you about having a very important visitor?'

'Would you like more. Such as something happening more dramatic than 9/11.' As with Hanan, Mahasheer collapsed into a blubbering mass of manhood.

'I could not help it.. They made me help them, I swear to Allah.' This time the Inspector threw an air ticket 'to Iraq' (via Tenerife) onto the table in front of Mahasheer.

'You recognise this? Your one way passage to Baghdad this evening unless you manage to persuade the Sergeant and myself otherwise.

Mrs Khaled and her son are at the airport this very minute. She lied and is paying the price. She flies to Iraq this evening. If you insist on lying you will be sitting next to her.'

'Tell me what you want. I will tell you everything. Please, I cannot go back to Iraq, they will kill me.'

'The choice is entirely in your hands Mahasheer. Help us and you remain in the UK. However, should you wish to remain you will give us information now. You will also give us information in the future which may be considered useful to the authorities. Do you fully understand? Any news relating to terrorists or such like will be passed on to us. You will work for us from now on. Are you positive you understand?'

'Yes sir, anything sir. I swear to you.'

'Right. Where is this man Mursi. What is he about to do. What car is he driving?'

'All I know is that he has gone to the North of England but I do not know where or what he plans. I do know it is something spectacular. He told me it would be broadcast world wide. As for his car, it is an almost new BMW. I know it is silver in colour but I do not know the model or the number. He has taken a friend with him, Anas Al Liby.'

'Where did he get the car from?'

'I arranged it. The car belongs to a member of the mosque.'

'His name and telephone number. He can tell us the model and number.'

'He is Abdullah Alabassi. I have his phone number in my diary here.' In his haste to produce the diary it fell to the floor. Picking it up he held it open at one of the pages for the Inspector to see.

'Here, here is his number and his address,' thrusting the small book into the Inspector's outstretched hand. Handing it to the Detective Sergeant the Inspector ordered her to contact Alabassi for details of the car.

'Once you have the information get it to Thames as fast as you can. It will help the men locate the terrorists. In the meantime hang on to the diary. I am sure Mr Mahasheer won't mind will you?' The DS hastened from the interview room to locate a telephone. Fortunately

Alabassi was home and after hedging for a time he eventually passed the information on. Remembering that she still had Stewart's card the DS decided to try his number direct. At the second ring.

'Stewart.'

'Sir, it is Detective Sergeant Holloway. The car you are looking for is a silver seven series BMW registered number …'

'Sergeant, you are an angel. This will be of enormous help. One more thing. Did you find out if the car has a tracker?'

'Oh God no sir. I am sorry. It just never occurred to me.' Damn, for some reason she had wanted to please Stewart and she had missed something obvious like a tracker.

'Don't blame yourself. You know what to do now. Get back to the owner and find out from him. If it does have a tracker I am sure I do not have to tell you what to do then. If it has a tracker we are pretty much home and dry. You have done well. I won't keep you, you have a lot to do.' As the line went dead Kate Holloway thought to herself, mmm, perhaps not such a bad laughing cavalier after all. He could have roasted her for not thinking about the tracker. Not having time to waste she dialled the Alabassi phone number again. After seven rings a recording machine came to life. Shit now what! There was no mobile number for him. Tearing back into the interview room she interrupted Inspector Bailey.

'Mr Mahasheer, I can not find a mobile number for Alabassi and his phone just rings. Do you know where I can contact him?'

'No, his wife has a Mercedes and they usually go to the shops on Saturday. They could be anywhere.'

'Do you know if the BMW had a tracker fitted?'

'I do not know what a tracker is,' pleaded Mahasheer.

'Bugger, I never thought of that. That would have been a huge bonus for us,' the Inspector added.

'OK Sergeant. Make tracks to find out if the car does have a tracker.' The weak pun earned a wry smile from the DS as she left to do as instructed.

CHAPTER 68

Saturday 16th February 1054 hours

'Butch, you two join me asap. I will be in the Museum car park.' Stewart had summoned his two aides.Within five minutes their car tore into the car park.

'Yes boss, what now?' asked Sundance.

'First thing. Presents for both of you.'

'Jeez new satphones. About time we had them up here in the sticks. Our mobiles are worse than useless.'

'They have been programmed with most of the numbers you will be using. Similar to your mobiles. I will give you the chargers before you go. Now down to business. Here is a list of phone numbers. The police, the rest of our people up Catterick way and Inspector Deptford. Here is a description of the car our two baddies are driving. Impress on them, especially the police, they are NOT to approach the vehicle if they see it. I don't want a load of woodentops panicking the two men into doing something prematurely. I want them to contact me and try not to arouse the terrorist's suspicion if someone is lucky enough to clock them.'

'A newish Beamer. Does it have a tracker fitted?...

'Give some of us a little savvy, you must be the twentieth person to say that. If the bloody thing did have a tracker and we knew about it we would have the sodding car by now, wouldn't we? At present we do not know about a tracker but we are giving it priority. The location of that car is the key to everything. Get cracking with your phoning and, I repeat, do impress on them the need for caution. No one is to approach them or alert them until I get there. That is, if someone spots

'em. I am going to drive to Catterick and speak to the CO in person. I will also meet some of our lads. It MUST be Catterick, that is the only likely target. Europe's largest military installation. A few thousand squaddies with a fair number of women and kids thrown in. If AQ manages to set the weapon off it certainly will be a huge boost to their cred in the Muslim world.' Stewart set off towards Bainbridge and ultimately Catterick Garrison leaving the two men busy telephoning using their new toys, reflecting that the money spent on satphones was money well spent. Much of Wensleydale is not kind to mobile phone users who, more often than not, find they have no signal. Passing through the picture post card hamlet of Wensley Stewart's phone sounded.

'Stewart, sir,' he responded having seen the DG's initials on the display.

'Ah Stewart. You have not been incinerated yet. I called to let you know we have a chap in from the mosque that our man was using. He is the one that put us onto the owner of the BM. You may be interested to know he has also given us the name and details of the helpful individual who gave Mursi the lowdown on the device.'

'Great news sir but until we find the bloody car that is not going to be very helpful to us. Did he have any info that we are not aware of?'

'We are in the process of locating the technical bod and dragging him in. Until we do that we will not have any more details. At this moment in time the man we have arrested is giving us names left right and centre. Once this present situation is resolved there will be a bucket load of interviewing and checking these other names we are being given. This bomb headache could be a blessing in disguise if all the information we are being given turns out to be solid gold. Your Inspector and Detective Sergeant can't stop the man from talking. The amount of beans he is spilling he could soon put Heinz out of business.'

'Thank you sir. I am en route to Catterick Garrison to meet the CO. I have decided all hands are to cover this area, apart from Inspector Deptford's crowd and they will continue checking on accommodation in and around Hawes for up to ten miles.'

'Good man. Keep at it. Oh, and Stewart. If the bomb goes off no need to phone me. I am sure I will hear of it soon enough. One more thing. Have you come up with anything other than the Garrison as a potential target? I am still not convinced that Catterick is their destination. It is so widespread that the bomb would not achieve the amount of publicity those two predict. I also rule out RAF Leeming and Menwith Hill. I will go along with you at present as you are the man in the field and we know the two men were in your area. Good hunting. I will get back to you if I have anything new.'

CHAPTER 69

Saturday 16th February 1149 hours, Thwaite

Mursi and Al Liby were finishing off a delightful lunch in the Kearton Guest House. Suddenly a bright patch of sunlight swept across the lower slopes of Kisdon, the incredibly steep hill behind Thwaite.

'Anas, look the fog has lifted. I will settle up and we will return to Hawes. Taking it off the map will put Al Qaeda firmly on the world's map.' As his car neared Buttertubs Pass his mobile trilled and he pulled into the side of the road. To his left the frighteningly steep hillside dived down to the bottom of the valley. Another few hundred yards and he would not have received the signal.

'Yes?'

'It is your dry cleaners. I have some information I felt you should be made aware of.' It was Mursi's contact from Bradford.

'Yes, tell me but no names remember,' ordered Mursi.

'Your female holiday companion has not returned home. We believe she may still be held for questioning.' 'I know this already so why ring me to tell me something I already know?'

'Because you will not know that the contact from the mosque was also arrested and taken to a police station.'

'If you discover any further information call me immediately. This is not good.' As Mursi closed the call Al Liby enquired.

'What is not good?'

'Now it seems Mahasheer has also been arrested. He does not know what we plan but he knows many of my contacts and the location of my flat. I dare not return there.'

'We still press on though?'

'Yes, we must. Such a feat is guaranteed not only to boost our recruitment numbers but it will show the world we are a power to be reckoned with.Another mobile was smashed after which he resumed driving over the crest of Buttertubs towards Stags and Hawes.

'Mursi. Is that not your friend from this morning?'

'Yes, I wonder what is going on. Surely they can fly now. That helicopter is vital to our plans.' Stopping near to the temporary helicopter pad Mursi climbed out and walked over to his breakfast acquaintance.

'Hi mate. No good coming for a looksee just yet. The bloody helicopter is grounded,' called out the crewman.

'What for? Surely the weather is good enough to fly now.'

'The weather is OK but when we checked the machine this morning there was a pool of fuel underneath it. One of the fuel pipes has split and we cannot get the replacement until tomorrow. So it means two more nights in our B & B and, fingers crossed, we will finish on Monday instead.'

'But will you fly on Monday?' asked a now agitated Mursi. 'No problem. The weather forecast is excellent for the next three or four days. A ridge of high pressure means the weather will be settled. The repair is straightforward so we will be back to normal ready for an early start on Monday. By then I expect you will be far away from here. Sorry you could not look round the chopper but these things happen. This contract has been jinxed for us, what with the weather and now this mechanical trouble.' Little did the mechanic realise these previous jinxes were nothing compared to the jinx lined up for him.

'We will have to see. I like the area and may be able to stay another day or so. If not, it was a pleasure to meet you.' Walking back to the car an alarmed Al Liby queried Mursi's decision.

'Surely we could set the timer and leave. I know I am stating the obvious but we stand out here. I think it would be wise to leave Hawes today.'

'No, I must have that helicopter in order for you to film the explosion from a safe distance. The British say that things happen in threes. This is our second set back, surely there can not be a third. I do agree we cannot stay in this area for another two nights but I do know of an isolated B&B. About fifteen miles from here.' Back in the car a thoughtful Mursi slowly drove down Stags Fell and into Hawes. Having decided to make sure the BMW was still parked safely in the Creamery car park. Passing through the old market place Mursi followed a car with a load of free range children bouncing about in the back. It turned into Gayle Lane towards the Wensleydale Creamery and signalled left to turn into their car park. Mursi was about to follow when he spotted two police patrol cars parked side by side.

'Is this British saying cursing us my friend, this is number three in about a matter of minutes. I must drive on.'

'Do you think we should abandon the idea? The police may have found the car. If we return we may walk straight into a trap.' Al Liby was becoming increasingly anxious.

'No, it must be something else. The car is not stolen so the police will have no reason to be searching for the car.' Had Mursi only known, the policemen WERE searching for the BMW but at that precise moment they were taking a comfort break and the opportunity to have a chat over a coffee and a sandwich. On top of which, the Creamery had a nice big car park.

'Remember, they have Mahasheer now and he may be talking to save his own skin.'

'I do not think so. There is not enough time for Mahasheer to tell them much. Certainly not sufficient time for them to have two police cars here so fast.'

'So where to now?'

'We will go to the B&B I mentioned earlier. They may have vacancies but if not we will find somewhere well clear of Hawes. It is a nice quiet road and we will keep low profiles until Monday morning.' Crossing the old bridge near the newly renovated Gayle Mill Mursi turned right, eventually motoring up the long and steep hill past Wether Fell. A crowd of paraglider pilots were doing their best to soar in the light westerly wind. Driving steadily Mursi eventually arrived at Starbotton, close to the village of Kettlewell. He soon spotted the sign he was looking for, leading to a quiet looking farm which catered for bed and breakfast travellers. Approaching the farmhouse he spotted a sign saying 'vacancies'.

'See Anas, our luck may be changing for the better. It is quiet and according to that sign we can also have dinner here so we have no need to stir until Monday morning.' By the time Mursi was out of his car a smiling farmer's wife was there to greet them.

'Good morning madam. We would like two rooms for two nights if that is possible. I see you also do evening meals. If so we would be delighted to sample your cooking which I am sure will be mouthwatering.' Mursi was at his most charming once again.

'It will be nice to have you stay. I have no other guests at present and I have just the two rooms. I can do you a snack now if you wish, and tea or coffee.' In mid-February two guests for two nights and all meals. Little wonder she was prepared to be most pleasant and accommodating.

'That would be wonderful. If you could show us to our rooms we will unpack and get changed as we plan to do a lot of walking over the weekend.' Remembering the hordes of walkers in the Dales, Mursi had fixed himself and Al Liby up with suitable hiking gear for all weathers. He was thinking how fortunate his foresight had turned out. What better way to keep a low profile than to disappear along the many miles of walks in the area. It seemed his luck was changing for the better. If only Mursi had realised that the British saying that things happen in threes was now working to his advantage. The occupants of the two police cars, having eaten, had a quick look round the car park and set off in different directions to look for the silver BMW. They had not realised, or bothered to look, if there was an overflow car park. Had they done so, and investigated, they would have found the missing BMW quietly resting there with its terrible cargo.

CHAPTER 70

Saturday 16th February noon, Catterick Garrison

'Good morning sir. The Colonel is expecting you.' An immaculately turned out Warrant Officer ushered Stewart into the CO's office.

'Hello sir, I am Stewart. Good of you to see me at short notice.'

'Not at all. I am grateful for your help. I only hope we can be of some assistance to you in return. What do I call you by the way?'

'Stewart is fine sir. It is vital that we locate the silver BMW. It seems incredible that it has not been found yet.'

'I feel pretty certain it is not in the environs of the Garrison. I have over one hundred and fifty men covering the entire location. It has been drummed into them to merely note where it is or the direction it is travelling. They are ordered not to make it obvious should they spot it but to radio in immediately. That is in compliance with your Director's wishes.'

'Thank you sir. I have eleven of my men liaising with yours and they have also come up with a huge blank. The North Yorkshire police are also doing their bit. Even though the vehicle has not been seen round here I can think of no other target. Sorry, Colonel, but I am afraid it looks as if this is the only likely spot.'

'I am sure your people have looked into other possible sites for these men to detonate the weapon. The only other likely place I can bring to mind is Menwith Hill. After all, from what your DG told me on the phone, the bomb was initially designed to create a massive output of EMP. Knocking out that place would certainly have a most substantial effect on our elint gathering.'

'Initially I felt it the most likely installation. The only niggles in my mind are the fact that the terrorists have been seen a few times in the Hawes neck of the woods and Menwith Hill is not too close. Secondly, Menwith Hill would not really have a worldwide impact and our two informants have stressed that the incident will be newsworthy, worldwide.'

'Mmm I see where you are coming from, so it is back to the Garrison. If there is anything you need, where I am in a position to help, please ask. I am anxious to see this unfortunate business resolved.'

'Thank you Colonel. There is one thing. My men will need food and accommodation. I prefer them to remain around here at present. If you can come up with something?'

'Consider it done Stewart. I have a vacant Sergeant's Mess which will more than adequately cater for your team's needs. It was due for redecorating and refurbishing but I can delay that a few days. Anything else?'

'Thank you Colonel. Yes, there is one more thing. Find that bloody car for me. Anyhow, I had better get out and about again. To do what, I have no idea. I am totally at a loss.'

'I do not envy you one iota but I have even more at stake than you.' Stewart bade the CO farewell and returned to his car. He sat deep in thought, feeling utterly frustrated. With such a massive search underway for that BMW, how could it remain undiscovered? On impulse he decided that, as the terrorists had been positively identified in Hawes, he would return there.

CHAPTER 71
Saturday 16th February 1203 hours, Stags Fell

No helicopter meant no stone delivery. No stone meant no work. Reluctantly the Ranger decided to call it a day. The volunteers began making their way down to the roadway. The quad bike and its trailer conveyed their tools and lunch bags to the improvised helipad.

'Hey mate,' a volunteer called out to the chopper engineer, 'what was you talking to that foreign bloke for?'

'Hiya. He was one of the guys at the B&B this morning. He wanted to have a close up of the helicopter,' replied the helicopter man.

'That was the bugger than nearly took my leg off,' complained the volunteer.

'Give over. He was miles away from your leg, you big girl's blouse,' called out another of the volunteers.

'I bet you'd have shouted the bloody odds if it had been your leg,' volunteer one retorted indignantly.

'What's all the excitement?' asked Tom Prescott, walking up to the rowdy group.

'This silly sod says a foreign bloke almost ran over his leg,' explained another of the workers, laughing at the other man's misfortune. Remembering the Board from the previous evening Tom enquired.

'What did he look like?'

'There were two of them. Foreign looking and coloured,' insisted the 'almost' casualty.

'Did he look anything like this?' asked Tom taking a crumpled photo of Mursi from his wallet. A photo given him some time previously by Stewart.

'That's the bloke. What are you up to Tom, do you fancy him or summats? Carrying his photo in your wallet. Didn't take you for a shirt lifter.' More guffaws erupted from the small group. Ignoring them Tom went on, 'are you sure it was this man?'

'I should cocoa. You don't forget a face as close as that bloke was to me. Anyway, what are you so het up about?'

'That was the bastard that murdered Jeb. What sort of car was he driving?' demanded Tom.

'Well why do you have his photo, You are not shitting me are you Tom? I know what you are like.'

'No way. His car! What make was it?'

'You are serious aren't you? It was a Vauxhall. Newish one and dark blue, nearly black. I don't know the model or any of its number.'

'Any of you others know the car?'

'Sorry Tom, we were too busy trying to manhandle the quad bike off the trailer. Are you sure they are the ones that did for Jeb?' Taking Stewart's card out, Tom decided to call him on his mobile.

'Jeez. No bloody signal, even as high up as this,' cursed Tom. It was unbelievable that with the such a panoramic view and the height of the road there was no mobile phone signal in that part of the world. Running to his car Tom called out to the Ranger, 'see you Monday morning.'

'Cheers Tom. Nothing doing tomorrow without the chopper,' the Ranger yelled back to him. Rumbling over the cattle grid Tom drove swiftly down the hill. Still no bars showing! He passed the public phone box opposite Simonstone Hall pub, noting someone using it. He continued into Hawes market place, where he stopped on double yellow lines and ran into one of the vacant phone kiosks there. He dialled Stewart's number.

'Stewart.'

'It's Tom Prescott. That bloody Arab...' A tap on the side of the kiosk caused Tom to turn and look. Stewart was standing there, grinning, his mobile to his ear. He crooked a finger to beckon Tom outside.

'Bloody hell that was quick,' joked Tom.

'What about the Arab?'

'He drove over Stags Fell less than half an hour ago,' gasped Tom.

'You are positive it was him? Did you see him yourself?'

'No but some of the other volunteers did.'

'What car was he driving?'

'A very dark blue Vauxhall, fairly new,' replied Tom.

'Hard luck matey. He is driving a silver BM so it was not him,' answered Stewart glumly.

'Don't you buggers ever listen? I showed them his picture and two of them recognised him. There was another guy with him in the car.'

'Tom, we know he is driving a silver seven series BMW.'

'Well, he has a bloody Vauxhall as well. Rick said it was this guy and if Rick said so you can take it as gospel.'

'Where is this Rick now?'

'Maybe on his way back to Masham. I told him I'd call back to make sure he had a lift as I was in a hurry to call you.'

'Come with me in my car and we will find him,' directed Stewart.

'I need to park my car somewhere off double yellows.'

'Leave it. I'll sort it later.'

'OK, if you say so,' replied Tom somewhat doubtfully.

'Right, which way now Tom?' Back that way,' Tom pointed in the opposite direction Stewart's car was facing. With that, Stewart carried out a tyre squealing turn, showing utter disregard for other motorists. His manoeuvre was to the accompaniment of those motorists blasting him with their horns.

'Bloody hell, that was close,' protested Tom as he directed Stewart back towards Stags Fell. The car had crossed the bridge near the cricket pitch when Tom called out, 'that's them,' indicating a car approaching about seventy or eighty metres away. At that Stewart flashed his lights and pulled directly into the path of the oncoming car, skidding to a halt. He leapt out of the car leaving Tom frantically unbuckling his seat belt.

'Here, what are you playing at? Daft buggers is it?' demanded Eric the driver.

'Which of you is Rick?' By then Tom had joined them.

'This is Rick,' pointed out Tom.

'What's up Tom?' enquired a worried Rick.

'This is what's up! The man you saw earlier. Tell me which one he is.' Stewart passed over the folder containing pictures of the ten most wanted. Turning the pages Rick stopped at one of Mursi's photos. Curious motorists drove past the two cars parked bumper to bumper, some of them cursing as they drove cautiously past.

'This bloke was driving and I think this was the other man in the car,' indicating Al Liby. This is very very important. Are you absolutely positive? And you can confirm the make of car they were in.'

'You asked, I told you. I know a Vauxhall when I see one and I told you these were the two men,' pouted an indignant Rick.

'Come with me in my car. Now.' Rick looked up questioningly at Tom.

'It is OK mate. Come on.' Tom reassured him.

'What about getting home?'

'I'll be clear then to take you back to Masham,' intervened Tom. The pair climbed into Stewarts car in time to hear, 'Butch, Sundance. The Museum car park as soon as you can,' as Stewart performed a one, handed three pointer, speaking into his mobile, completely disregarding the oncoming traffic.

CHAPTER 72

Saturday 16th February 1247 hours, Hawes Museum

'Yes boss, what now?' asked Newman.

'This man is Rick, or Richard Brown. Tell these two what you told me.' After Brown had re-told his story.

'You two get phoning again. Pass on the details of the Vauxhall. What I'm wondering is, have they planted the BMW already? If so where in Heaven's name is it? When you inform the others about the Vauxhall remind them to re-double their efforts to locate this damned Beamer. It could well be ticking away at this very moment.'

'I've remembered something else,' interrupted Rick.

'Spit it out then,' snapped Newman.

'Is there anything else you have just happened to remember?' The tension was beginning to affect all of them.

'Those two blokes stayed at the same B&B as the two helicopter men.' This revelation put a glimmer of hope into Stewart.

'Which B&B?' And to Newman, 'get Inspector Deptford here.'

'I don't know which B&B but the chopper man was still up at the helipad when we Left,' added Rick.

'Into the car. Show me where. You come too Tom.' Stewart's foot was hard down as his car crested Stags Fell. The helicopter engineer was about to climb into his van. Once again Stewart repeated his demented driving act by skidding to stop alongside the van. The bemused engineer walked over to Stewart's car.

'What's this Grand Prix stuff in aid of?' Stewart thrust his ten most wanted in front of the man's face.

'Have you seen any of these men before?' Very quickly the engineer picked out both Mursi and Al Liby.

'Good man. They are wanted for murder. I want you to return to the B&B to see if they are still there. If you see them do not alarm them in any way.'

'Bugger alarming them. It is ME that is alarmed,' responded the engineer.

'You will be in no danger. If they are there, find some excuse to go out again and tell me. Do not give them any indication that you know what they have done. Is that clear?' demanded Stewart.

'I can check but I am sure they booked out this morning.'

'We will stay behind you. As soon as you have checked let me know immediately.' Following some way behind the van, they saw it pull into the private car park. Stewart drew to a halt some way past the B&B. Within minutes the engineer came out of the front door waving to Stewart. Walking towards him Stewart was greeted with.

'No good mate. They booked out this morning. The owner is not back yet and I can't tell you anymore. This is the car they were in and its number. It might help.' Handing Stewart a piece of paper he had written 'silver Toyota, registered number...'

'Oh well, he is learning fast. At least he gave a false make and number. I felt things were going too well. Thank you for your help. Someone will call by shortly to take a statement.' Back in his car Stewart spoke.

'I just knew it was going to be another dead end but we have to try. The pair have flown the nest once again. Do you have any other revelations up your sleeve Mr Brown?'

'No sorry, that is as much as I know. Tom says they are the ones who did for Jeb, is that true?'

'We are pretty certain it is that pair. I want you to wait until someone has also taken statements from you two.' Stewart's mobile trilled.

'Stewart.'

'Hello, Inspector Deptford here. I understand there has been a significant development.'

'You could say that! I'd like you or your people to interview some witnesses pretty quickly.' Stewart then passed over the details of the two helicopter men, Tom and Rick and the B&B owners.

'Will do. I'll have someone speak to Mr Prescott and Mr Brown right now, I am in the Museum, car park.'

'I will be with you in two minutes Inspector. Almost done you two. Just two calls to Make,' aside to Tom and Rick. His first call was to the DG.

'Sir. The two Arabs have ditched the BMW and are now using a Vauxhall. Would you have someone grill the mosque chappie even more. It would be nice to know the model and number of the Vauxhall. I now feel Catterick is not their target after all.'

'I will get back to you.' The DG had gone. As one call ended Stewart tapped in the direct number for the Catterick CO.

'Hello sir, Stewart here. I am calling to let you know our two men are now using a dark blue Vauxhall. No other details at present. I firmly believe the Garrison is NOT now their object. I also believe the BMW and its 'package' are in their final resting place. It really is imperative we find that car fast.'

'Thank you Stewart for letting me know. We will remain at Red Alert until the BMW is traced. I assume your men will still be our guests.'

'Yes sir. Until we locate that car, or the balloon goes up, we will remain in this part of the world. Whatever they intend doing with that device is not going to be too far away from here I'm afraid. Both distance and timewise.' With Catterick seemingly out of the equation Stewart was faced with his headache of once again trying to figure out what the intended target was. The bummer was that no one could come up with any suggestions that would indicate a target of world wide newsworthy importance. Had they missed something? There simply was no other high profile target. Someone had even mentioned York or Ripon Cathedrals. Both of them magnificent and splendid in their own right, but Stewart was convinced they did not fit the bill.

CHAPTER 73
Saturday 16th Feb1627 hours, Starbotton

Due to the heavy overcast cloud the light was fading quickly as Mursi and Al Liby walked up the lane towards their B&B. Their walk had lasted about three hours.

'That walk did me much good my brother. A hot bath and then our evening meal.' They reached the front of the farmhouse to be greeted by the cheery farmer's wife.

'Hello, did you both enjoy the exercise? You can leave your boots here in the conservatory. It is heated but they don't look too wet at all to me,' pointed out their hostess.

'You really are too kind and thank you for the loan of your map,' responded Mursi.

'You are welcome to hang on to it if you plan on walking again tomorrow. Did you find anything interesting?' asked the helpful lady.

'We did very well and followed your advice. We managed to reach Kilnsey Crag,' replied Mursi.

'My, you two boys did do well. That will give you a good appetite.'

'We called for a coffee in the nearby pub and saw a wooden structure you call 'stocks,' explained Mursi.

'Oh yes, they were used in times gone by to secure people who had committed some sin or other. You need have no fears. They are not used these days. Here I am going on, holding you up. Now off you both go and have a nice hot bath. Your dinner will be ready on the table at seven prompt.' Chuckling to herself the landlady bustled off to sort out the evening meal.

'We are hungry already and looking forward to it,' called out Mursi to the lady's ample rump as it disappeared along the passageway. Some hours later the two terrorists were sitting in the lounge in front of a welcoming log fire and enjoying a cup of freshly perked coffee. The walk had made them comfortably weary and the wonderful meal had rounded off their day very nicely.

'Well, my friend, I feel really comfortable and at ease. The leg of lamb almost melted in my mouth,' Mursi said to Al Liby.

'Yes it was delicious and I could not say no to a second helping of home-made apple pie with hot custard,' sighed Al Liby and continued.

'It must be a good life for our hosts living is such a scenic place as this. The apples came from their own trees and even the meat from one of their own lambs.' Rising to his feet, Mursi said, 'you know what Anas? I am going to bed now. It is still early but I feel sleepy. I will see you at breakfast my friend.'

'Goodnight to you my brother. I will also 'turn in' as the British say. I feel today has turned out better than I expected. I will see you in the morning, Inshallah.'

CHAPTER 74

Saturday 16th February 2053 hours, Catterick Garrison

Stewart eased himself into a comfortable armchair in the Sergeant's Mess, which was conveniently not in use by the military. He cradled a large malt in one hand. He had been joined by the CO, who would normally require permission before entering a Sergeant's Mess, normal army etiquette. The police officers, Stewart's own men and Butch and Sundance were also there. A morose atmosphere hung over the room. Despite Herculean efforts that damned BMW and now the damned Vauxhall had still not been discovered. They had to be under cover somewhere.

'So, Inspector, the visit to the B&B owners was a wasted exercise,' from Stewart.

'Yes, Stewart, but it was better to check and be sure. You never know, it might have worked out better. It is the basis of good police work. Check everything slowly and methodically. Don't worry, we will find the car. We MUST have a break soon.'

'Mmm Inspector, I hope we find the bloody bomb before it finds us,' chipped in Sundance.

'If I may?' interjected the CO.

'My men will continue searching for this BM throughout the night. We have already completed four very thorough searches of every possible place within a radius of about six miles of the garrison. We will continue searching until we know it is not a threat to us here.'

'I am utterly baffled. The North Yorkshire constabulary will also continue their search. It simply has to be undercover somewhere,' opined Stewart.

'I can categorically confirm it is not in any of our buildings on the garrison. All possible accessible locations have been searched. In addition, no one can obtain access to the military sections without passing through a manned control point. Every single vehicle on camp can be accounted for. That car is not in our secure boundary. I must confess to feeling a little more confident that Catterick is not the target and that all the staff and families here are not in any specific danger,' added the Colonel.

'One thing is certain. Very soon we shall all know,' said Stewart, grunting as he pushed himself to his feet. At least there is some comfort that the poor bastards close to the detonation will not know a thing about it. I do not know about the rest of you but I am heading for my bed. It seems a month ago since I left London early this morning. We will meet here at eight gentlemen. Goodnight sir,' Stewart nodded to the CO, 'and thank you, again, for accommodating so many of us at such short notice.'

'I shall sit here and nurse my malt a while longer. Night, Stewart. I will also join you here in the morning,' muttered a very thoughtful and troubled Commanding Officer. Nodding again, Stewart left for his room amidst a chorus of 'goodnight's' and 'me too,' every single one of them concerned about what the morrow would bring.

CHAPTER 75
Sunday 17th 0758 hours, Starbotton

'Good morning gentlemen. Did you both sleep well?' enquired the beaming landlady as she placed a 'full fry-up', minus bacon, on the table before the two Arabs.

'Excellent thank you. I slept like a tree,' replied Mursi.

'A tree?' queried the landlady.

'Oh I know what you mean. Not a tree, but like a log.'

'Ah yes. I apologise. I still have much English to learn.'

'Nay, your English is very good indeed. You speak it really well. Anyway you tuck in and call if you need anything. I shall only be in the kitchen.'

'I am sure we shall be fine,' said Mursi to the lady's beam as she scurried away to the kitchen. Sometime later, hearing the two men talking, their hostess returned to the dining room.

'Could you manage some toast now. I baked the bread myself early this morning.'

'Yes, I could smell your bread as soon as I woke up. It made my mouth water. I can not speak for my friend but I could not eat another thing. Any more and I would not be able to walk today,' answered Al Liby. Mursi, with a mouthful of food smiled pleasantly and waved his hand to indicate he could not manage any toast either.

'Have you decided where to go today? If you like I will prepare you some 'pack-ups'. I mean sandwiches and so on. I have two flasks you can use for hot tea or coffee.'

'Dear lady, you are too generous.'

'It is no trouble at all. I will prepare you both a snack. Do you have any particular request or will you leave it to me?'

'I am sure we can rely on your good judgment. We will go to our rooms and prepare for our walk,' said Mursi.

'I will have them done in a jiffy. Do you prefer tea, coffee or my home made soup in the flasks?'

'Soup sounds a delightful suggestion. What a good idea.' Some twenty minutes later the landlady called up the stairs to inform them that their pack-ups were ready. In the conservatory the two terrorists put on their hiking boots. The plastic bags containing their sandwiches wrapped in tin foil were soon stowed in their day sacks.

'Looking at the map, I thought we might set off towards this lake called Malham Tarn. It is quite a way but it is a nice day so what do you say Anas my friend?'

'It looks to be a long walk but we can set off and see how we feel,' replied Al Liby looking at the map over Mursi's shoulder. A little after noon the two men lowered themselves wearily onto the ground. They had been walking steadily for almost three hours. The last half hour had involved a fairly stiff uphill climb. On opening their flasks the two men discovered one of home made soup and one of coffee. They decided to try the soup first, together with crisp chunks of the home made bread. Maybe because they were eating out of doors, picnic style, the soup tasted especially delicious. The first cup was closely followed by a thick sandwich containing succulent slices of onion and crisp Wensleydale cheese. Their landlady had, once again, exceeded their expectations. Resting in the lee of the louring hills the men leisurely finished off their delicious repast before rising stiffly to their feet to begin the long trek back, the thought of a nice long soak and another gourmet meal awaiting them, the men considered it had been a most satisfying day. All thoughts of what the morrow would bring, gone from their minds.

CHAPTER 76

Sunday 17th February 0811 hours, Catterick Garrison

About the time the two Al Qaeda men were beginning their breakfasts the men hunting them had assembled to hear Stewart give his briefing.

'Good morning gentlemen. I trust you slept well and enjoyed your breakfast. I am sure it is not necessary for me to point out what is first on your menu. Find those cars! Do you have any questions before you are assigned your tasks?'

'Yes sir, I have a question.' A self conscious, young, police officer stood up.

'I can see you are one of Inspector Deptford's men. Name please and question.'

'PC Crane sir. Why is there nothing on TV, radio or in the papers about these two men and their cars?'

'A good question officer. There are certain aspects of this case that a few of you are not aware of. I cannot reveal those details at present but the news blackout comes right from the very top. These men are well aware that, as known terrorists, they are wanted men. What we MUST not alert them to is the fact that this is the biggest covert manhunt in history. Which makes it all the more amazing that we have not come up with the men or their cars. I am afraid this is not a very satisfying answer to your question but it is all I can give you at present.'

'Very well sir, but it does seem strange,' added the constable sitting down.

'I spoke to the DG this morning. We have no further info on either of the cars. We still do not know if the BMW has a tracker. Returning to the point so ably made by the constable, with full media coverage we would have located them by now. Regretfully, for reasons only a handful of you know of, media cover is out. I do not have to tell you the police have had no luck overnight either. Two of my men will assign you your tasks. If nothing turns up we all meet here this evening at seven. If that is OK with you sir?' Directing the question to the Colonel. Rising to his feet the Colonel spoke.

'The military is more than happy for you to use these facilities for as long as is necessary. It would help, this evening, if you could finish your evening meal by eighteen-thirty hours. This will allow us to release the civilian staff on time. If that time is acceptable to Stewart.' Stewart nodded his agreement to the Colonel.

'On behalf of all the new personnel I would like to thank you for the extra workload that has been forced upon you and the cheerful and willing manner in which you carry out these arduous duties.' The Colonel obviously appreciated the fact that the men were doing their damnedest.

'Thank you Colonel. Butch, Sundance, pass out the work schedule please. Good morning gentlemen. See you back here this evening. Remember the Colonel's request for you to finish dinner by eighteen-thirty.'

CHAPTER 77
Monday 18th February 0809 hours, Catterick Garrison

'Good morning again gentlemen. The only good news is the fact that, so far, we have not yet had the expected catastrophe,' announced Stewart to the assembled men.

'Last night I was on the phone to the DG. The information I am about to give you is NOT to leave this room. In addition to causing unprecedented panic, any person or persons divulging this information would spend a considerable part of their lives at Her Majesty's Pleasure. The DG now feels that if you know the real reason behind the search it might spur you on to even greater efforts.' Stewart paused for a moment looking at the gathering before him.

'These terrorists are, indeed, wanted for a most brutal murder. Despite this the murder pales into insignificance compared to the real reason we want these two men. They have, for want of a better description, a suitcase bomb. The bummer being this is a nuclear device. In plain English gentlemen, these men have in their possession, an atomic bomb.' Loud gasps and exclamations erupted from the remaining members not already in the picture. As Stewart raised his hand for silence a man stood up.

'Sir, a question if I may.'

'Of course. PC Crane if I remember correctly.' answered Stewart. A wag, one of Crane's colleagues, aside to Crane.

'Watch it mate your card is marked. They know your name.' This raised quite a few laughs and helped take some of the tension out of the situation.

'Yes sir. In fact two or three questions,' said Crane, pleasantly surprised that Stewart had remembered his name.

'Do I assume this bomb is portable? If so how heavy is it and what is it's expected yield? Finally, what amount of damage it is likely to cause?' Blushing furiously Crane resumed his seat.

'Very well done Crane. An excellent set of questions. We know the weapon is of low Yield, between half and two kilotons. The Russians have told us that they suspect this particular bomb to be about one kiloton. As a comparison the Hiroshima bomb was about fifteen kilotons. As for damage, there are so many variables. The initial blast will, obviously, be extensive. The residual fallout may, in fact, be more of a problem. A lot depends on the site they place the weapon to operate it. What we do know is the fact that these men brought the bomb with one aim. To do as much damage as possible. The man, Mursi, has let it be known that their operation will eclipse even 9/11. We strongly suspect it will be in this part of the world as they have been seen a few times in the last few days in and around Hawes. The only likely target we can come up with is this camp.' Stewart paused to let this latest information sink in.

'Any further questions? No. Very well. I had the North Yorkshire Police work with the Tourist Board to prepare a comprehensive list of accommodation. I am convinced the men must have stayed within easy reach of Hawes. In addition to keeping an eye out for the cars ALL of us will concentrate on B&Bs, hotels, self-catering properties and even caravan parks.' This time there were no groans or complaints. Every man fully realised the true gravity of the situation.

'If you come across them it is imperative you do not alert them to the fact that we are interested in them. Fob off the owners of the accommodation that you are looking for sheep rustlers or something. Or whatever else people do to sheep in this part of the world?' This brought more laughter from the group.

'Seriously, pay no attention to the wanted men but drive off and get a message to me fast. Right, Butch and Sundance have lists of addresses for you to work through. The Colonel has kindly allowed us full use of the Army switchboard in order to telephone some of the more outlying places. I have increased the radius from Hawes to twelve miles. If nothing by the end of the day we rendezvous here at nineteen hundred, after we have eaten. To remind you. I know some of you have families not too far away. Much as you feel tempted to contact friends, relatives and families to warn them to leave the area, you will NOT do so. An important factor is that we do not know the intended target of this weapon. Therefore, you might be advising relatives to move to the danger area. Above everything, this must remain the most closely guarded secret of your lives.' Looking at the grim faces Stewart sensed they would cooperate fully. The men went to where Stewart's two side-kicks were handing out lists of accommodation addresses. Perhaps today would see the searchers having more luck! Once all the sections had been assigned their tasks Stewart called out.

'Right ho gentlemen. Let's go get 'em.'

Chapter 78
Monday 18th February 0945 hours, Starbotton

'Thank you madam. An excellent breakfast. If you prepare our bill I will settle up with you,' stated Mursi.

'I will just take this phone call if you excuse me a moment. I have your bill ready for you. I added four pounds each for your packed lunches if that is fair with you.'

'That is most generous of you. The snack went down very well indeed. Here you are' said Mursi handing over the money for himself and Al Liby.

'You have given me ten pounds too much,' protested the farmer's wife, holding the phone to her ear and speaking quietly into the mouthpiece.

'I won't be a moment, I am saying goodbye to my charming guests,' aside to Mursi, 'it is my eldest son. He is a policeman, you know.'

Slightly alarmed, Mursi quickly replied, 'Please take it. It is for you. We would be most offended if you refused it. This past few days have been one of the most enjoyable periods in my life for a very long time. Good food. Exercise. Fresh air and no worries about our work before us.'

'Well, if you are sure? Here is one of my brochures if you ever find yourselves this way again. I would be delighted to accommodate such nice, polite gentlemen as yourselves.'

'Be with you in a moment John,' she said to her son on the phone.

'If ever we make it up here again we would be most happy to stay with you. I am sure both of us have put on weight from your delicious meals.'

'I am so pleased you enjoyed your stay. Drive safely. Have you far to go?'

'We thought we would spend a few days looking round York. Thank you again, we will collect our bags and be on our way. Quickly Anas, we have a lot to do today.' Once out of her earshot Mursi said, 'let's get away. I appreciate the police are not specifically looking for us, but all the same, we can't be too careful.' As they hurried down the stairs with their bags the landlady was continuing her previously broken conversation with her son.

'Oh your dad will be so disappointed. We both will be, we looked forward to seeing you today. Overtime, you say searching for two Arabs suspected of murder? I had two lovely foreign gentlemen stay with me the past two nights. So polite and charming, they even paid me ten pounds extra.' Once a copper always a copper. Despite her protestations he gave a description of the two men and the car they were thought to be using.

'Oh, my God, you must be mistaken. It can't be them,' cried out the landlady. At that moment Mursi and Al Liby were passing the door with their bags. Hearing the woman's cry of anguish Mursi asked her what was wrong. Seeing the look of horror on her face he guessed it was something to do with them. If Mursi had doubts before her face confirmed his worst fears. Even as she called out to her son Mursi was striding rapidly towards her. He wrenched the phone out of her hand and smashed it against her head. She stumbled across the breakfast table sending crockery flying. Blood streamed from the nasty gash on her forehead. Pushing herself up she turned towards Mursi, a bread knife in her grasp. He stepped towards her as she lunged and slashed his upraised arm with the razor-sharp blade.

'Aaaghh.' Yelled Mursi blood pouring from a deep cut above his wrist. By now Al Liby had joined the fray to try to control the wildly lunging woman, her vicious slashes causing each man to leap back. Al Liby grabbed the only thing to hand, which happened to be a dinner fork. Not great against a bread knife. The two men circled the desperate woman. Mursi tore down the heavy window curtains and threw them at her, giving Al Liby the opportunity to grab her knife hand. Despite this she fought like a wildcat, kicking and trying to twist her wrist which still held onto the knife. A sudden twist and she was free. She stabbed at Al Liby who instinctively jabbed the dinner fork into her face.Screaming, she collapsed to the floor. The fork sticking out of her left eye. Before she could move out of the way Mursi brought his foot crashing down onto the fork, stamping it deep inside the woman's eye. Her body gave several huge shudders and then she lay there completely still. Catching their breath, Mursi snatched up a first-aid box off a side table.

'Anas, see if there are any dressings in here.' The box was well stocked and Al Liby applied a dressing to staunch the flow of blood from Mursi's arm.

'It needs stitching,' said Al Liby.

'It must wait. Hurry now. Her son will realise something is wrong and will have alerted the police. You drive, my arm hurts like hell.' Hurriedly flinging their luggage into the car they tore down the lane to turn left at the main road. Towards Hawes!' Some minutes later the initial panic wore off and the two men began to relax a little.

'I feel restored after our weekend, and look at the sky. Not a cloud in sight. That, my friend, means the helicopter will be flying today,' explained Mursi.

'I am concerned about the BMW after seeing two police cars there,' Ssid Al Liby.

'I am also concerned about that woman's son, now he realises who we are.'

'Do not worry Anas, Allah will guide and protect us. This is a very quiet road and we are well clear of the bed and breakfast place now.'

'Park away from the Creamery and I will walk down to the car park. I will have a careful look round. If I take the camcorder I will look like a tourist doing some filming.'

'Very well, Midhat, my brother but please be very careful, warned Al Liby. As Mursi approached the top of Wether Fell, Al Liby called out.

'Look, you were correct. The helicopter is flying.'

'I am not at all surprised. They have lost a lot of time with fog and the breakdown. They need to catch up as helicopters are very expensive to operate.'

Driving into Gayle, Mursi crossed the small bridge and parked his car in Gayle Lane. He was some way from the Creamery next to the gate leading to Beulah Bank, a pathway on the Pennine Way. Also popular with local people walking their dogs. With his camera hanging from its shoulder strap Mursi walked into the Creamery car park. He had a good look round and could see nothing untoward. Entering the shop he purchased a couple of different flavoured varieties of the famous Wensleydale cheese. Walking back outside he pretended to film the front of the creamery. With the camera to his eye Mursi ambled along towards the upper car park. Still nothing looked out of place. He walked towards the BMW 'filming' as he walked. Standing next to the car it looked exactly as when he had left it forty-eight hours earlier.

A van and two other cars were also parked nearby but no one elese was about. Mursi waited a few moments longer then pressed the button on the electronic door opener in his pocket. The indicator light flashed and the car gave a little beep. Opening the boot he quickly lifted a corner of the sheet from one of the cases. He had rehearsed the arming procedure so many times he could do it eyes closed. Even though everything was labelled in Russian he had had it translated AND explained to him. It was also a very simple system. First he turned the mechanical timer to indicate two hours. He intended using the remote radio transmitter but just to be on the safe side he would use the mechanical timer as back up and the transmitter overrode the timer. So even though set for two hours he could detonate the device instantly. So, timer set! Next turn the operating system to 'both'. The control unit had four positions. Number One was the Off. Number Two for the mechanical timer. Number Three for the remote transmitter and Number Four for either timer or remote. Mursi slowly turned the control switch to Number Four. Lastly the 'power on' switch. His fingers trembled with excitement to such an extent That he had difficulty in pushing the switch down to the 'On' position. His first attempt resulted in his finger slipping off the switch, but at last it clicked down. A green light began pulsing away. The device was armed.

Mursi had begun the sequence for Al Qaeda's greatest coup. In two hours at the most, much less if he used the transmitter, The town of Hawes would pass into the history books, as would Al Qaeda.

CHAPTER 79

Monday 18th February 1017 hours

Driving towards Hawes, Stewart's sat phone vibrated.

'Stewart.'

'Sir, North Yorkshire Police HQ. One of our constables was speaking to his mother who runs a B&B.'

'Get on with it man. So what.'

'Whilst speaking to his mother, it is believed the two men we are looking for attacked her. He heard the fight as he was on the phone. Our men will be there about now but I thought it best to contact you immediately before anything is confirmed.'

'Where was this?'

'A place called Starbotton near Kettlewell. We are having roadblocks in the surrounding area as we speak.'

'Keep me fully informed.' With that Stewart closed the call and immediately began phoning Butch and the police inspector working with him.

Monday 18th February 1020 hours, Stag's Fell

'Tom, where do you want this next load?' asked one of the volunteers as the helicopter laboured up the valley. It was carrying yet another heavy load of stone suspended below it in a cargo net. In the absence of the Ranger the others looked to Tom for guidance.

'Tell them to drop it about twenty feet in front of us. I think we shall only need another half dozen or so loads.'

'OK Tom.' Holding a handheld transceiver the volunteer yelled into it to let the crewman know where to lower his net. The noise was deafening as the helicopter entered a hover precisely where the stone was needed. The vicious downdraught whipped up small stones and dust, almost blinding the workers on the ground. The volunteer with the radio waved the chopper away accompanied by vigorous 'V' signs to the crewman, who, in turn, returned the gesture with a wide grin across his face as the helicopter turned away for yet another load.

'They work well those two Tom. They are saving us a lot of backache by flying the stone right where we need it.'

'Yep. It would be a bloody pain having to carry it in the quad bike trailer. This way we only handle it once. It is saving us work and time,' answered Tom Prescott. By the time the helicopter re-appeared with a further load the volunteers had just completed laying the previous load. They worked quickly and carefully to make a safe and durable path. The original had been seriously eroded over the years by the thousands of feet crossing the high fells.

CHAPTER 80

Monday 18th February 1240 hours, Hawes

Mursi had set the clock ticking. He had actually put into motion what would turn out to be Al Qaeda's biggest coup ever. Suppressing his wild excitement he ambled slowly back to his car parked a little way up Gayle Lane. As he exited the Creamery car park an emergency vehicle's siren split the air. Unnerved, Mursi began to almost trot towards his car. It had been a trap after all. He was determined that they would not get him before he detonated the device. An agitated Al Liby flung the passenger door open for Mursi to get in.

'Quick Midhat, get in. I will drive. I TOLD you it was a trap but you would not listen. Those two police cars were obviously onto us.' Mursi dived into the passenger seat, feverishly trying to open the glove compartment to get the remote transmitter.

'What is it? What do you want?' called out Al Liby as he shot off towards the Creamery car park to do a U turn and getaway.

'The remote. It is in here. They will never take us alive. I will not be stopped now.' Al Liby was almost at the Creamery car park entrance when he realised the siren was coming from a rapidly approaching ambulance.

'WAIT. STOP,' he yelled to Mursi.

'It is not the police but an ambulance.' The ambulance whooshed past, lights flashing and siren blaring. A police car was following at high speed, the occupants not even giving Mursi's car a single glance.

'It must be an accident, Allah be praised.' muttered Mursi, a sheen of nervous perspiration moistening his hair line.

'All is well my brother. It is time we took over the helicopter. You continue to drive to the helipad.' Al Liby drove carefully through the ancient market place which was crowded with pedestrians making the most of the pleasant weather. He turned into Hardraw Road and followed the twisting road before turning right to towards Thwaite. In front, an old Land Rover was laboriously making hard work of towing a trailer up the hill. Sheep's heads could be seen poking through the wooden slats. Suddenly a police car appeared from nowhere. Lights and siren on. A shiver passed through both men. Al Liby could not pass the old Land Rover due to oncoming traffic and another two cars were close behind. His only option was to drive on. Mursi retrieved the transmitter from the glove locker and switched it on. Ignoring them, the police car accelerated past and rocketed over the top of Stags Fell.

'Phew, Anas. I can't take many more of these scares.'

'What now?' wondered Al liby.

'Drive on as normal towards the helipad.' Still behind the aged Land Rover with its trailer they cleared the top of the hill. The police car was parked in the middle of the road. A policeman was in earnest conversation with the helicopter engineer and pointing frantically in the direction of Wether Fell. The engineer could be seen speaking into a handset. The helicopter was approaching from the west with a further cargo of rocks and stone. It suddenly swooped low near the helipad, releasing its heavy load. It turned in its own length and flew low and fast towards Wether Fell. By now Al Liby was close to the helipad where he had no choice but to stop behind the farmer's vehicle. The policeman raised his hand and walked briskly to the Land Rover where Mursi could see them talking. Seconds later the policeman returned to his car, quickly turned round and headed back the way he had come. The farmer set off again with his load of sheep. Still unable to pass him Al Liby was obliged to drive slowly behind. After about half a mile the trailer indicators flashed to the left. Al Liby was about to drive on past.

'Pull in behind him, I will try to find out what is going on,' ordered Mursi. The farmer was about to lower the trailer gate as Mursi approached him.

'Good day to you,' called out Mursi.

'Nah then,' from the gruff farmer.

'I wonder, do you know what all the excitement is about back there.'

'Aye.'

'Would you mind telling me please?' asked a frustrated Mursi.

'Owd this while I unfasten the catches.' Reluctantly Mursi held the filthy tailgate, doing his best to avoid the fresher deposits left by the sheep.

'Right, I've got it. Let go,' ordered the farmer.

'The police car. What had happened?'

'Oh aye, you was asking about it.'

'Yes please.' By now Mursi was becoming even more frustrated with the apparently slowwitted farmer. He lowered the tailgate to the ground and a dozen sheep trotted down to the freedom of the moor, obviously not troubled by their journey as they immediately began nibbling the sparse grass. Without speaking the man raised and secured the tailgate once again.

'One of them paragliders has had an accident. Silly buggers. The Air Ambulance is tied up with a multi-car pile up on the A1. The police wanted this chopper to take the lad to hospital.'

'Oh I see. Thank you. Do you know if the helicopter will be away very long?'

'No idea. Nowt to do with me. I reckon they won't get back today if they go to Northallerton hospital and they are needed on standby.' With that the man climbed into his Land Rover and U-turned back towards Hawes.

'Anas, quick. Back to the Creamery. I need to stop the timer.' Mursi explained the problem as they drove.

'Midhat, please. No. Let's just drive and get away from here. I am not at all happy with all these hold ups. I have a bad feeling.'

'All will be well. There is no need to worry. I must have the helicopter to film the event.'

'Midhat. I would follow you to hell but please, just this once. The bomb is set. Let's just go and leave it at that. Please reconsider.'

'NO, my mind is made up. If you wish to leave you may do so but tomorrow I shall have the helicopter. If necessary I will do the filming myself.' They drove in silence back to the Creamery where Al Liby coasted to a halt. Mursi approached the BMW cautiously but everything seemed normal. Having a final look round he quickly opened the boot. He turned the main switch to off and set the timer back at zero. Closing and securing the boot he walked steadily back to the second car.

'See, Anas. All is well. Now let's find somewhere to stay the night.' Mursi directed Al Liby to Ingleton where he turned left on the A65 towards Settle.

'There Anas, that looks ideal and the sign says it has vacancies.' Mursi had spotted a property set back from the road and pretty well obscured by bushes. The car turned into the drive and Al Liby drew up close to some bushes.

'Good day to you. I wondered if you had two rooms for my friend and myself?' Mursi enquired of the elderly man who had answered the door. The man had two rooms and they were more than welcome to stay. Once again Mursi's luck was holding. They had found a safe haven for the night and the car was pretty well concealed behind the bushes. Even though they had acquired it legitimately Mursi still exercised caution in everything. A further advantage was that the owner offered to cook an evening meal if the two travellers were interested. Not only that, he also kept in a supply of bottled beers should any guests wish to enjoy a glass of ale.

'Thank you kindly. We would both be delighted to take advantage of your kind offers.'

CHAPTER 81

Monday 18th February 1255 hours, Stags Fell

'Sorry lads. No chopper again today. By the time he delivers the casualty to hospital and gets back here he will need to refuel. With that bloody hand pump it takes an eternity. On top of that the police have asked if he will remain on standby until the air ambulance is available again. So that is it for the day. Sorry,' explained the engineer.

'Can't be helped. So what do we do now?' enquired the Ranger.

'You told me earlier that you will need another five or maybe six loads. It will be too late today so I suggest we get an early start in the morning. The forecast is good so we will be able to fly first thing. I can be ready to go around about 0830 if that suits you?'

'It'll have to do. Not a lot we can do about it in the circumstances. I will arrange to have some volunteers here by then.'

'Fine. I will refuel this evening and I will be all set as soon as you say the word.'

'Cheers mate. Are any of you lot not available in the morning?' the Ranger called out to the volunteers. Three of them assured the man that they would be available.

'Sorry, I can't help first thing tomorrow. I have a dry stone wall to fix where some silly bloody motorist knocked it down,' explained Tom Prescott.

'Pity about that Tom. You are pretty clued up as regards sorting out the right rocks for the pathway.'

'Aye, mebbe, but I do need to earn my daily crust. I reckon I shall only be a couple of hours and it is only in Hawes so I will come up when I've done and see how you are doing.'

'Thanks Tom. I appreciate all you've done so far. I'm going to call it a day. Nothing else we can do without that chopper. Bye you lot. See you 0830 sharp.' With that the Ranger climbed into his van and drove off.

CHAPTER 82
Monday 18 February 1815hours, Catterick Garrison

'I won't keep you from your evening meal too long. Unfortunately, as most of you are aware by now, the mother of one of your constables was murdered in a most cruel and vicious manner. It seems most likely that the crime was carried out by the same people we seek. Despite roadblocks and intense police activity our two men have, once again, vanished into thin air. For once in my life I am totally baffled. It is just incredible that the BMW has still not been located, nor the Vauxhall with the Arabs. It is as if they have disappeared from the face of the earth. I just KNOW, in my bones, it is in this area,' stated Stewart.

'Oh and before you ask, Crane, there will be no mention of it in the press or on TV.'

'What more can we do?' asked the Police Inspector.

'We will simply have to carry on checking accommodation. I am certain they stayed somewhere fairly local to Hawes. People keep seeing them in that area so it follows that they must be around this area. Another matter that baffles me is WHY they have not yet used the bomb. Never, in all my years have I encountered such a puzzle as our two Arabs have placed before us.'

'Is there some special Muslim celebration due, are they waiting for that to use the weapon?' asked Constable Crane.

'You certainly do ask some interesting and sensible questions Crane. However, my people in London have already gone down that road. Muslims are always having some special day or event to celebrate but we feel there is nothing of importance due within the next week to justify such a delay.'

'You still feel they intend operating the device around Hawes or Catterick?' proferred the Colonel.

'I have this itch in the back of my neck that tells me that YES they intend using the bomb not too far from here. I realise it is not based on any logic but in my bones I know it. That is my opinion Colonel.'

'I ask because as you stated yourself, it seems just impossible for them and their car to vanish into thin air. Could they not have left Yorkshire for some big city? Birmingham, Glasgow?'

'As I said Colonel, I KNOW this is the area. From tomorrow we increase the radius of accommodation checks to twenty miles from Hawes.'Loud groans accompanied this announcement.

'I know just how you feel gentlemen. I, personally, visited fourteen premises from our list today. It appears that every other property offers accommodation, I never dreamt there were so many places. The Police and Tourist Board staff are, at this moment, finalising a list of every type of accommodation up to the new radius. They are doing a fantastic piece of work collating all the properties. Another important factor. Not every property is registered, not that they have to be. I just pray that our two heroes are using registered accommodation. Butch and Sundance will assign you your areas so you can get an early start. I will also help with these checks. Anyone, anything else?'

'I appreciate the North Yorkshire Police are keeping a look out for the car. Have the details been passed onto neighbouring forces?' one of the policewomen asked.

'That is an emphatic yes. The search originated in London and has been passed to every police force and other concerned departments right from the word go. Which is why I am astounded that this damn BMW has not yet been located. Personally, I believe it to be hidden under cover until they decide they are ready to use it. We do know they were last seen in a Vauxhall. That, also, has not been located. Any more? If not let's go and eat.' Everyone wandered out to the dining hall. Many of them intending to take full advantage of the reduced drinks prices in the bar afterwards.

'This is a right bugger Stewart. I feel sorry for you and your people,' sympathised the Colonel.

'You are putting such an effort into it with little or no reward so far.'

'It goes with the territory I'm afraid. Our work is very like the police. Lots of shoe leather often leading to nothing. Quite often we spend months on an investigation or surveillance to be thwarted in the end by Human Rights and Brussels or The Hague.'

'Tell me something I don't know. Political correctness gone mad and favouring the crook instead of the victim,' said the Colonel.

'Don't let me keep you from your meal. Remember, if there is anything we can do from my end you only have to ask.'

'Thank you Colonel. I will be happy to find where our two terrorists have spent the past night. Assuming we do discover they stayed reasonably local to Hawes it will prove I was correct and their target is in this vicinity.'

'Goodnight Stewart. You had better eat now. You look well and truly bushed.'

CHAPTER 83
Tuesday 19th February 0755 hours

'Help yourself to fruit juice and cereals if you wish. Do you have any particular requests for your breakfast? I have kippers, a full British breakfast, omelettes with various fillings,' pointed out their landlady.

'Do you know, I quite fancy an omelette. What fillings do you have?' asked Mursi.

'The menu lists the various fillings for you to choose from. I recommend a creamed mushroom filling. It is one of my own favourites.'

'Then we will follow your recommendations and try the creamed mushrooms. Is that OK for you?' Mursi asked of Al Liby.

'It sounds delightful and I really could not face another one of the full fried breakfasts.'

'I have brought in a pot of tea but if you prefer coffee I can soon do that as well.'

'Tea will suit us admirably.' Once the lady had disappeared into the kitchen Al Liby asked, 'what is our programme for today? I don't imagine I can talk you out of trying to use the helicopter?'

'No, we shall use the helicopter for the filming. The weather is clear so it looks like a good flying day. At last today will see our mission completed. Further conversation came to a stop as the landlady re entered with two plates of omelettes.

'Well, Anas, I think it is time we settled up and got on our way. I will ask for the bill.'

'Well gentlemen what did you think to the omelettes? Can you manage toast now?'

'We were both most agreeably surprised. It is certainly something I will try in the future. It really was most tasty. Neither of us could manage another bite thank you. We would like to be on our way so could you prepare the bill please?'

'All ready for you' announced the landlady lifting a folded sheet of paper from her apron pocket.

'It was a pleasure having you stay and if you are ever up this way again you would be most welcome.'

'It is most kind of you madam,' Mursi said, 'and here is a little extra for your hospitality,' handing over an extra five pound note.

'That is most generous of you, thank you. Have a safe journey. Have you far to go?'

'Yes, we plan on visiting friends in Glasgow. That is why we wish to be on our way.'

'It is an easy drive from here. Mostly motorway up the M6,' advised the landlady.

'Yes, we did look at the map. Well thank you again. We will get our bags and be on our way.' Within ten minutes they were back onto the A65 heading for Ingleton, and subsequently Hawes. A light drizzle was falling. Fortunately for them no roadblocks, the police being convinced they had slipped through the net and were well clear.

'Midhat, if this weather continues the aircraft will not fly today,' pointed out Al Liby, fervently hoping that Mursi would agree to use the timer and scrub the chopper idea.

'Anas you worry too much my brother. I feel today that Allah is with us in our quest.' They drove on in silence until, a mile outside Hawes Mursi pulled onto a small layby at the side of the road. From here they had a perfect view of Stag's Fell.

'Look, Anas, the helicopter is flying. I told you Allah was on our side. Now do you believe me.'

'I have faith but I am still not happy about attempting to hijack that helicopter. I can not put a terribly bad feeling from my mind.'

'You drive from here. If the car park looks quiet drive straight up to the BMW so I can set the timer.'

'As you wish Midhat, but you know my feelings.' As it turned out the Creamery car park was very quiet so Al Liby drove slowly into the upper car park where the BMW was standing. Climbing out of the Vauxhall, Mursi had a quick glance round. All seemed quiet. He opened the boot of the BMW and repeated the arming procedure for the device, setting it for a three hour delay. With one final satisfied look at the two containers he closed the boot. He was about to return to the Vauxhall to carry out the final stage of the task, the acquisition of the helicopter in order to have Al Qaeda's greatest ever coup on film. Suddenly a head appeared from the opposite side of the dry stone wall. Mursi was momentarily taken aback. It was a face he recognised.

'You, you bastard. I'll have you for what you did to Jeb!' Roared Tom Prescott. Coincidentally the dry stone wall he was repairing just happened to be right next to Mursi's parked BMW.

CHAPTER 84
Tuesday 19th February 1002 hours, near Kettlewell

'If it wasn't for the overcast sky this would have been a lovely ride out.' One of the policemen assigned to Stewart had driven over the top of the fells and was not far from Kettlewell.

'I reckon that Stewart bloke is up the Swanee. If that car and those Ayrabs had been in this part of the world they'd have been found by now,' added his comrade, PC Crane.

'Let's find somewhere in Kettlewell to have a bite and a drink,' suggested the driver.

'I second that proposal my good man. Ah, just a mo. Go up this driveway, we may as well check this B&B out. It is off the road and it is on our list.'

'OK will do. Then we find a café. I've seen enough B&Bs to last me a lifetime. I will never ever stay in one again.' As they approached, a pleasant faced lady was walking towards the house carrying a basket of freshly laid eggs.

'My what have I done now? Two handsome policemen come to arrest me.' Climbing out of the car the two policemen stretched their legs.

'No madam, I am afraid it is nothing as exciting as that. We are looking for a couple of men and wondered if they had stayed with you over the past few days,' explained Crane. With that he held out two photographs of Mursi and Al Liby.

'Why goodness me, yes. They stayed with me on Saturday and Sunday. Two of the nicest gentlemen you could ever wish to meet. They also tipped me very well. What have they done?' Both policemen's mouths fell open. Crane was the first to recover his wits.

'Please look carefully. You have no doubts in your mind that it was these men, did you also see what car they were in?' demanded Crane.

'I never forget a face. It was them and they were in a dark blue Vauxhall.'

'Did you get the number of the car? Did you see what model it was? When did the men leave? Do you have any idea where they were going after they left here?'

'Whoa, slow down young fella. Best come into the house and I'll tell you over a nice cup of tea and some of my freshly made hot scones.'

'This really is urgent,' protested Crane.

'Tea, young man, now let's get inside.' They were soon seated with a steaming mug of tea and a delicious warm scone smothered in melted butter.

'Now what do you want to know about my two foreign guests?'

'Did you notice what model of car it was and the registration number?' asked Crane.

'Definitely a Vauxhall. Don't ask me what model as I have no idea. Nor its number.'

'Thank you. How long ago did the men leave and have you any idea where they were heading next?'

'They left Monday morning nice and early and were heading for York.'

'Terrific but how do you know they were going to York?' asked Crane's colleague.

'I asked them where they were going and they told me. I even suggested places for them to visit.'

'Would you mind if I used your telephone please? I'll pay for the call.'

'Use it by all means and don't worry about paying, so, tell me what did they do?' Ignoring her question, Crane dialled Stewart's number from the list of contacts.

'Stewart'

'Good morning sir, PC Crane here. Are you well?' A devilish streak compelled Crane to delay passing on the good news.

'Crane. It is nice to hear from you but I am busy and you ought to be. Finding our two friends is paramount, or had you forgotten?'

'Oh them,' said Crane offhandedly.

'Yes THEM Crane. Now what can I do for you?'

'Oh, I knew there was something Sir. The two men. We have found where they spent Saturday and Sunday.'

'Crane, you lovely, lovely man. Where for God's sake?'

'A Bed and Breakfast at a place called Starbotton just outside Kettlewell. Not much to tell. The car was a Vauxhall, no further details. They left early Monday morning telling the landlady they were going to York for a few days.'

'Ah, I knew they had stayed not too far from Hawes. This proves I was right.'

'Sir, they should be In York now,' said Crane.

'A red herring to throw us off the track. They will have headed back towards Hawes.'

'But sir, surely that is what they want you to think. It may be a bluff.'

'No Crane. All along I felt this was the target area. I will pass this on to the rest of the team. Well done you two. I don't think we will gain anything by my visiting the place. Get what further information you can. We need to know where they stayed last night. I am going to move all the team to check accommodation that side of Hawes. I bet my bottom dollar they spent last night around there.' Stewart had closed the call Crane replaced the phone saying, 'oh yes goodbye to you sir and three bags full.'

'What was that about three bags full?' his fellow colleague asked.

'Stewart. No goodbye or anything. One minute he was there the next he was gone. Talk about people skills.' Once again Stewart's bedside manner had upset one of his aides. The landlady could offer no further useful information so the two left and drove the short distance into Kettlewell to enjoy a bar lunch and a pint, Crane still feeling miffed by Stewarts apparent rudeness.

CHAPTER 85

Tuesday 19th February 1053 hours, Thames House

'That is a start, I suppose, but we really need to know where they are now, not where they were last week.'

'I know that DG but it proves that they have an interest in this area. Whenever someone has ID'd them it has been not too far from Hawes. Our people have missed something in this area. I am confident it is not the Garrison, RAF Leeming nor Menwith Hill.'

'We have covered everything that we consider may be of interest to AQ but there simply is no other worthwhile target that is of sufficient propaganda value.'

'I have had some sticky ones before but this beats everything. Nothing makes any sense. No trace of either car, the men or the device. The sixty-four-thousand dollar questions. WHY are the men still hanging around here, and equally puzzling, what are they waiting for?'

'I am sorry I cannot offer you more Stewart but the Yanks are doing all they can, as are our equivalent departments in France and Germany. They fear they may be next on AQ's hit list. We have a lead on the technician that checked over the device for Mursi. Once we nab him perhaps we can squeeze some answers out of him. The PM has authorised us to use any means necessary to obtain this information, and I do emphasise ANY.'

'Right-ho sir. I will keep you abreast of any developments here. I just wish bloody Allah would put the boot in against AQ for a time and give us a hand up. We could certainly use some divine assistance.'

CHAPTER 86
Tuesday 19th February 0941hours

'OK boss, that is everyone contacted and assigned to searching south and west of Hawes. I just hope you are doing the right thing,' Sundance was speaking to Stewart.

'It can't put us in a worse spot than we were. No one saw hide nor hair of them round here and young Crane has confirmed they were staying in that area. I am positive we shall locate them around there. They are also using the blue Vauxhall, so where the bloody hell have they hidden that Beamer, find the Beamer and I bet my boots we find the device.'

'Butch and I are approaching Kettlewell now. We will check isolated B&Bs here and then work back along the A65 towards Ingleton. The rest of the guys should all be here by then. In fact we are going to have a word with the landlady where the two stayed. She might be able to point us in the direction of other out-of-the-way places.'

'Good idea. Her local knowledge might help and these B&B people tend to pass customers on to others if they have no room. Keep in touch.' Well before ten in the morning the police and Stewart's team were steadily working through accommodation in the newly allocated area.It was about ten when one of the search team pulled into a quiet driveway.

'Good morning sir. Sorry to bother you but I wonder if you could help us?' Desperately trying not to sound too dejected, Inspector Deptford with one of his constables had called at the umpteenth residence that did accommodation.

'Certainly Inspector, what can I do for you?'

'We are trying to locate these two men' explained the Inspector as he produced photos of Mursi and Al Liby.

'Why what have they done? Nothing bad I hope.'

'We just need to speak to them sir. Now, have you seen them?'

'I have, indeed, seen them Inspector. Those two men stayed with us last evening and left this morning on the way to Glasgow.' Getting over the initial shock Deptford asked, 'can you tell me any more about them? Their plans, their car details.' Aside to the constable with him, 'contact Stewart, now.'

'Not really. They were both very nice and polite. They said they were going to visit friends in Glasgow. Left about nine-ish if I remember correctly. They were driving a very dark blue car but I did not notice the make.'

'Stewart for you sir,' said the PC passing over the mobile.

'Well done Inspector. I knew it. I knew it. Do you have anything else?'

'Not yet sir. We only found out this very minute but I thought you would want to know immediately.'

'You did right. Where exactly are you? This time I will come there myself. I want to speak to the proprietor.' Passing over the directions, the Inspector then suggested that the proprietor showed them the rooms the two men had used.

'Very well. The rooms have not been cleaned yet as my wife and myself are going to the cash and carry and having lunch out. The rooms will be as the exactly as the men left them.' As the Inspector looked round the last room, a screech of tyres heralded Stewart's arrival.

'Ah, that will be my boss. If you would come with me sir we will go and have a word with him. I know he will want to speak with you.' A smiling Stewart had walked straight into the house without knocking.

'Morning Inspector. You are the proprietor?' Without waiting for confirmation Stewart went on. 'Did you hear any of the conversation between these two men or anything else that will help us locate them?'

'I told the Inspector all that I knew. The men were polite and no bother whatsoever. As he paid me one of the men said he was on his way to Glasgow.'

'Nothing in their room's Stewart. Even the waste bins have not been used. I had a good poke round before you got here,' advised Deptford.

'I don't think we will get any more here. They are one step ahead of us again,' said Stewart rubbing his chin, deep in thought.

'I am calling off the accommodation check for today and want all the team to meet me back at the Garrison for six pm. Until then, all of you drive round looking for that damned Vauxhall. We need to rethink this. I am utterly baffled.' With that Stewart swept out without a word of thanks, or any farewell to the proprietor. Preparing to leave, Deptford thanked the proprietor for his patience and assistance.

'That bloke's a bit rude isn't he? Sorry I could not help more. Is it OK to clean their rooms when we get back, just in case we have other guests this evening?'

'I apologise for him. He is from London, you know. However, he has a lot on his mind I'm afraid. Yes, you can do the rooms. No point us fingerprinting or anything else. Thank you again.'

'Bye Inspector. Oh there is one thing. Silly really but when I went to collect their dirty dishes I had the impression the two men were going on about a helicopter. They shut up when they realised I was there. Probably nothing at all.'

CHAPTER 87
Tuesday 19th February 1001 hrs, Hawes

For an instant Mursi was rooted to the spot. Prescott leapt over the wall savagely striking out at the Arab with the mason's hammer he had been using. The blow struck Mursi's upper arm. A loud crack indicated the bone had broken. The terrorist fell onto the ground, calling out in agony. Remembering Jeb's battered features spurred Prescott on in a wild rage. He launched himself astride Mursi's chest and raised the hammer to smash it into the man's skull. At that precise moment Prescott felt a blinding pain at the side of his head. Al Liby had booted him viciously behind the right ear. Prescott slumped to the ground unconscious.

'Help me up Anas, quickly,' ordered Mursi, his right arm hanging uselessly.

'Up you come Midhat. To prevent your arm moving too much I am going to place your hand in your jacket pocket. This might hurt.' Al Liby manoeuvred Mursi's hand into the pocket. Despite doing it carefully, Mursi cried out in pain.

'That may help a little. What do we do now?' Overcoming an attack of nausea, Mursi leaned on the car.

'We will bundle him into the boot of the Vauxhall. If we leave him here someone will soon come across him.'

'But what about your arm? It is clearly broken.'

'Help me get this dog into the car,' snarled Mursi half crazed with pain. With a struggle Prescott was soon manhandled into the large boot.

'Use that parcel tape to bind and gag him securely.' In no time at all Al Liby had Prescott trussed like a parcel ready to be delivered. The Arabs had been fortunate in that no one had heard the commotion and they were still the only people in the upper car park.

'The timer is set Midhat. We should abandon the plan to use the helicopter.'

'No, no, no! We are going to take that aircraft.' Pain and frustration were beginning to take a hold of Mursi.

'Drive up that hill and park on the grass verge so we can observe the progress and watch for the helicopter to land and refuel.'

'But Midhat, it might be ages yet,' pleaded Al Liby.

'No, Anas. If you recall, the engineer said they were only taking on a small amount of fuel in order to carry a heavier payload.' At the top of the Thwaite Road Al Liby pulled onto the verge some distance from the improvised helipad. Soon afterwards thuds could be heard coming from the boot. Quite obviously Prescott had come round.

'Lie still or I will silence you for good,' shouted Mursi, starting to climb out of the vehicle.

'Midhat, look. The helicopter looks as if it is coming in to land.'

'I told you so Anas. They will refuel now and when they are done it will be ours.' The helicopter touched down and the rotors whirled to a stop. A fuel pipe was connected to its tanks and someone could be seen operating a small hand pump from a barrel.

'Very soon now, Anas, you and I will become living legends in Al Qaeda. Hawes will be devastated by the bomb in the BMW. You will have recorded it all on film.' Opening the car boot Mursi looked at Prescott.

'Shortly you will be dead along with hundreds of other worthless infidels like yourself.' Prescott could only kick in vain and grunt obscenities.

'No one will hear you my friend and in a short time it will not matter in any case.' As he spoke Mursi delved into his travel bag and pulled out two well worn but very deadly Beretta Model 34 automatics. He pointed one at Prescott's head and pulled the trigger!

CHAPTER 88
Tuesday 19th February 1013 hours

'Things are looking up at last.' Stewart was on his sat phone to the DG.

'I feel vindicated in that it seems to prove they plan on using the device around here.'

'I am afraid you may be correct. I still think it is likely to be the Garrison. I am reluctant to advise the CO to evacuate the base as it would create untold panic.'

'We know they are still using the Vauxhall and talked about going to Glasgow but I have discounted that. The damned BMW is the fly in the ointment,' said Stewart.

'Yes, like yourself I believe Glasgow was mentioned as a blind. By the way the 'so called' technician Mursi used was still denying any knowledge of the affair. Even though Mahasheer ID'd him. However, I feel that very shortly he will change his tune. I ordered Carter and Killoran to take over the interview an hour or so ago.'

'Jeez boss, I don't fancy being in his shoes. Those two are bloody animals.'

'Needs must, Stewart, and the PM did authorise any means to obtain information. If that device detonates, one side effect will see the PM and this Government out on their ears. You can bet our PM wants to hang on to his job with all its perks and questionable MP's allowances.'

'OK sir, I'll get back to work.'

'Wait. I have another call.' Stewart could hear talking but could not distinguish what was being said.

'Stewart, an update. Carter and his chum were successful. Apparently after having a wet towel placed over his face and more water poured onto it the man saw sense. He is not fully coherent yet but has indicated he will cooperate one hundred per cent.'

'Poor bastard. Waterboarding. I am not surprised. I experienced that during training. I swear I honestly believed I was about to die,' said Stewart.

'Yes, it is quite an experience I believe. However, once I have something I will call you, bye Stewart.'

With that the DG was gone.

CHAPTER 89
Tuesday 1017 hours, Stag's Fell

'Right-ho that'll do. Enough to complete the last couple of trips and get me safely back to Yeadon,' the pilot called out to his engineer.

'OK boss, I'll put the empty drums in the van and remove the barrier tape round this site. I'll see you back at Yeadon.'

'Good, I need to drain my radiator and then I'll get off,' answered the pilot as he proceeded to pee behind the helicopter. Some distance along the road Mursi laughed out loud at Prescott's terrified expression as the firing pin came down on an empty chamber.

'You will wish you had never met me Inglesi,' laughed Mursi. Prescott furiously mouthed a stream of obscenities at Mursi who could not understand them due to the tape across his prisoner's mouth. Prescott continued cursing as the boot lid slammed shut again.

'They have finished fuelling. Time for us to go my brother. Put this pistol in your pocket. I also have one. I have the remote control and the camcorder is on the back seat. Drive quickly so we take them by surprise.' The pilot was adjusting his clothing as a dark blue Vauxhall slithered to a halt in front of him. In a trice Mursi and Al Liby were out of the car and had their weapons drawn and covering the pilot and engineer.

'You, into the aircraft,' Mursi ordered out to the pilot.

'Piss off I know who you are,' he retorted. Crack!! Mursi had put a bullet through the engineer's foot, he fell to the ground groaning.

'Would you care to reconsider?' smiled Mursi.

'I have no time to waste. The next slug will smash his kneecap.' Seeing the injured man writhing in agony on the ground was enough to persuade the reluctant aviator to climb aboard. Mursi sat in the front next to him whilst Al Liby sat down behind them preparing the camera.

'Start up and take off.' The shot had been heard by the volunteers high up on the fell. They cautiously began hurrying down the steep path to find out the reason for the shot, watching as the helicopter lifted off the hillside and flew to the south, instead of towards the west where it should have been headed.

CHAPTER 90

Tuesday 19th 1007 hours

'Sir, Deptford here.'

'Yes Inspector what can I do for you?' enquired Stewart.

'Just as you left here the owner said he overheard the two men arguing about a helicopter. As soon as they realised he was there they shut up until he had removed the dirty dishes. He heard their hushed voices as he left the room again.'

'Why a helicopter of all things? What on earth can that mean. If, in fact, it means anything to us. Have you any thoughts on it Inspector?'

'Well, Stewart, they have Army choppers based at Catterick.'

'Mm back to the Garrison again. I wonder if they plan on trying to hijack one from there. Thank you Inspector, I will contact Catterick.'

Two minutes later. 'Colonel, Stewart here. I understand you have helicopters attached to the Garrison.'

'Of course. Anything from a Lynx to a Chinook. Why do you ask?' After he had related Deptford's message to the Colonel, 'Stand by Stewart. I will call you back,' ordered the Colonel.

Almost immediately Stewart's phone warbled. 'Stewart, I just spoke to the CO of the helo flight. There is NO way anyone could get to their aircraft. In any case, two are flying now as part of an exercise. One is stripped down for routine maintenance and the others are well guarded and protected.'

'Thank you Colonel. The helicopter conversation may be totally irrelevant but with those two one can never be certain of anything.'

'There is one thing, Stewart. When our birds fly they file flight plans and are notified of any other flying that may take place in their area. Apparently they have been warned to keep an eye out for a private helicopter operating on Stags Fell.'

'Stags Fell. The name rings a bell. Is it near you sir?' Stewart asked.

'A short flying distance. Stags Fell is on the hill overlooking Hawes.'

'Bloody hell. I remember it now. Thanks Colonel.' Closing the call, Stewart raced towards Hawes using his hands-free phone system.

'Butch, Sundance. I want you two in Hawes as fast as you can. Contact the rest of the team and do it fast. I want everyone there. Now.' Speeding towards Hawes Stewart's phone vibrated again! This time the caller ID indicated the DG.

'Sir?' queried Stewart.

'Ah Stewart. Regarding Mursi's technical adviser. He began talking to us and suddenly died from a massive heart attack. So inconvenient. Carter and Killoran really do become over enthusuastic about their work. I must speak to them about it. Sorry, but no more help from this lead. In the meantime his body will be found in his bed where he quietly passed away in his sleep. Once we have him moved back to his own house.'

'Bugger, so no further help there. Thank you sir for letting me know. Speak later. I'm a tad busy right now,' answered Stewart as, driving one-handed, he passed a stream of vehicles on a bad bend to the accompaniment of flashing lights, horns blasting and finger signs.

CHAPTER 91

Tuesday 1021 hours

'You won't get away with this,' shouted the pilot over the noise of the engine.

'A vain hope my friend. We already have,' said an elated Mursi. Taking the helicopter had been a piece of cake. His broken arm almost, but not quite, forgotten.

'Fly towards Wether Fell, over there,' pointed Mursi.

'I know where Wether Fell is,' retorted the pilot, his voice full of anger. As they neared the fell Mursi pointed his finger to the right.

'Descend towards Dodd Fell. When I give the word dive down quickly behind the hill. Anas, start your camera.'

'It is running Midhat.'

'Both of you put these goggles on,' directed Mursi passing over the welder's goggles. Neither of you look in the direction of Hawes.'

'I won't be able to see with these on,' grumbled the pilot.

'You will see enough. It is only for a few seconds until I give you the order.' The Creamery was in sight and Mursi was satisfied the helicopter was nicely positioned to dip below the brow of Dodd Fell. He carefully took the remote from his pocket with his good arm, gripped the top of the aerial in his teeth and pulled it fully out. The remote was switched on. A steady red light came on and the remote was set to send the fateful signal.

'Anas, direct the camera. Use wide angle. Do not open your eyes. Pilot, when I shout "Now" dive quickly.'

'What is the purpose of doing that,' queried the disgruntled and very reluctant airman.

'If you value your eyesight or even your life you will do as I tell you.'

'My God you madman. You must have some nuclear device and

the goggles are to reduce the effects of the flash,' exclaimed the pilot in full realisation of what he was about to be a part of.

'Remember, there is nothing you can do to stop it now. All I have to do is press this button. Even if you decided to crash you would be too late. You should know my friend and I are willing to sacrifice ourselves. Enough talking. Standby, standby. NOW.' As Mursi pressed the transmit button the pilot dived behind the hill. Self preservation and the fact that he knew no one could stop Mursi being sufficient motives.

CHAPTER 92

1024 hours Stags Fell

As Stewart powered over the crest of the road he saw a group of people gathered at the helipad.

'What happened?' he demanded.

'The two men you want have just flown off in that helicopter,' explained a volunteer.

'They also shot the engineer.'

'Did you call for an ambulance?' asked Stewart as he bent down to look at the wounded man's bloody foot.

'No signal, but in any case we only arrived here about the same time as you.'

'Very well, I will do it in a moment. Look in the van, there must be a first-aid box.' Prioritising was high on Stewart's list as he pressed a speed dial button!

'DG, Stewart. The stakes have literally now gone sky high. The two men have commandeered a helicopter near Hawes.'

'Right, I will contact RAF Leeming to see if they can scramble a fighter. If that chopper approaches a big city, or even Catterick, I will ask the PM to order it shot down.' The helicopter could still be seen in the distance to the south when a loud banging drew their attention to the Arabs Vauxhall. One of the volunteers operated the boot lever.

'Well, Mr Prescott. You do keep some strange company,' drawled Stewart. This elicited more kicking and mumbling from Prescott as the men slowly lifted him from the car boot onto the ground. At that moment Stewart's mobile sounded.

'Yes. Very well DG but Leeming will have to move its arse before that chopper sets off for Catterick.'

'Ouch.' A yell of pain from Prescott as someone pulled the sticky tape from round his mouth, removing a fair amount of hair as well. Still too stiff to stand, Prescott called out.

'Be buggered with Catterick. The bastards are going to nuke Hawes. I heard one of them say so. They need the helicopter to film the explosion and also make their getaway.' Stewart's sat phone was in operation again.

'DG. It is NOT, I repeat NOT Catterick but the town of Hawes itself. Have Leeming scrambled a jet, there may still be time to shoot the helicopter down.'

'So the weapon must be close by. Listen,' ordered the Director General.

'Hey, Stewart. I think I know where the device is,' yelled Prescott, 'I am sure it will be in a car in the Creamery car park.'

'And I bet it's a bloody Beamer. Just a second DG. We think we may know where the device is located.'

'Excellent, but listen. Our boys have got the operating details from the AQ technician. If you can reach the device in time there is a simple ON/OFF switch. Just put it to OFF. The switch is situated immediately below a green light.'

'I remember from the photos. I am on the way now. Would you like to give the Colonel the good news.' Some of the feeling was back in Prescott's legs as he hobbled around.

'In my car Tom. Direct me to the car park.' As he spoke he was calling Butch.

'Location, Butch?'

'Entering Hawes. Approaching a filling station on our right.'

'Go to the Creamery top car park. The Beamer should be there. Look in the boot. If the device is there all you have to do is switch it to OFF. You will recall the photos. Now MOVE IT.'

Chapter 93
Airborne over Dodd Fell

Mursi pressed the button on the remote whilst the pilot executed a diving turn to the Left, dipping behind the fell. A look of sheer disbelief and horror came across Mursi's face. There had been no detonation.

'Climb again,' he screamed at the pilot, 'Anas continue filming.'

'I am filming Midhat there is plenty of space left in the camera.' Frantically Mursi repeatedly stabbed the button. The remote seemed to be functioning correctly. A steady red light changed to green indicating the instrument was transmitting.

'Fly closer damn you,' the pilot was ordered but still nothing. A press of the button showed a steady red changing to a steady green, but still no explosion.

'Closer, closer damn you,' Mursi was in a frenzy now and for once in his life not thinking clearly. Even Al Liby began to fear for the man's sanity.

'Midhat, we must go now and make our escape. The timer will work OK and do the job for us,' begged Al Liby. The helicopter was still slowly flying towards Hawes whilst Mursi pressed and re-pressed the operating button.

'Midhat. We must leave now. You said, yourself, that Allah was smiling on us. Let the timer do its work.' As if awaking from a dream he realised that Al Liby was right. He gave the pilot new directions.

'Ha, ha, so your plans did not work. Typical Arab cock-up. I worked with your lot for years in the Middle East. Fucking useless bunch of ragheads,' guffawed the pilot.

'Silence your mouth or I will throw you out. I can fly this aircraft myself.'

'With a broken arm? Now that is something I'd love to see,' grinned the pilot. The timer would work perfectly. He had set it for three hours at a little before 10am. By 1pm Hawes would be no more. It was intensely disappointing not to have it on film like the airliners when they flew into the Twin Towers. However, there would be massive TV and news coverage. The world would know what he, Midhat Mursi, had done to advance the cause of Al Qaeda.

'Fly lower,' Mursi directed, suspecting that the RAF would have mobilised a fighter after them. Heeding Mursi's instruction the pilot flew at treetop level, he knew full well, that even as low as that, his transponder would be flashing out on Air Traffic radar sets. During Mursi's tantrums the pilot had carefully operated his transponder. Aircraft show up on radar screens and a transponder gives a flash. The Controllers would soon realise what was happening and then vector the Royal Air Force fighter onto them. Less than twenty minutes later Mursi pointed to a small field near Otley, 'there. Land there.' Doing as he was told, the pilot touched down gently on the soft grass. He fully expected Mursi to shoot him but instead Mursi whacked the man behind the ear with the butt of his automatic. The pilot slumped over the controls, unconscious. To make certain the helicopter would not be able to fly until repaired, Mursi smashed the communications console. Al Liby helped Mursi down from the helicopter and the pair disappeared amongst the bushes and trees. They emerged from the undergrowth into a huge car park. It had very few cars and Mursi quickly spotted the car he had arranged to meet them.

'You made it my friends,' said the driver. His voice was drowned out by the thunderous roar of a low flying fast jet.

'Yes, my friend. Let us go quickly. I fear that aircraft may have been searching for our helicopter.' The driver eased out of the Golden Acre car park onto the A660, Otley road. The driver was soon entering the outskirts of Bradford. Once there the two terrorists soon disappeared into the Arab community. A doctor, sympathetic to the cause, administered morphine to Mursi whilst he reset the broken bone and splinted it. He also cleansed the nasty knife wound at the back of

Mursi's wrist. Mursi had refused hospital for obvious reasons, ignoring the doctor's well meant advice. After all, nothing was going to prevent Mursi being amongst the first to see the television newsflash!

CHAPTER 94
Hawes, Creamery Car Park

Butch and Sundance hurtled into the main car park, scattering startled visitors.

'There, yelled Butch,' pointing to a sign that indicated the overflow car park.

'The bloody Beamer. I bet the bugger was here all the time,' exclaimed Butch as Sundance braked to a halt alongside the BMW. The most hunted car in Britain had probably not been hidden at all. Simply left in a car park. Where better to lose a car? Only a handful of other cars were parked there. People had just secured them and were heading slowly towards the Visitor Centre. The two men leapt out of their car and Sundance yanked the door handle of the BMW. Locked.

'Bastard. It is locked.' He shouted. Butch quickly opened the boot of their car and trotted towards the locked car with a small crowbar in his hand.

'Shift yourself. I'll soon have this open.' To Sundance's surprise, instead of jemmying the door the short crowbar shattered the Driver's window. Butch had his hand inside in a flash and opened the door. At that moment Stewart, guided by Prescott, slid to a halt inches from Butch.

'Hey up boss you nearly had your car up my arse,' as he operated the boot catch. Sundance had the boot up and was pulling a couple of car rugs off something they were concealing. He flung them to the ground to be confronted by the nuclear device. He was about to move the switch to OFF when he looked at Stewart.

'The honour is yours sir.'

'Fuck the honour just switch the bloody thing off before we are all attending harp playing classes.' Doing as he was told Sundance leaned forward and flicked the switch to off. As the lights went from two greens to a green and red the relief was palpable. The tenseness seemed to drain out of everyone. For once even Stewart's sangfroid was absent as he breathed a huge sigh of immense relief, his hands showing the slightest tremble.

'Phew, that is a damned relief and a half,' sighed Stewart.

'That was what we saw in that underground bunker,' confirmed Prescott who had limped towards the car.

'I can't believe that those two cases make up an atom bomb with all its power and destruction.'

'What cases and what is that ridiculous comment about atom bombs to do with chasing a couple of murderers?' queried Stewart to Prescott.

'That fucking bomb...' Tom's voice trailed off as he realised the implications of Stewart's comment.

'This bomb never happened, do you understand?'

'Yes, point made but what about the two bloody Arabs who murdered my mate?'

'They are not a priority any further as far as I am concerned. Neutralising this device came before everything. The police will try to locate the two Arabs,' replied Stewart.

'I'll tell you one thing. At least I had the pleasure of breaking the arm of one of them,' added Tom Prescott.

'Why? What do you mean?' Sundance asked.

'I was working the other side of this wall when I heard them. I jumped over and clouted the bastard with my hammer. I definitely heard his arm break.'

'Good for you,' laughed Stewart,

'but you can be sure he will not be visiting any hospital to have it set. I will have Inspector Deptford organise routine hospital checks just to be on the safe side.'

'Served the bloke right. The other one gave me a right boot full to my head. I reckon I shall have this headache for days,' grumbled Prescott.

'Ah that reminds me. That poor bloody engineer will be

wondering where his ambulance is. You had better go for a check-up yourself Tom, and thanks again for everything. Butch, you phone for an ambulance. I have some phoning to do.' A few seconds later Stewart could be heard.

'This morning's work should earn you your KT. Sir.'

'Splendid, splendid. I will get onto the PM and Home Secretary. Give my congratulations to all involved.'

'Really, it is thanks to the man standing in front of me but I will give you all the details later. I'd like to call the Colonel at Catterick now sir, if there is nothing else.'

'Any news on the two men?' asked the DG.

'They flew off in the chopper so we have no idea. I can tell you we believe Mursi was given a broken arm by our local hero here, Tom Prescott.'

'Is he with you now Stewart? Put him on for a moment,' ordered the DG. Stewart beckoned Prescott over.

'The man wants a word with you.'

'Hello Mr Prescott, I understand you played a vital role in locating the men we were seeking and the er, er, device. You also managed to wing of one of them.'

'Yes the device! I know about that and as for the man I hit, I wish I'd killed the sod for what he did to my friend.'

'I am sure many people have your precise sentiments over the men. We will be in touch to thank you officially for the part you played. Unfortunately, because of the nature of the incident the full story will never come out. However, once again thank you for your help in putting us on the trail of the murderers.'

'I'm not concerned with thanks, I'd be well satisfied if you caught the two bastards though. Oh, and a couple of Aspirins for my head would not go amiss.'

CHAPTER 95
Saturday 1st March, Heathrow Airport

'Final call for passengers travelling on British Airways flight BAO 155 to Cairo. The gate will be closing in ten minutes.' The metallic and almost incomprehensible voice echoed round the airport. A very overweight and obviously wealthy Arab led his two wives past the shortening queue of economy class passengers directly up to the First Class checking-in desk.

'Good evening sir,' smiled the attractive check-in lady. The man merely smiled politely and handed over three Egyptian passports and three first class tickets. A porter wheeled a trolley piled high with a mixture of Louis Vuitton and Prada travel bags. He placed them onto the scales and turned to the Arab.

'There you are sir. All done and dusted.' Without a word the Arab handed over a crisp new ten pound note.

'Thank you sir. Most generous,' said the porter cheerfully marching off in search of another customer.

'You and your wives can board now sir,' the girl at the check in desk informed him, handing back the various documents. Almost laughing out loud the Arab gave a nod of his head to his two wives. Looking straight ahead he strode off to board the direct flight to Cairo with his two wives obediently in tow behind.. They passed through security with no hassle whatsoever. Mind you, had they heard the comments from the security staff they may well have smiled to themselves.

'Bloody rag heads. Get away with murder because of our politically correct Mandarin's. groused one of the men to his lady colleague.

'Yeah I agree. In the old days the Arab women would have to show their faces whether it offended them or not,' said the security lady.

'Mind you, seeing some of their faces perhaps it is better to keep them hidden. Right ugly old cows.' Both security staff chortled as they prepared to vet the next passengers in line. The flight was uneventful and landed practically on time in Cairo a little before midnight local time. The weather was pleasantly warm after the cold and damp of London. The Arab led his wives from the airport to a waiting limousine.

'It worked well, my friend. So very, very easy. Luckily those infidels dare not ask to check beneath the niqab or ask you to raise it. Yet even in some of our own Arab countries the security insist on comparing the face to the passport photograph but not the weak and stupid British,' laughed the large Arab.

'I do not expect we will be able to use this system for much longer my brother. The British police already know that at least one male Arab murderer passed through airport security dressed in such a manner. I will be glad to get out of these ridiculous women's clothes and back into some proper men's garments. My arm is itching like mad in this cast and it is has been killing me all through the flight.'